HAIRDOS
of the
MILDLY
DEPRESSED

HAIRDOS
of the
MILDLY
DEPRESSED

· · · · · · · · · · ·

a novel by

DOUG
CRANDELL

Distributed by Macmillan

This is a work of fiction. All of the characters, companies, organizations,
and events either are the products of the author's imagination or are used
fictitiously and are not to be understood as real.

first edition

Designed by Jason Snyder

Library of Congress Cataloging-in-Publication Data

Crandell, Doug.
  Hairdos of the mildly depressed : a novel / by Doug Crandell. —1st ed.
    p. cm.
  ISBN-13: 978-0-7535-1378-1
  ISBN-10: 0-7535-1378-1
  1. Brothers—Fiction. 2. Hair—Fiction. 3. Georgia—Fiction. I. Title.
  PS3603.R377H35 2008
  813'.6—dc22
                                                              2008019179

10 9 8 7 6 5 4 3 2 1

For my mother,
Doris May Crandell

Acknowledgments

A book always comes to life thanks to innumerable people. Second-grade teachers, a parent, a group of supportive fellow writers; the person who ends up with his or her name on the cover is just a way to simplify credit. Anyway, I'd like to thank my junior high school English teacher, Mr. Swan, who helped me understand the power of words. A big hunk of gratitude also goes out to Tod Citron, the best day-job boss a writer could ever have. In addition, Dr. Steve Hall, an old friend and fairly funny guy, deserves a little something, too. I embarrassed him at the Southern Voices 2008 in Birmingham, but it got lots of laughs.

If I didn't have Kennedy Crandell and Jennifer Molton around, always wanting me to feed them and drive them places, I wouldn't know what to do. They are wonderful girls with sweet hearts, even if they always make me pay at restaurants. Walker Lane is also important to me, and I'd like to acknowledge his work. Here's to keeping the farm fenced and cleared and the chores done. Walk! Nancy Brooks-Lane is my loving first reader and my companion. More than anyone, she deserves my gratitude for an unfailing abundance of support. Without her, I would never have taken up writing.

Also, my agent Robert Guinsler has kept his faith in me even when I didn't have any left. He's a smart and dedicated advocate. Ann Espuelas has pushed me to become a better writer, and done it with grace and sensitivity. Amy Hitt made sure I remembered my little fella, Terry! Ken Siman at Virgin Books is a consummate professional with a great sense of humor to boot, not to mention a boatload of patience. Thank you Robert, Ann, Amy, and Ken for your guidance.

Finally, I've had the good fortune of meeting lots of fellow misfits over the past year, a development that provides me with a great deal of satisfaction. To them I say, "Let's never fit in!"

Hair is the first thing. And teeth the second. Hair and teeth.
A man got those two things he's got it all.

—James Brown

PART I

· · · · · · · · · · · · · ·

One "I found Jesus. She's changed my life," Compton Orville said to his brother, Brad. Compton leaned into the wooden fence behind them, the splintered wood sagging a bit under his weight. A trio of cardinals fluttered from one leaning post to another, dusk creeping over the dry land.

"Wouldn't it make more sense to call her Mary or Madonna?" Brad said.

Compton just laughed and shook his broken head, as he sometimes referred to it. "No, no, no, Half Pint," he said.

Brad watched Compton now, the frail lopsided body. He touched Compton's arm, steadied him.

"She isn't her own mother. She's not the mother of Jesus; she is Jesus," said Compton, a serene expression on his face. He batted his big green eyes at Brad, licked his lips, and brought a broad smile out into the sticky heat. "You need to talk with Jesus, Half Pint. She could do you some good."

Brad nodded, noticing for the thousandth time how full his brother's hair was, how utterly paltry his own was in comparison.

Barn swallows dipped to the ground to pluck invisible insects from the dust. The air smelled of mown hay and diesel fuel exhaust from where the rural was turning into the suburban. There was a silver ribbon of creek in the front, and pastures on each side of the driveway, but all around them was excavated earth and homesteads in demolition.

Compton pulled a pack of Juicy Fruit from his shirt pocket. He fumbled and dropped the first stick, did the same with the second, and then a third before he handed Brad the whole warm bundle. "Would you get that for me, Half Pint?"

Brad stared at his brother. They stood near the back fence where the land receded and a jungle of privet shot up. From where Brad and Compton were, it looked like it might simply slide off the knoll and disappear. Brad sorted through the gum pack, collapsed like a tiny accordion, wet and mushy, as Compton slowly stooped to retrieve the lost sticks. He stood and wiped the dust off each one, tucking them gently into his back pocket where they'd melt into a sticky putty when his brother dried his jeans. Brad handed Compton a new piece, peeled away from the foil like a banana.

"Thank you," Compton said. This was their routine after dinner: a walk, a chew, some conversation about the day. It was talk that Compton likely wouldn't remember, or would do so selectively, reciting bits of it over breakfast in the morning, where once again he'd urge Brad to go with him to meet Jesus.

The sun was sitting in an orange ball behind a spinney of flimsy pine trees as they chewed the gum and Compton slurped extra saliva back into his droopy mouth. His body was palsied and it seemed his face was slightly quivering all the time. Brad could smell Compton's Speedstick, the same scent he used before the beating. Off in the distance, cars idled at the stoplights that had steadily encroached upon the farmland. When they were kids, the whole area was fields of green dotted by red barns, but now, as they chewed the sugar out of their gum, cars honked and chirped, a newly developed rush hour.

Out of the corner of his eye Brad spied on his brother. Compton was four years older, and Brad believed five times as handsome, even now, though Compton was unrecognizable from the man he used to be. His face was smoothly shaven, brown hair combed back, full and shiny, his olive skin contrasting with the curious flickering of his green eyes. Compton turned fully toward Brad, his body fighting him all the way.

"What's the matter, Half Pint?" As he spoke, the gum got away from Compton and slid out of the weak side of his mouth; he made no attempt to stop it, and Brad couldn't tell if he even knew it was gone. Brad scrutinized his brother's right eye, the one that seemed unmoored in its socket. The eye steadied to a slow twitch. Compton smiled gently, an act that reminded Brad of the vulnerability of a baby trying to pick up a Cheerio.

"Nothing's wrong, Compton. I just worry about you is all," Brad said, hearing his brother's shallow breathing under the incessant thrumming of crickets. Compton stumbled closer to him, his right leg dragging in the parched dirt.

He was shorter after the accident, as if the metal bar had actually driven his vertebrae together, pounded him down by three inches. "What's really wrong?" he said.

Brad moved off the fence and out of the light, the clapboard fence behind them throwing deep shadows. "I just told you, Comp. I'm worried," said Brad. "This thing with the woman you think is Jesus."

Compton looked into the distance; he tried to shove a hand into his pocket, then stumbled, grabbing hold of the fence. "The problem with you," Compton said, "is that you've got no faith in love, Brad. If you ask me, all you need is a really good blow job from a woman who doesn't desire wedlock."

It was almost dark as they moved toward the house, a lone sheep bleating down the road, most likely from Old Man Tyler's place. He was the only other fool left on the county road, his sheep and cattle and ten-acre garden enclaved by towering, four-story 500K Vernacular Homes.

Compton thought the development was something evil that should be stopped, a plight on the rolling landscape. Most of Brad's time was spent trying to distract his brother from the spread of the suburbs, the march of subdivision progress.

The nightly routine was ending, the gum had been chewed, and Brad was proud of himself for not letting the conversation become hostile. On the front porch, Compton said, "Let me get that for you, Half Pint," as he shakily held the door open. The inside of the house smelled musty. They had a water problem in the basement, a leak in the foundation that needed attention. Things were sprouting down there. Brad didn't like to turn on the cellar light because it meant facing the problem. It was dark and scary even to be on the third step, which was the farthest Brad had been able to descend since they'd moved in. After the accident, though, the only place Compton would agree to live was here; he'd told Brad it was the old family house or the nuthouse, nothing else.

Brad sniffed the air. "What is that?"

Compton shrugged his shoulders, then smirked. "That's the damn basement, Half Pint."

"No, I smell smoke," said Brad. He jogged through the dining room to the kitchen, the floorboards creaking. Compton followed him, dragging his body.

Brad ran to the stove and yanked a smoldering pan off the gas burner. The acrid smell of blackened steel made the air difficult to breathe. Brad tossed the hot pan into the sink and doused it with water from the faucet. Smoke hissed into the air. He threw the window open and waved the air before his face. "Damn it, Compton!" he said as he took his brother by the arm and led him into the dining room. He sat him down in a chair and pulled one out from the table for himself. He sat with his legs spread like an umpire.

"What the hell were you cooking?"

Compton hung his head some, scratched his thick hair. "I believe that was going to be a soufflé of some sort. Maybe a tort."

"Don't you remember the rules? You can only use the microwave when I'm not here."

"But you were here," said Compton, eyes popping open, finger raised, objecting.

Brad rubbed his head, then his face. He sat for a moment in the chair, listening to the pan pop in the sink. He was tired and ready for bed. Compton touched Brad's shoulder. "Okay, Half Pint. I'm sorry. I'll stick to the nukery."

Brad stood up and pushed the chair under the table. "Come on," he said, offering a hand to Compton. "Let's just get some sleep."

Compton nodded and pointed to the floor. "Gotta get that basement taken care of, Half Pint."

Brad escorted his brother up the stairs. When they reached the top, a small pop of gas erupted from Brad's rear end. "Excuse me," he said to Compton.

"I'd say so, Half Pint," Compton said, pinching his nose. "You're as rotten as the incredible, inedible egg."

two They went to their rooms. Brad rolled onto his side in the bed, thinking about how his parents would dance on Christmas Eve, tipsy on eggnog. His father, a short but nicely built man, educated in the life sciences, liked to whisper into his wife's ear while they swayed to a rough-sounding 45 of "Strangers in the Night," then switch to something contemporary, like "Love Train" by the O'Jays. When Brad and Compton were kids, they'd listen from the bottom of the stairs, stowed

away behind the door jam. It was as if the whole house were an orches-
tra, blowing and then inhaling, playing the music of anticipation. Brad
drifted off to the memory of the old sounds.

But at nearly three a.m. he was awakened by the same thoughts
that always formed the cold, jagged edge of his sleeplessness. Where
is Compton? Is he safe? Has he escaped again toward town, walking
unsteadily along the berm, his pajama bottoms slipping down his butt,
crack exposed to the oncoming headlights of Old Man Tyler's wasted
son's Toyota? Brad had installed a complicated series of deadbolts and
keyed lock sets on the doors that Compton seemed to be able to crack
all too easily.

Brad swung out of bed and crept down the hall toward his brother's room. Sometimes, it was comforting to know he had to take care of
Compton; he liked to watch him sleep, when the night offered a break, a
time to feel grateful. But not tonight. From the doorway of his brother's
room, Brad saw that Compton was splayed out on his bed with the covers wrapped around his torso. As Brad watched him breathe, a pang of
hurt in his throat made him swallow harder. He knew he'd not get back
to sleep until it was almost time to get up again.

He switched off Compton's light by his bed and nearly stooped
to kiss his brother's fine, small forehead, but stopped himself. A therapist, the man whom Brad's last girlfriend had asked him to see to save
their relationship, warned Brad to refrain from getting all his emotional
needs met by caring for his brother like a child.

"He is a child," Brad told Dr. Chandler. "He can't tie his shoes or
brush his teeth without reminders. If that's not a child I don't know
what is."

"That's right. You don't know what a child is. You can't know
unless you become a parent to a child of your own, which is what you've

told me is one of things you'd most like out of life. And if you don't allow Tracy some room to breathe, you won't have any of that."

Brad had been diagnosed with depression, not entirely clinical, but mild, and still significant—enough, the doctor had said, to interrupt his major life activities. Since then, Brad took antidepression pills called MegaWell, the warning labels on which said you might get everything from sexual dysfunction to constipation. His favorite was: "Taking this medication may induce a false sense of well-being, and rectal leakage." How, he thought, could you believe you were happy and secure if your rear end had sprung a leak? Brad suffered, unfortunately, from one of the most common side effects—burping and flatulence. Still, the pills were self-fulfilling; if he forgot to take them, he'd worry, feel doom when he was brushing his teeth or be wired with despair at work when people chatted about awful TV shows. So he took the pills, but his belligerent belches could find their way out from his stomach with no more warning than an eye blinking, and the same with the farts.

Brad stood in the murky light next to his brother's bed and listened for his breathing, then allowed his fingers to barely touch his brother's warm head. He turned and crept out of the room.

He went toward the bathroom and switched on the light, careful to keep the door from squeaking on its rusty hinges. Compton was a light sleeper nowadays; he'd jump up from his bed at the slightest noise and throw on anything, a sheet worn like a cape, the drapes yanked from the window and cinched around his skinny waist, or even a bath towel inexplicably worn around his head like a baby's bonnet. When they first moved back in, this happened often; after pulling on layers of whatever clothing he could lay his hands on, Compton would appear at Brad's bedroom door like a child about to play in a blizzard, underwear stretched over four pairs of sweatpants.

In the mirror, Brad surveyed his baldness. At age thirty-three his head looked to him as if it had started to molt. The worst part, he thought, as he plied the crown of his head, the skin oily and tight there, was how much the hair loss made him look like a man in his fifties. He'd stayed in good shape, watched what he ate, but the head, the head looked superimposed, Photoshopped. His hair loss had started early; by the eighth grade the sides were receding.

Now in the bathroom, years later, the light bright, a moth circling the globe where others had died and piled up, Brad scrutinized his head. He swatted at the moth. "Mom would be mortified to see that," he muttered to himself. He should clean out the light fixture, but nowadays he just couldn't seem to muster the energy to do much else than oversee Compton.

Brad opened the closet door and reached behind the stack of ratty towels. He patted around until his hand touched the plastic bag. He ushered it out into the open like a ticking bomb and slowly peeled the bag open, afraid the sound would bring Compton running down the hallway.

The thing in the bag (and that's how Brad had started to think of it, as the "thing") seemed to move some when he took it out of the bag. It made him think of a muskrat pelt. The thing had arrived Priority Mail two days earlier, and for two straight nights he'd fiddled with it, inspecting the weave and texture. There was a DVD to be viewed before even attempting any kind of adjustments, but just like when he was a kid, opening a new board game or a Hot Wheels track, Brad couldn't wait to get things going; his patience for reading instruction books was not like his father's or even Compton's back in those days. Brad wanted first to look over the product—possess it before reading about it. In that way, Compton was like something new, too; Brad had not yet cracked the cover of Living with Your Brain Injured Loved One. The book sat on the oak desk in their father's study, along with the last newspaper his father had been reading the day of his death. Leaving the desk as it was had been their mother's idea, and when she died not a year later, Brad and Compton drank beers in the study and thumbed through all the books. That was before the beating, and it was the old Compton who said, blowing dust from The Attraction of Wildlife to a Country Manor, "I guess we should start gathering their stuff together and hold an auction. It would be the easiest way."

Brad hadn't been able to speak, his throat lodged with grief, as Compton nonchalantly speed-read two then three pages, licking his thumb. In the end, they decided to hire out the job and agreed that once all the household items were sorted and compiled into neat lots, they'd get quotes from two auctioneers, but the months slipped past and then it was too late. Brad got the call on his cell phone from a state trooper who told him he'd better hurry. "Your brother might not make it."

Brad smelled the hair system, the thing, actually brought it to his nose and inhaled. It reminded him of something a pervert would do. Under the light it appeared to be a mortician's prop, as if the filet of hair could be used to make a departed loved one look spiffier than they had in life. Brad placed it on top of his head. Resting there the thing appeared wounded, like it had crawled to that very spot to die without a fight.

He rearranged it, using a comb to bring the bangs into some semblance of order. The whole shebang: the piece, special adhesive tape, instructional DVD, and organic hair gel that was purported to leave "your new hair with full body and luxurious sheen, yet soft and manageable too," all of it cost nearly $300 with shipping and handling. In the mirror, if he stood back a few feet, the piece looked authentic. It matched his dark brown hair at the sides of his head and blended in lengthwise

Brad turned his head from one side to the other, inspecting his profiles. Down the hall, he heard a footstep, followed by a dragging sound. Compton was up and he never knocked anymore, just burst in, that is if he'd gained enough momentum to do so, otherwise it was a sluggish entry, as if he was purposely trying to move in slow motion. Brad listened as his brother's leg dragged along the carpet, creating static electricity, which was something Brad would have to get used to, he figured. For months now, most every time Compton touched Brad, he got a little shock. Compton would say, "Sorry, Half Pint. Too much energy in these bones I guess." The shocks were starting to irritate Brad, like a roommate's nasal drip.

Brad plucked the hair system from his head and shoved it into the bag, rushing to hide it behind the towels. He felt like a kid again, concealing his Playboys in the exact same spot where the thing now hid. Brad wasn't sure how necessary being covert was; Compton tended not to notice most things, although sometimes he might casually mention seeing something that was in fact extraordinary. "One of those guys who has seizures," he said to Brad recently, telling him about another patient at his adult day care, Paradise Club, "died today at Paradise. He was just twenty-nine. He liked that show where the two twin boys live in a hotel." Compton had said this as if it were a weather statistic. At other times, a little bird lying dead outside a nest might bring him into a teary-eyed diatribe about the state of the environment.

Brad pretended to be brushing his teeth, applying toothpaste to his Oral-B, even though he'd already done it, flossed and gargled, too. The bathroom door creaked and slowly opened, inch by inch, taking forever.

Finally Compton pulled himself in, heaving his body so close to Brad's that their hips and shoulders touched. Brad spit and rinsed and wiped his mouth on one of their mother's hand towels. It still had the Bowman College seal on it, a toothy alligator, the embroidery frayed.

"What is it?" asked Brad, turning from the sink. Compton didn't answer, just stared at Brad, and for a few moments that's all they did, look at each other.

"Come on, Comp, let's go to bed," said Brad, noticing how small his brother looked in his pajamas. "Compton," Brad said louder, as if talking to a deaf grandmother, "what is it?" Compton reached out and took his brother's hand. Brad thought he might start crying. It was a side effect of the meds and of the accident, the doctors explained; his brain had been most severely damaged in the frontal lobe. Compton blinked in the bathroom light and smiled; it was the same grin he'd always had, a part of him that had stayed, even after the brain damage. If Brad didn't know better, they could be back fifteen years ago, high and drunk, whispering after a long night of partying at Bowman, careful not to wake their parents.

"I just wanted," Compton said, "to make sure you are going to be there tomorrow, Brad." He rubbed extra spittle off his mouth and grinned again. Brad smiled back, experiencing one of the moments when he actually felt fortunate to be taking care of his brother. A nursing home facility had been offered, but Brad never considered it.

"I'll be there, Comp. I promise," Brad said as he led his brother down the hall to put him back in bed, resisting the urge to put his arm around him.

"Because it's important you're there, Brad," said Compton, pulling his ruined leg behind his torso like a ball and chain.

"I know," said Brad, now thinking of his hairpiece back in the bathroom, his mind drifting a little. He patted Compton on the back.

"Listen," said Compton, stopping right outside his bedroom door. His voice was curt and intense. "I mean it, Brad. We've got some things to talk about. Real life things." Compton's cheeks had reddened and his eyes held the extra tears of strain.

"Okay, okay, Comp," said Brad. "I hear you. I know it's important and I won't miss it." He was partially lying; he would be there, as always, but he doubted it would be anything more than the usual. Your brother needs to work on his social skills. For instance, he interrupts people when they are speaking.

Compton rubbed his eyes, hard enough that they made little squishing sounds.

"Don't do that, Compton. You know that's bad for your cornea. The doctor told you so." Normally, this kind of reprimand would turn into a full-blown argument, but Compton was tired and Brad was beginning to know better than to push things further. Compton kept rubbing his eyes.

Once Compton was back in bed, Brad stood in the doorway watching him, his fingers on the light switch, feeling like his father, without nice hair, of course.

"Brad," said Compton, his head jutting out from beneath the covers. "Don't forget about tomorrow, okay?"

Brad switched off the light and whispered into the dark, "I won't forget." His stomach gurgled as he went toward his own bedroom, wondering whether wearing his hair system to Compton's meeting tomorrow would be a good idea or not. He stopped again in the bathroom and swallowed the MegaWell pill he'd forgotten to take before bedtime.

three Brad waited in the car for his brother. He leaned across the seat and unlocked the passenger-side door. This was another of their routines: Brad drove Compton most every day to his program at the Paradise Club. The morning sun was golden, lumbering between hot and hotter; it was the kind of slow day Brad had always loved out here.

The pastures were still, the slow-moving clouds accentuated by a few birds calling from the tops of the high poplar trees

A distant roar bellowed from across the road. At the end of the lane, heavy-duty machinery crawled about like clunky automata, the operators unseen, sitting in low-rider seats, moving earth, making way for another subdivision. Dust kicked up in blood-orange swirls, as the dry, hard clay was pushed into towering mounds. A drought, the worst this part of Georgia had seen in decades, had left the ground like cement, the ditch mallow, and pasture grass as friable as kindling. Lately the small creek out front, where a sturdy bridge their father had built stretched over the languishing silver ribbon of water, had become somewhat polluted. The runoff from all the construction, and the increased traffic, left plastic soda bottles and bits of Styrofoam cups, fast-food wrappers, and beer cans stuck in the sandy banks, strewn along the thick tangles of fescue. The sight of any of these made Compton, in his post-trauma worldview, nuts. He'd even started a group called Eco-Greenies at the Paradise Club.

He looked at his watch as he sat in the car waiting for Compton. From the house Compton stumbled from the front door, his shoulder dipped even more from the strain of toting his insulated lunch box, a hairbrush in his hand. Brad packed it every night, putting in the items Compton liked: baby carrots, a small bag of Real Hot Bar-b-que Chips, and two bottles of flavored water, black cherry. Compton refused to eat real meals since the injury; he'd acquiesce only time to time, when something struck him as not really an entrée.

"Good morning, Half Pint," said Compton, as fragrant with Speedstick as ever. He pulled his bad leg into the car and his heavy foot thudded against the floorboard, bumping Brad's coffee.

"Compton, could you please quit calling me that," Brad said, trying to balance the steaming cup.

Compton ignored him and moved closer to his brother as if about to kiss him. "It's a wonderful, targonic morning, Half Pint!" Compton said, rubbing his hands together, fidgeting in the seat.

Brad registered the made-up adjective, "targonic," and weighed it against their history. Compton had always had an extraordinary vocabulary. He knew the Latin roots of words and could translate other languages without much trouble, even though he'd never formally studied them.

Brad buckled his brother in. He glanced in the rearview mirror, where at the end of the lane a backhoe spewed oily exhaust into the clear blue sky. He hoped Compton would be too busy with his good humor and morning routine to notice.

"What's got you in such a good mood today?" asked Brad, putting the Sentra into reverse, backing up, and making a U-turn.

"Oh, Half Pint, how could a man be in a bad mood when it's the first day of the rest of his life?" Compton wiggled, smiling his half-grin. He pointed toward the sky through the windshield. "Just because it happens every day doesn't mean it's not a miracle."

"What are you talking about, Comp?"

"Please don't call me that, Brad. The full name is Compton Horace Orville, if you don't mind." Compton jabbed his brother in the ribs, laughing through a cough.

"What," Brad repeated slowly, pinching the bridge of his nose, his foot still on the brake pedal, "makes today so special?" The car eased forward as they started over the bridge.

"Oh, you'll see, Half Pint. You'll see," said Compton. Brad thought of gunning the motor and flying over the bridge so Compton wouldn't notice the trash in the creek, but it would only put Compton's ire fully on the construction across the road. Brad braced himself as Compton looked out the window and down at the creek.

"Those dirty sons-a-bitches," Compton said, his unsteady gaze taking it all in. The creek looked like a can of restroom trash had been dumped into it; the banks were strewn with what looked like ticker tape. Some kind of packaging was floating in the stagnant water. Brad sped over the bridge and down the lane.

"It's just because of the drought, Compton," Brad said calmly, hoping to encourage good self-control like the PT/OT/speech/behavioral specialist had told him to do. "Your brother," the young woman had said, "will follow your lead like a robot. If you are patient and relaxed, he will be, too." It was, in fact, a load of horseshit. No matter how Brad reacted in their day-to-day interactions, Compton had not once taken a single cue from his brother.

"No it's not, Brad," argued Compton, his eyes now glued on the heavy machinery toiling in the clouds of red dust as they waited at a stop sign.

"Why don't you find that jazz station you like," Brad said, willing himself to be composed and peaceful. In front of them the traffic was not only thicker these days, it was also exponentially more dangerous. Or was it because since Compton's injury Brad thought of the almost endless ways one could become brain injured?

A truck with a Confederate flag blew by, jacked up and sounding every bit like a race car, the wheels as tall as a man. Trash from the ditches flew into the air, gliding back down as dust and smoke swirled over the windshield.

"Great," Brad said, mostly to himself. Even before he knew what was happening and what he was doing, Brad was grabbing instinctively for Compton's arm. For a person with a traumatic brain injury, and moderately impacted gait performance, Compton could slip away in an instant when he wanted to, even if it took most of his energy. He was out of the car and starting across the road, his stronger arm waving wildly in the air, his entire body lurching. He was yelling at the machinery operators, who couldn't possibly hear him over the deafening motors. Brad sprinted into the road and pulled his brother into the ditch.

"You dirty motherfucking fi-fi fuuuuuh!" shouted Compton. Brad held on to him until the road was clear, Compton swearing the whole time.

Back inside the car, Brad managed to get Compton buckled back into the seat. It was late now, and Brad would have to rush to drop Compton off at the Paradise Club and make it back across town to his office.

"You can't do that, Compton. You can't run into the road like that," he said, trying to keep his own voice steady. Compton's roan hair hung in all directions, and he was drooling onto his polo-style shirt. He wiped at it, sniffling.

"I'll get it," said Brad, reaching for a napkin in the glove compartment. He cleaned the spot from Compton's shirt and began fixing his brother's hair. He thought of his own hair—the thing, the hairpiece—now packed away in his briefcase. He was fairly certain he wouldn't wear it today, but still, he had the conversation with himself. If not now, when? It was the mantra on the packaging. Compton tolerated the primping for a few more seconds then jerked the brush from Brad's hand. He began to brush at his hair himself, almost ripping some of it out where the curls had stuck together.

"Not so hard," Brad said, looking at his watch as he checked the road again, ready to turn from the lane. Compton began to cry, still fixing his hair.

"What is it, Compton?" Brad said, his voice tight. Compton shook his head and tossed the brush to the floorboard.

"Today is a special love day," Compton finally said, blowing his nose into the same napkin Brad had used to clean him up.

"Is that some kind of theme today at the club?" asked Brad.

"No," said Compton, looking at Brad with his old wry expression, as if he thought Brad was a little on the slow side himself. "I mean today is our special, special love day. Peaches and me."

"Oh," said Brad, distracted. He was tempted to honk his horn at the driver ahead of him, an SUV the size of a land barge, creeping along, looking at all the signage posted at the various subdivisions in progress, probably jotting down price ranges and builders' numbers. The lots out here had been selling before a single truss had been raised, but lately more and more auction announcements in the paper gave way to foreclosures. The license plate on the SUV read: "Ohio, Birthplace of Aviation" and under that, "One Nation Under God." Brad tried to fight the word "Yankee" from entering his mind.

"Pay attention, Brad," said Compton, his mood swinging back toward the playful. "Today is Valentine's Day in the summer. It's love's purest hour." Compton winked. "Trust me, bud."

Brad laid on the horn until the SUV pulled over. As he passed by, he noticed that the driver was a middle-aged black woman. She mouthed, "Sorry," and Brad couldn't shake the feeling of being a total ass.

In a few miles they passed Kyle Tyler riding a minibike in a field. The guy was addicted and had a mullet. He'd been arrested so many times for DUI that the state had prohibited him from owning or driving a car for ten years. Now, as he hopped over ruts in the field, his black hair fanning out behind him, all Brad could think of was scalping him. Only a fool would wear his perfectly good, full head of hair like a nineties country music star. Kyle whirled around in a circle as Brad stopped at the four-way. For a long moment he watched him in the dusty field, as Kyle stopped and tilted back what Brad guessed was a beer. "They shouldn't even let him own that thing," Brad said, but Compton didn't answer; he was busy staring dreamily into the distance.

Everyone knew Kyle made something illegal inside his father's barn, but most of the people who had known the guy had moved away, sold their pieces of property to developers. Now, Whitchfield County sheriff's deputies tried raiding the place about every month, but someone had been tipping Kyle off, and even though they scoured the barn and house the cops only drove off with their ears ringing from his dog Curty's rabid barking.

Brad pushed the pedal to the floor and sped away. In the rearview mirror, Kyle was giving the sky a thumbs-up, his thick hair like a helmet as he mounted his squatty hog.

Compton slept the rest of the drive to the Paradise Club. He wasn't getting enough sleep at night, Brad thought. They were both restless these days, waking in fits and starts, most nights more like small naps interrupted by a series of intense if not beleaguered interactions. So Brad was surprised when Compton woke up immediately as the car rolled to a stop under the aluminum awning of the day program, alert and smiling. "I'll see you later today?" Compton asked.

"Of course," Brad said, remembering the treatment planning meeting. "I'll be back."

Compton nodded and started to get out of the car, one side of his body ignoring him. "Good. There are some things we need to talk to you about." He was nearly at the front sliding doors of the Paradise Club before Brad registered exactly what his brother had said. Compton had never used the word "we" when talking about his treatment plan meetings; if anything, he'd hardly acknowledge that the meetings even took place. Sometimes the staff let him attend, and he'd sit quietly with his hands on the table, head down. Compton looked so vulnerable, his body language conveying everything, that he, too, was deflated at how his brain had let him down. "We," Brad said out loud as he pulled away from the curb, stopping halfway down the drive to let Compton's fellow program participants cross. An enormous man with buckteeth waved at him as if they'd been friends since the dawn of time. "We," Brad said again, turning his brother's words over in his mind. Maybe it meant that Compton was taking some responsibility for his own time. The people crossing in front of Brad's car seemed to take forever, some of them shuffling the same way Compton did. A woman with clown-red hair flipped him off, and he drove away slowly, muttering, "We."

four   It was close to lunchtime. Brad was on his way to the restrooms to put on the thing. As he rounded a corner, a young secretary, too young for him, he realized, but nonetheless perky and cute, stopped him. They'd started having friendly interactions, with Brad trying hard not to stare at her pretty, oval face.

"Hey," she said, flashing a smile. She asked Brad how to bill mileage reimbursement on a form.

"I can help you with that," he said, drinking in her scent, something fruity, the smell of a young woman who'd only recently stopped using cola lip gloss. She leaned in close to pay attention as Brad showed her where to print her trips. When she said thank you, smiling again, maybe even flirting a little, Brad felt a small toot escape his clenched rear end.

"You're welcome," he said, praying that the gas would stay put. But an awful odor crept in between them. The secretary crinkled her nose as Brad tried to use idle chitchat to distract her. "Did you see how bad traffic was today on Seventy-five?" he asked, while the woman took a half-step back, looking around her, apparently searching the area for a rotten lunch item.

Brad's face throbbed red. "I mean, it was bumper-to-bumper out there," he said, his bottom tighter, trying to stave off another little deadly bomb to no avail. The secretary scrunched her face. She turned and walked away, as offended as if Brad had groped her. He said below his breath, "Sorry."

His embarrassment still pulsed along his face, his heart beating rapidly as he slipped into the restroom with his briefcase and secured himself in a stall. "Fucking pills," he mumbled to himself as his stomach churned.

Brad locked the stall door and retrieved the thing from his briefcase, along with a handheld mirror that had been his mother's. He was aware that if he had a heart attack at this precise moment, a co-worker might assume—when they wrenched the dainty mirror from his hands—that he was indeed a "confirmed bachelor." That's how they would say it here, he thought as he fumbled with the hairpiece. They'd be genteel about it. The owners of Watsons Convenience Store, Inc., where he worked, were fourth-generation southerners. Walter Watson looked just like his great-grandfather, whose picture hung on the boardroom wall. Walter's son, Toby, a muscleman who'd married a former Miss Georgia, looked the same. Strong-jawed, with deep-set, blue eyes and, of course, blessed with the thickest of black hair, styled to convey privilege Brad would never attain. Not that he wanted it, the handed-down company with all its social perks, but still. It seemed Toby's type always had hair, and lots of it.

Toby was Brad's boss's boss. Brad despised having to speak with him. According to Toby, everything was "super excellent": a new franchisee, the new office space, or the bridge named the "Walter P. Watson the Third" bridge, over State Road 92 near the west entrance of the college. He had a persistent sniffling condition, like what you might get from cocaine abuse, but was in fact due to his carpet allergies. The entire new office complex had wooden floors and sleek polished marble, nowhere for allergens to hide, constructed that way by the Senior Watson so his boy wouldn't suffer. Toby was a few years younger than Brad but carried himself like his father, the president, shoulders thrown back, his torso open toward the crowds, and chin tipped to indicate a vision. He once told Brad that he was "super excellent" when Brad had accidentally hit a hole-in-one at the stupid company picnic, held at the huge children's game palace the Watsons also owned. Brad had plucked his ball from the cup, set right under the mouth of a red, white, and blue hippo. Toby watched him and then spoke.

"Hey, don't you have a retarded brother? Hangs out by the city square? Yeah, at that program?"

Brad couldn't tell whether Toby's inflection indicated at least a small amount of sincerity.

"That's right. He lives with me," Brad said, instantly wanting to grab the cologne-ridden Toby by the collar and lay out just how Compton Orville's brain, even after being pulverized, could outthink Toby's wee little medulla, compute circles around his paltry cortex.

Toby said, "Huh," rubbing his chin, like his daddy did. "Well it sure is nice to see real family values these days, I mean the way you take care of him and all." Then he walked off, probably to make sure the guy with a retarded brother didn't want to keep talking. For the rest of the inane staff party, classic rock blaring over the Bose speakers, Brad lashed himself for having said, "That's right," agreeing that Compton was something he wasn't. That night, Brad brought home Compton's favorites: creamed corn and yeast rolls, apple pie, and mashed sweet potatoes, nothing that could even come close to an entrée.

Now in the restroom stall, the hair system seemed to lay down against the crown of his head much better than it had last night. Brad adjusted it and paused to consider whether he could get away with wearing it back to his desk. Sheila, his secretary, or rather the secretary for all the field supervisors, might even like the new look. Brad had a thing for her, even though she was married. He loved to listen to her whisper into the phone with her husband, giggling a throaty sort of passion, as she licked her lips and told him she loved him. She was older than Brad by more than five years, almost forty, but from what Brad could make out from the phone calls, she and her husband lived a life of complete bliss.

Someone opened the restroom door and Brad listened as the faucet blasted water. The man sniffed and spit into the trash or the sink, Brad couldn't see. Brad slowly removed the thing from his head, irrationally afraid that whoever it was might burst into his stall and point at his head and heave with laughter, calling others to join in. Before he could stop it, the hairpiece fluttered out of his hand and to the floor just under the partition, roosting like a hairy turtle a few inches outside the stall. Brad bit his lip. "Shit," he mouthed. If he made too much noise, the person would spot the rug on the floor, but if he didn't move fast enough, the same thing might happen. He crouched down off the toilet, trying not to think about what staph infection he was opening himself up for. He could see the man's pant legs, the shiny shoes. Brad pawed at the hairpiece just out of his reach. The man started whistling, then his cell phone rang. Brad calculated the distraction and went for it, nearly crawling completely out from under the stall to snatch the hair. He reversed the move and stashed the hair back inside the briefcase, thinking only of how he would scrub his hands until they burned.

"Hey, babe," the man blared into the cell phone. Just because it's little, Brad thought, doesn't mean you need to yell into it!

"Let's meet over in Spalding County. It's safer." There was a pause, as the man listened, his feet fidgeting, scuffing the floor. He was sniffling.

"All right, babe. Can't wait to see you. I know. We'll talk about all that. Okay. Super excellent. Bye."

Brad brought his knees to his chest, sitting on the toilet as if he were in high school, sneaking a smoke. The faucet gushed again as something hard, probably wads of hocked-up spit, smacked the back of the waste can. The expensive shoes grazed the marble as the man walked toward the door and left, the space now buzzing with silence.

Brad waited a bit and made the decision. He'd attend Compton's meeting with hair. Men with hair had a woman, and apparently sometimes two. The image of Jennifer Hunton, the woman he was to marry, pored into his mind. He couldn't recall a day in recent memory when he hadn't thought of her. Compton had betrayed him, slept with her nearly a decade ago, a brother's treachery lost in a damaged brain. Could you ever forgive someone if that same person couldn't remember they'd wronged you? Brad stood up and straightened his suit. He was grateful for at least some of Compton's memory loss, but bitter also; his brother had beaten him at the game of moving on, a sibling rivalry lost inside a damaged brain. If only Brad could forget it, too.

As Brad left for Compton's treatment team meeting, Sheila winked at him and told him good luck as he passed her desk. She was the one who had taken the frantic messages over the past year. She was the person who knew better than anyone how complex keeping Compton out of trouble could be. As he waved back at her and popped a smile, Brad thought, "That I am in love with her, she doesn't know." The phrase "in love" probably wasn't right either, he knew that, too.

"Don't forget, Brad," Sheila said, "you've got a three p.m. meeting with the zoning board about the new store going in at Wheeler Street," her flawless face looking at him with wide eyes, mouth set toward her one dimple. Just what the world needs, Brad thought, another convenience store that will be out of date before the last tile is laid.

Sheila swiveled in her chair and went back to the computer, her brown ponytail swaying.

"Okay," said Brad. He left through the sliding doors and walked across the black pavement to his ratty Sentra, worn and ugly on the inside, the vinyl sticky from all the cups of sugary coffee he and Compton had spilled on the morning drives to the Paradise Club. In the parking lot, the Watsons, father and son, had special spots reserved for them. Each drove whales, XL Yukons, both black, with the company logo plastered on the sides.

Brad took the scenic route, crossed over Tarheel Bridge and past the brown pastures with real estate signs erected at the fence lines, the word "commercial" printed across the billboards. He took a shortcut using Sandy Plains Road. Before long, the car emerged from the dry countryside. Brad peered through the window at vacant strip malls and boarded-up anchor stores, only to drive just a bit farther where he saw a new collection of retail stores, Wal-Mart and Target resurrected and open again in a newer block of shops. One solitary, enormous oak tree had been purposely left in place, built around, its roots tucked neatly under fake brick pavers. These days, Brad was told, as part of his training, it takes only one tree left untouched to make the shopper feel connected to the natural world.

Brad pulled off at one of the competitor's convenience stores. It was all glass and chrome, spacious, but stocked with low-end food labels. "The trend," President Watson had told the assembled staff at the company gathering, "is to offer the consumer private label grocery items at the same place they buy gas."

Brad jaunted into the Jiffy-Mart! and walked briskly into the bathroom. He realized he was starting to think of "the thing" as his own hair. On the DVD, the makers of the hair system had tagged this phenomenon "Identity Acquisition," meaning, the narrator said, that "the wearer of such a fine hair system will begin to see the hair as his hair, as part of who he is."

In the mirror, he looked pleased. After ten minutes of messing with the adhesive tape and the styling gel, he thought his hair looked natural. It was odd for Brad to be feeling positive, but that's what gave him more energy as he carried his briefcase to the Drink Island and prepared a mixture of Fortress Energy Drink and diet soda in a 64-ounce megacup. As he paid, Brad watched the young woman behind the counter, seeing whether she would notice his thick coif. It was a little itchy and it felt like he was wearing a mashed baseball cap, but Brad sensed it was secure, which was his biggest concern—that it might fly off like on a bloopers episode on TV. The clerk gave him his change and chimed out a hello to the four people who pushed their way into the store, not one seeming to notice Brad's new do. He hopped into the Sentra and sped onto Memorial Drive.

five   The parking lot at the Paradise Club was cobbled and broken, pieces of tarmac turned over like charcoal briquettes, tufts of grass pushing up between hundreds of cracks. Brad yanked the emergency brake and took a deep breath. With the engine off, it was instantly hot in the car, the summer drought brutal. Brad checked to see whether there were any other people in their cars, waiting as he was to go inside. There weren't, so he pushed down with both hands on the hairpiece, making sure the adhesive tape was secure.

It'd been nearly six months since Compton stopped the violent outbursts. The doctor had said to expect them, that his moods would swing like a pendulum. Brad was warned that the law might be involved and that these were simply the issues involved with a brain-injured person. "More and more we are seeing our brain-injured patients ending up inside the correctional system," a social worker told him at the hospital discharge meeting. "That's not where they belong. We want to prevent that from happening to your brother." She handed Brad a pamphlet for the Paradise Club and told him how to make an appointment via the hotline number. The woman's hand brushed his during the exchange of the paperwork, and Brad thought for a moment about asking her out, but her desk held several photos of her and a man.

Early on, Compton's anger was usually directed at himself; he was irritated and seemed ready to beat his busted brain back to how it used to be, quick and sharp. But over several months, he seemed to accept his limitations, grow into the way his mind and body now operated. It was like he reveled in the extra time he needed for nearly everything, as if some hidden pool of calm patience had been unearthed during the beating. If Brad allowed himself to recognize it, he would call his brother "wise" now, a term he'd never associated with Compton before.

Smart as hell, yes, even brilliant, but in the past Compton was rash, driven to experience the world in a rush. Now it seemed he was content with savoring moments, enjoying the very same everyday tasks he used to brush aside as a waste of time. The other idiosyncrasies, like his problem with eating entrées and his out-of-control rage at the developers, were maddening, Brad thought, but at least he wasn't in jail. As Brad grabbed his briefcase and opened the car door, he thought he wasn't sure he liked how easily Compton gave in to the disability.

In the conference room, there was a squadron of staff sitting in a semicircle, each with their version of a legal pad. The room smelled of Pledge and erasable markers. This was the worst part, Brad thought. He would have to listen to each staff member recount his brother's misdeeds over the past month. Some kept their head down and merely mumbled through their observations: client tried to touch a female's breasts, client was noncompliant during lunch, client used several curse words during the demonstration on how to clean a toilet, and the list went on and on. But others would sit up straight and stare directly at Brad's face. He assumed this was some new technique taught in the more modern social work degrees at the university, because the intense eye contact was generally found in the younger staff members, the ones who sipped Starbucks coffee as they flipped through their scribbled case notes, the paper crisp and indented.

For nearly forty-five minutes, Brad listened or pretended to. His hair didn't seem to attract attention. No one said, "Wow, you look great, Mr. Orville," or "For your own sake, take that off and restore your respect." It was as if the staff wanted to rush through the regular talk to get to something awful. Brad braced himself, thankful that a fan was at his legs, blowing cool air.

The program director, Mrs. Tantum, excused everyone except

a younger woman with "Donna Welsh, MSW" printed on her name badge. Brad noticed she wasn't wearing a wedding ring. The program director had an odd expression on her face; her lips were pursed, as if trying to contain a smile, but she seemed a little scared, too. He was nervous as they looked back and forth at each other; he had the idea that this might be some kind of "Scared Straight"-style intervention about his hair system.

"What is it?" he managed to say, hands crossed on the table, back erect. He felt himself blinking too much and tried to stop.

The two women looked once more at each other, scooting their chairs closer to the conference table. For a moment the two women looked almost like little girls playing dress-up. The program director cleared her throat, her earrings jingling. "Mr. Orville," she said, her hands white at the knuckles, "I'm afraid we've got some news that will come as a shock to you." The MSW nodded in agreement, clearly using her active listening skills probably honed at Bowman College, where Brad and Compton's parents once taught agriculture and sociology.

Out in the hall Brad could hear his brother; it sounded like he was upset. Brad stood up to see what the problem was, but the director beat him to the door. She popped her head out the crack, Brad behind her. He could hear her mumbling something, probably giving another staff member a command, but Compton only got louder. "I'll be the one to tell him, damn it!"

"What? What is it?" Brad said, the room growing hotter. He wanted to push the director out of the way but resisted the urge. "What's going on?" he said, willing himself to use the same voice he did when meeting with the contractors Watson hired to build the stores, calm and direct. Mrs. Tantum turned and shut the door behind her, apparently keeping

Compton from barging in. There was mild kicking at the door and then an anonymous voice from the hall: "Peaches is on break now. Let's go have a pop with her." Brad heard his brother's foot dragging the floor as Compton made his way toward the canteen.

"Please, sit back down," said Mrs. Tantum, her face flush. She smoothed her suit jacket and sat.

She folded her hands and looked Brad in the eye. Somewhere an air conditioner kicked on, blowing an icy breeze over their heads. "Your brother, as you know, has taken an interest in a woman named Peaches. He calls her Jesus?"

"Yes, I know. I'm sorry he keeps bringing people to the program. I'll talk with him," Brad said, an audible sound of relief escaping his mouth. He knew that Compton had gotten into the habit of bringing new "friends"—people he met on the street, at the park, in the grocery store—into Paradise, installing them as clients sooner even than the staff seemed to notice.

"No. That's not it. Your brother…" She turned toward the MSW and gave her a nod. Was she being trained? Brad noticed how fair her skin was, and that she wore a tangy-smelling perfume.

Donna Welsh piped up. "What the director is trying to say, Mr. Orville, is that Compton and Peaches got married last week. They went to the courthouse last Wednesday afternoon and came back with the license." She handed a piece of crumpled paper to Brad across the table. He turned what was apparently a marriage license over and looked at the back, half expecting to find some type of indication that it was a novelty item, like the fake newspapers with your very own contrived headlines they bought at the state fair as kids.

The director spoke again, her face whiter now. "It's legal and all.

We called the probate court about it as soon as they showed up here and spread the news, but because they are both their own guardians, I'm afraid there's nothing we can do." She swallowed. Brad was unable to speak, his throat tight and dry.

"Besides, there's more," the director continued, seeming to have gained confidence. She walked to a small window that looked out onto the smoking area. Brad tried to speak, staring at the piece of paper in his hands. It had a coffee stain right where the name Orville was printed.

"Compton and Peaches, which is her real name, by the way," Mrs. Tantum paused and bowed her head as if to pray, "they are going to have a baby." The a.c. died down and the room grew hotter.

A baby. Compton was married and was going to be a father. Was going to have to take care of a baby. Something in Brad was weighted down with the familiar sense of betrayal. The hairpiece was just another part of what felt artificial, something there but not talked about. Brad saw the future before him like a dark wall, edging closer and closer, fixing to squeeze the life out of him.

"Mr. Orville?" asked the director.

"Huh?" Brad said, but it didn't feel like it came from him. Air was simply being forced from his lungs.

"Peaches is an African-American woman." The director watched him for a response, her eyes somewhat squinted.

Brad frowned. "Why would that matter in the least bit?" he demanded, his face instantly red. Before Mrs. Tantum or the MSW could answer, he stood up, pushing his chair back with some force, the back of it slapping the wall with more impetus than he'd wanted.

"You people disgust me," Brad half shouted.

"I'm sorry, Mr. Orville," said the director. "But to some, it would matter. To others it might be the largest concern. Believe me, I'm married to a man from the Middle East. Here," she motioned to the world outside the windows, "it does seem to matter."

"Sorry," said Brad, the anger draining out of him. The director was looking at him with what he thought might be concern. She murmured something else, approaching his side of the table, something about the whole thing being hard to digest. Brad imagined a foot-long sandwich or an entire cake.

A wife and a baby to take care of, Brad thought, the words thudding around his brain like bowling balls. He thought of Jennifer Hunton, his own lost marriage, and it fueled another bout of anger. Compton was brain injured, and still, he got a wife and a family.

Before he realized what his body was doing, he was in the hallway, confused and reckless feeling.

And then he was shouting, again the words coming from some place inside over which he had no control. "Compton! Compton! Get out here now!" he felt like punching someone. The hairpiece itched mightily and he longed to rip it off.

The director was beside him now, then managed to place herself directly in front of him, holding him by the forearms. "Mr. Orville. Please. Relax."

Brad bit his lip and frowned. "Where the hell is my brother?"

"Compton is not on this side of the building." She lowered her voice. "I will go get him and Peaches. Please return to the conference room where we can talk about this rationally."

The thing on top of his head was feeling damp, heavier. It smelled, he realized, standing there watching the eager, serious eyes of the director, something akin to shoe polish or rubber cement. He thought of when he and Compton were kids, and they'd build model airplanes or mess with a chemistry set that required goggles and rubber gloves.

Their bedroom smelled like dry leaves and formaldehyde. They listened to KISS and AC/DC while they mixed potions and pretended to be rounding up classmates for lobotomies.

For a moment, as Brad stood there blankly looking at the director, he sensed he might be losing it. His hands shook. A few of the program's attendees had gathered around, sensing something might happen that would make the day mildly interesting. Mrs. Tantum tried to guide Brad back to the conference room. He pushed her off and headed toward the exit, the young MSW looking on, as pale as if she had spotted Big Foot.

"I'm due back at work. Tell Compton I'll see him later," Brad said, his hands jittery, mouth lolling like his brother's. He held his hand over his mouth, as if about to puke. Outside, Brad hurried past a group of smokers and down the sidewalk toward his car. The sun pounded the parking lot, heat waves coming off the ruined pavement, the vapors making cars look as if they were melting. Someone hollered, "The radio just said there are forest fires starting."

SIX Once he had driven several miles away from the Paradise Club, Brad found an empty lot in front of a strip mall that only five years ago had thrived but now sat desolate and weedy. He peeled the hair system carefully from his head as though he were slowly scalping himself; the tape pulled at his skin. Brad wasn't ready to wear the piece to work, and might never be, he thought, anxiety thrumming in the pit of his stomach. He wasn't sure what Sheila or the other staff at Watsons would say. He could imagine Toby pointing at his head, saying, "Super excellent," the entire office staff gathering around to take a gander at the hairpiece themselves. The accountants might find it helpful, a symbol that they, too, could look better, improve on themselves. The women in Sheila's secretarial pool might even be brazen enough to ask to touch it, passing it around like some new item from Mary Kay. Brad knew the marketing department, men younger than him, hipper men, would view the hair system as a prop, something to stimulate their thinking around a funny advertisement. They'd ask Brad to star in it, his one line as he sported an obviously bad rug: "Bring you and your little friend into any Watsons store and get a family discount!"

Now he tucked the piece into the plastic baggy, staring dumbly down at it in his lap. He hit the steering wheel twice with his fists, rapid-fire punches. "Fuck!" he screamed. The saliva at the corner of his lips reminded him of Compton. He shook his head, then straightened in the car seat.

Brad snorted air and took a deep breath. He put his seat belt on and placed the hair system inside his briefcase. Outside the car, more heat waves shimmered off the blacktop. "I'll just have to take control is all," he said to himself. "He can't be a father. He couldn't possibly be." He sped out the lot, heading for work.

On the drive back Brad took a longer route, trying to calm himself. He passed the Whitchfield Botanical Gardens, tangles of ivy climbing the white brick, quadrants of lush shrubs, sprinklers spraying silver. Their parents used to bring Brad and Compton there when they were kids, and the sight of the neatly manicured hibiscus plants brought the memory of his mother and father to him with a pang.

The Orvilles had been married more than forty years when Sarah died just six weeks after Milo. He'd been diagnosed with a brain tumor and was gone in two months. Sarah tried to keep the farm and her teaching going, but in the end she gave up, wanting to be with her one true love, at least that's how Brad eulogized her at the spreading of her ashes.

That Compton would become brain injured just a year later would've seemed absurd to everyone in attendance. He didn't offer a personal eulogy at either funeral, but instead read Seamus Heaney poetry, smiling at the crowd from under his dark sunglasses. If Brad remembered correctly, there were two women with his brother at his mother's funeral, a blonde and a brunette, skirts instead of dresses, but he could never set that notion rightly in his head, so he assumed he was wrong.

Brad steered the car through a busy intersection on the outskirts of town. Classes were letting out at Bowman, and the sidewalks were teeming with kids who looked like they should be in the ninth grade. He stopped at a pedestrian crossing and saw in his head his parents again, working in tandem at their own garden as the sun tried unsuccessfully to sit; the entire horizon glowed golden, crows filling the air over the corn, glinting dark green in the strong sunlight. Milo Orville could tell the temperature outside by counting the number of cricket chirps per minute; he knew how to splice plants to bloom exotic flowers and what bark made the best parchment paper; he could play melancholy folk songs on a harmonica he'd made himself. Their mother told the boys she'd fallen in love with him at the same college at which the Orvilles eventually became tenured; she wanted to marry him because when Sarah Grady asked Milo Orville for directions to a building on campus he drew a map that looked like it was ancient, precise and elegant. "It was as pretty a thing as I'd ever seen," she told the boys as they sipped peach tea made from their very own trees. "Like a piece of art."

Brad shook his head as if to clear it, realizing the cars behind him were passing by in annoyance, probably, but none of them had honked or even acted angry as they cruised past his open window. In this town, their university was something holy; it was the anchor of a southern concern, of a county trying with all its focus and attention to shrug off stereotypes.

Brad accelerated, thinking about how best to deal with his brother, now married and a baby on the way. He pondered what they'd say to each other, how the conversation would go, how it would probably turn into an all-out battle, as it usually did. He realized that he had no idea what to say to his brother, no idea at all.

Another fight entered Brad's thoughts, but he pushed it back, seeing once again only his fiancée's clothes in a heap near the bedroom door, Jennifer Hunton running down the beach after him, Compton, too, both wrapped in blankets. Brad sped through a changing light.

He parked the car and got out at what appeared to be a small field by the side of the road. Another little stop before heading home, just some extra time to think. The dirt was moist from the water sprinklers and mulched with grass and twigs. Brad walked in the space where he knew the new Watsons convenience store was set to open. In a few days this same patch of earth would become concrete and rebar; the gas pumps were already in place, and the building would be built quickly, too, in less than two weeks. Brad squatted and scraped the ground with a piece of wood, thinking about the trees they used to climb just beyond a lone stand of honeysuckle. He'd come here to think when he was a kid, not telling even Compton about the plywood platform he'd tacked way up high in an oak, a secret assembly of limbs that only Brad knew how to climb.

Near a Dumpster something sounded, a rustling of paper, minor clanging, a small bell maybe. Brad looked up to see an old man clad in what appeared to be deflated white balloons. Brad stood, squinted. The man dragged a tattered and enormous suitcase on rollers; it was held together with gray duct tape. He stooped and plucked something from the ground, gave Brad a mild wave.

"Can I help?" asked Brad.

"You're not open yet are you?"

"What?" asked Brad, his hands in his pockets, discreetly trying to find a few bucks to give to the guy.

"I said," the man called over the noise of a cement truck passing, "you don't open up until the store's actually built, correct?"

Brad fingered some bills in his pocket. "Right, it doesn't open for a couple of months. I meant, can I help you, you know, like some money maybe?"

The man moved closer, pulling his bulging suitcase along, white tufts of pearly hair springing from underneath a baseball cap. Brad saw that the deflated white balloons were actually a great number of plastic grocery bags, and they fluttered as he approached. Up close, the guy was actually clean-shaven and orderly. Something about the way he stood before Brad didn't fit. The only dirt on him was a large stripe of black across his left cheek; it looked like paint. "Sure," he said. "That'd be great."

Brad handed the man a five-dollar bill. "My name's Brad."

"Preston," said the man, sticking out his hand. They shook. Brad wondered what Compton would do. He'd probably have the guy at the Paradise Club within the hour, through intake and fed, a whole host of services in place.

"Why the bags?" Brad asked, pointing to Preston's chest, where a clump of ten or so stuck out of a raincoat. The guy had to be sweltering.

"I just pick 'em up. Best way to carry the things."

Brad nodded.

They stood quietly before each other. "Well," said Preston, "I better get back to work. Thanks for the cash." He circled Brad, hauling the suitcase like a mule to a wagon. He rambled over a shoddy area, then past a towering magnolia tree; it would be gone once they started the full construction. Brad watched as Preston climbed a hillock and eased out of sight.

The late evening sun dappled the clods at Brad's feet. He looked around again, trying to place the history of this land within its present demolition; it was like staring at an optical illusion, things came into focus, then disappeared. In the distance the construction rumbled on, the clap and thud of wood trusses going up. He drifted toward the car and put his hand to the door. The metal handle was warm, and as he plopped behind the wheel he realized the theoretical freedom a man like himself owned; he could do a thousand things with this moment, go as far as he'd like without a child's broken heart or a wife's disapproval. The world was fragmented; you were known in some of it and lost in the rest. But, Brad thought, at least Whitchfield County was becoming a place where a person could become lost.

As he backed up the car, he witnessed a sky as silver as a twenty-fifth anniversary, and it gave him the words he would use on Compton.

seven Brad pulled into the driveway slowly. It was hard to tell how long Compton had been sitting on the porch, the woman called Peaches beside him. Ducking to look through the windshield, trying not to be too obvious or intense, Brad thought that maybe Compton and the woman had walked all the way from the day program, leaving, then, right after he'd left. Sometimes a bus dropped Compton off or he would hitch a ride with a fellow attendee. Once he said, "A schizoid person drove me home today." He paused and rubbed his chin at the sink. "No," he said, "that's not what you're supposed to call them." Other times, more recently, he had started to call himself and others he'd met with TBI "Broken-Heads."

Compton rose from where he sat on the rocking chair and hobbled toward the porch railing; he stared at the car, as if about to salute it. Peaches didn't move from where she sat on a bench.

Brad saw that she had a lit cigarette hanging at her side, the smoke coiling to her slim shoulder, as he approached the front porch.

"Hi," she said as she stood up, a smile exposing a nice set of teeth, something Brad didn't expect. She stood and patted her flat stomach. "I guess you heard we're gonna have a child," she said.

Brad rolled his eyes, but didn't mean to. Compton glared at him. Brad rubbed his hand over his face. The heat rolled in around the three of them, swarming the porch in humidity. A fly buzzed from Brad's bald head to Compton's feet, then up. Peaches swatted at it, and when the fly landed on Brad's head again, she said, "It's on your skin up there now." She pointed with her cigarette, the ash growing like an ugly gray worm.

"Sit down," Brad said to Peaches, pointing to where Compton now sat on a garden bench. A child. They were going to have a child, Brad thought. The image of a disabled baby being born came into his head: weeks in intensive care, followed by early intervention and special education. He shook his head to clear it; he knew this made no sense, either biologically or probably even genetically. His brother hadn't been born the way he was, and he wasn't sure what was wrong with Peaches. She seemed only to be small, maybe a little addicted to nicotine, but if there was some more organic problem, it wasn't visible, either in her petite limbs or in the manner in which she spoke.

"Sure," she said, planting herself next to Compton, wrapping her arm under his and placing her head on his shoulder. They looked like they were about to have their picture taken at a dance.

"Here's the answer to the situation you two have gotten yourselves into," said Brad, loosening his tie.

Compton kissed the top of Peaches's head.

"Pay attention, Comp. Listen up here," Brad said, knowing as he spoke that he sounded like a gym teacher. Brad felt a headache pulsing in his temple, along the brow. A strong whiff of the basement mildew wafted through the open door to the house. Brad leaned to look inside. "Why is the basement door open?" he asked, looking directly at his brother. He intended the question to drip parental control, some kind of authority.

Compton didn't hesitate. "Because I showed Jesus the problem. We're going to fix this place up, get it ready for the baby. We can't have that moldy down there making the little one sick." He stood, his bad leg crumpling slightly under his weight as it did when he was especially tired. At the sight of this, and of the perspiration soaking his brother's shirt, Brad realized that the two had indeed walked all the way from the day program, most likely using the unsafe fescue ditches, crossing intersections that the sprawl into the exurbs had made as treacherous as whitewater rapids.

Peaches flicked her cigarette into the dry yard.

"Don't do that," Brad scolded, stomping down the steps. He bent and picked up the smoking butt, held it like a poisonous asp in his hand as he jogged back up the steps to the porch.

"This is dangerous," he said, using his best instructive voice, "this is flammable." Brad mashed the cigarette into an old potted plant, where there was only a clump of black loam.

"Sorry," said Peaches, shrugging her shoulders. "I didn't think about that. You're right, Mr. Orville." She fiddled with her nails, looking embarrassed. Brad felt bad for a moment, thinking maybe he'd been too hard on her. There was something about Peaches that was very likeable, even though it had been only a few minutes that he'd known her. She was sweet, you saw that right off. But he still had to talk some sense into them.

"That's right," he said. "You two haven't thought about anything except yourselves." He pointed at Compton, then at Peaches. "And that's going to stop right now."

Compton's eyes filled with the kind of anger that they had as kids. More than most brothers, they'd ended up in fistfights, quarreling over everything from whose turn it was to ride the minibike to calling dibs on driving the old pickup through the orchard.

"Don't point at my wife, bucko!" said Compton, taking a step toward Brad.

Brad bit his lip, counted to five, let out a long breath. It was no good.

"Shut up, Comp. Just shut up," he hollered. The machinery toiling across the road had begun to fade as the dusk crawled in. Brad grabbed Compton by the arm and tried to push him down on the bench.

Peaches turned her small head from side to side, bird-like. "Don't," she said. "We can all work this out if we just respect each other's feelings."

"Get your fenneled hands off of me!" Compton yelled. He pushed back against Brad, and for a moment they stood face to face, staring.

"That's not a word, Compton," said Brad, taking Compton by the shoulders, turning him around, trying to seat him. Compton elbowed Brad in the ribs.

"You all should stop," said Peaches, holding her stomach, tears in her eyes. "Some people wouldn't even think you're related!" she said shakily before collapsing into sobs, covering her face with her tiny hands.

Finally, Compton wrestled free, pushing Brad aside. Brad backed down the stairs.

"I'm taking you two to a lawyer. You'll get this annulled." Brad pointed at them both as if holding them at bay with a gun. Compton tried to comfort Peaches, patting her little puff of hair.

In the dusty yard, Brad turned a full circle, then took off walking at a fast clip, crossing the bridge, not daring to look down at the litter. He began to lightly jog along the driveway, heading toward the construction area across the road.

Brad watched as the sun completely died behind the tree line, the darkness as thick as the heat. He plopped down on a barrel and blew out air. Even at this distance, he could see that the porch light of the house was on, faint shadows moving about. He imagined another possibility, one where he was simply home for a visit, Compton, too, their parents still alive. Both brothers had young women on their arms, lips shiny with gloss, but it took too much energy to keep the fantasy going, so he looked up at the stars. As kids, they'd sprawled with their parents on soft quilts, preparing to watch whatever night sky event Milo had been anticipating: meteor shower, eclipse, some obscure planetary setting. "Mars won't be this close to Saturn for another forty years, boys, that means you'll be in your fifties," he'd say, pouring them steaming cups of apple cider from a silver thermos.

"Shit," Brad said blandly. He rubbed his bald spot and stood up again. One more try. Compton usually handled things better the second time around. Sometimes he even apologized about his behavior. Brad skulked back across the development field, down through the ditch and across the road. As he walked up the driveway, the nighttime sounds were thick, crickets and tree frogs almost quacking, bats dipping down out of the darkness, only flashes of movement, the swish of their path, like black falling stars. Boys, bats use echolocation to determine where an insect is, much like when you shout into a canyon. A plane droned overhead, lights blinking. In the distance, a lone dog howled. Along the fenced pasture the yellow eyes of a tomcat gleamed when a car rushed by.

To his surprise, Compton and Peaches were still on the porch, thumb wrestling of all things, laughing, a can of pop between them. They didn't look up as Brad hauled himself onto the porch again.

Brad sucked in a deep breath. "You have to give the baby up for adoption. I can't afford to take care of all three of you, and besides, the baby needs two parents that can really provide for it." The words came out like bullets.

Compton stood quicker than he should have been able to. "That's just like you, Half Pint! You don't want me and Jesus to be married or have a baby because you have no faith!" Compton surged toward Brad and took a very weak swing at his head. He missed him by more than a foot, his slack fist slicing bleakly through the humid air.

"Compton, calm down. It's the only thing that makes sense. If you two want to be married, that's fine, you can see each other at the program, but we're not moving her in here and leaving me with the burden of a baby and two people that can't take care of themselves, let alone a child."

Peaches stood, too, and shivered, then mashed her cigarette out on the porch with her tiny foot. Brad frowned. He couldn't imagine the small woman would ever make it through childbirth. He wanted to yell: it wasn't only about a wildfire. you're pregnant. don't smoke!

Peaches's clear eyes roamed over Brad's face. She allowed her gaze to linger; it was an empathetic expression, purposeful, as if she could help—somehow. And for a moment, Brad almost wanted to believe her. He looked away.

"Get out!" yelled Compton, pointing toward the field of construction equipment. "You don't have to stay here. I'm the oldest, not you." He pulled Peaches to his side. "This lady loves me and I love her. We'll be married for fifty years and you'll still be nursing your wounds."

Brad took a step back, astonished. Even before the beating, they'd never spoken directly about Jennifer. Not once. Brad wasn't certain if Compton now even knew that he knew. In this latest world in which they found themselves, Brad secretly feared he'd never be able to use it on his brother, something that before he'd always had in his back pocket, a tool that would allow him moral superiority. Now, the force of Compton's statement, the confidence it had, made Brad long for his older brother the way he used to be, wish that he would once again swagger instead of waver, purse instead of slurp, quote novels rather than sitcoms.

Compton stepped toward the house with Peaches clutched at his side; Brad couldn't help thinking of a lame rooster and a bantam hen. Compton fumbled opening the screen door, the whap hitting him on the back instead of the jam.

"Now if you don't mind, my wife and I are going to retire. It's been a long day," he said through the screen door, the gray mesh filtering the porch light. He blew Brad a kiss, a taunt he'd used in the past. The couple disappeared into the darkness of the doorway, and Brad was left on the porch with a cold sweat and anger, and the dread of a man alone and doomed. A moth fluttered around the ocher light spreading from the utility pole. "This isn't over, Compton," he muttered, sounding like a child even to himself.

Brad swallowed. "Acting tough isn't going to change my mind," he called, lifting his voice louder with each word, thinking it would help.

The light in Compton's bedroom flipped on and Brad could hear giggling, then Compton's voice: "Mrs. Orville, would you let me carry you over this threshold, darling?"

Brad sat down on the bench. The radio in Compton's room began hooting sweet jazz. Brad clutched his ears and bent over, staring at the ground, only darkness. His head felt naked now without the hair system, naked and wicked.

eight For two days Brad acted as if nothing had changed. He dropped off Peaches and Compton at the day program and made dinner at night, a smile plastered on his face, never bringing up that a strange woman now lived with them. He'd asked a staff person at the Paradise Club if they knew anything about Peaches. He was told she'd come a long way with her recovery, but he didn't know what that meant, and they didn't get any more specific. He imagined a meth addiction. The woman leaned into him and whispered, "She does have sticky fingers, though."

On the third night of Peaches's stay with them, Brad served spaghetti. Compton watched as he ladled out the pasta, looking at Brad with what could only be taken as admiration. Finally he stood up and hugged Brad slightly. Brad nodded and filled their plates with more spaghetti, which Compton ate, apparently less concerned about the definition of an entrée now. "Thank you, Bradley," Compton said, and the ease and naturalness with which he spoke reminded Brad once again of what his brother used to be like—funny and smart-ass, all at once. Back when Compton still sold radio airtime to small businesses in a ten-county area, he'd tell Brad: "We should just sell that damn place and be done with it. Neither one of us is ever going to live there. Besides, we could get a pretty good penny if a professor from the college wanted to be Thoreau. That is, if they don't turn it into a parking lot first."

The spaghetti sauce made a red ring around Compton's mouth; he'd flicked a great deal of it onto his shirt as well. Brad started to say something, thought of maybe tucking a napkin into Compton's open collar, but he didn't want to risk a confrontation.

Besides, Brad was harboring a new plan, one that would involve covert tactics and, if he allowed himself to admit it, even a bit of utter deception. He was biding his time, and for now—tonight, at least—there would be peace in the household.

A bouquet of purple coneflowers sat on the table, inside one of their mother's many vases. Brad chewed, examining them. A bow had been poorly tied around the bottom of the vase, hanging loosely. As he looked closer, Brad realized the bow was made from a bolt of drapery cloth that his mother had used to decorate pillow cases, line pot holders, a floral pattern that seemed to go on and on.

As Brad finished, pushing his plate away, Compton stood and started to clear the table with Peaches following his lead. She smiled at Brad as she removed his plate. Brad watched as Peaches nabbed a pewter bottle opener from the table with a furtive pluck and shoved it into her pant pocket so quickly that he thought he might have imagined it.

"I made dessert," Peaches said as she refilled Brad's glass, pouring too much, the glass overfilling, and spilling some onto Brad's lap. "Oopsy!" tittered Peaches. "Look what I did!"

"Don't worry," said Compton, "I'll get that."

"No, I'll get it," said Brad, still distracted by Peaches's apparent theft. He'd half hoped that the reference the person at Paradise had made to Peaches having sticky fingers had something to do with her love of some sort of Hostess snack.

As Compton bent to wipe the floor, he almost collapsed, swabbing the mess, his eyes bulging, the wild one going white. He finished the floor and started to pat at Brad's crotch where the wine had spilled. "Excuse me, Half Pint," he said. "I swear I'm not trying something."

Peaches giggled.

"Stop it," said Brad, trying to take the hand towel away. Compton nearly fell into Brad, losing his balance.

"I can do it," insisted Compton.

"Geez, Comp, let me get it, will you," said Brad, snatching the dish towel from Compton's hand. He wiped at the spill on his pants, letting out a long breath. Tonight was supposed to be peaceful, he reminded himself. Keep it cool. "Thanks, though," he murmured. "For trying. I appreciate it."

Peaches approached the table with a pie and Brad saw that it was pumpkin. It was midsummer and hotter than Brad could remember, but she'd baked an autumn treat. He realized now that she must've prepared it sometime earlier and popped it into the stove before he even started dinner. The entire time Brad had cooked the spaghetti and made the salads, he had been smelling the pungent spices from the pie, thinking he was going slightly loony, imagining how the kitchen had smelled back when Sarah worked in it.

The top of the pie was perfect, ginger colored. Compton beamed. "That's some tasty tart!" He playfully pinched Peaches's bottom and she swatted him.

She cut the pie and served it, a large wedge for Brad. Brad tried not to let her small hands, vulnerable and obviously hard worked, touch his heart, but it was difficult. He swallowed and told her, "This looks real good, Peaches," and she smiled.

The three of them took bites, each squirreling their faces up immediately.

"I did something wrong," said Peaches, half smiling, pushing her plate away. "Sorry."

Brad could tell immediately the pie had an extravagant amount of nutmeg. His tongue was instantly numb, and his mouth held the flavor of scorched liquid soap.

Compton didn't flinch; in fact, he dug into the pie more. "I think it's delicious," he said, his mouth full. Peaches laughed and shrugged her petite shoulders. Brad fought a smile. He watched Compton devour another slice, Peaches now sitting in his lap. "I baked it from memory," she said. "I guess I should find a recipe for it."

Brad's tongue felt swollen as he stood up. He went to the sink and drank a full glass of water. Still at the table, Compton said, "Yummy to this boy's tummy." Brad watched as he kissed his wife full on the mouth, and Brad realized that he was smiling himself. He looked away and bit his lip, watching as the water swirled down the drain.

Focus, he told himself. Focus. It was time to get his plan going, which involved bringing a psychologist to the house for a sort of secret assessment of Compton's and Peaches's skills, something that might form a report for a judge to review. Brad gulped down another glass of water, watching out of the corner of his eye as Peaches, who now stood at the kitchen counter, tucked two silver spoons into her back pocket.

When Brad got to work the next day, he heard the latest rumors and avoided Toby Watson Jr. as they passed in the hallway, pretending to be engrossed in paperwork as he walked. The word was that a huge development was going in somewhere in the county and that the Watsons were working secretly and diligently to get the scoop from the Whitchfield County commissioners, particularly a younger politician named Dean Birdsong, a descendant of the ubiquitous Birdsong family, a clan that had lived and governed in the county since just after the Civil War. Brad went to high school with Dean; they'd played on the baseball team together, but that's been more than fifteen years ago.

At lunch, Brad walked down the hall toward the restroom, as office doors opened and shut softly, their gentle clicks indicating that important behind-the-scenes meetings were taking place, power brokering, too. If he'd seen right, Commissioner Birdsong's SUV was in the parking lot.

Brad dried his hands and looked in the mirror. His shiny baldness seemed chrome-like. Along with the new plan to deal with Compton and Peaches, Brad let another idea bang around inside his head: how to best use the hair system to begin seriously dating. Surely if Compton could find a woman to marry, he could, too. After the mess with Peaches and Compton was taken care of, put to rest, kiboshed, he'd take full advantage of his new hair. Brad wet a paper towel and scrubbed the shine from his dome, but it didn't work. The skin there was tight and in perpetual gleam. He gave up and left the restroom, thinking about his phone conversation earlier in the morning with the psychologist Dr. Banter. They'd set a time to meet, that evening, which would be fine except that the doctor had night blindness and would need to be driven to the Orville home.

It was all about timing with Compton, Brad had said. The therapist had scoffed. "We'll play this on our terms, not theirs." The comment had worried Brad; still, if he was going to make a move, he couldn't wait, and, after all, Banter's Web site stated he was an expert in disability issues.

In the hall, Sheila seemed to simply materialize. "Oh," she said, somewhat breathless, "there you are. The folks at the Paradise Club just phoned. Compton was in a fistfight. They've taken him to the emergency room. Apparently he needs a few stitches in his head, but he's all right." Shelia winced and handed Brad a folder. "Also, the Watsons want you in a meeting in twenty minutes with Commissioner Birdsong."

"Why?" asked Brad, his eyes squinty.

"I guess because you work here and know the area where the new development is going in."

"No, I mean," said Brad, his face red, "why did Compton get in a fight?"

"I don't know, hon. I think they said something about his wife. So it must be that he thought someone was his wife," said Sheila.

"Yeah," said Brad, not contradicting her.

"He'll be fine, Brad. I'll call the hospital in a little while and check on him. The program's bus will take him home. Apparently he's got some peaches, too, he wants to bring home. That's what the nurse there said." She shrugged her shoulders, used to Compton's unpredictable behavior.

"Okay, thank you," said Brad, hands fumbling with the paperwork in the folder. He read the top sheet, smelling Sheila's perfume. She watched him.

"Hey," he said. Sheila was already nodding. "This is just on the other side of our house."

"Yes. That's why they want you in there. That and I think Birdsong mentioned he knew y'all." She tilted her head and listened. "I think that's the phone." Brad noticed her shiny lips, red and perfect. "Read that," she said, pointing to the folder in his hands.

"Crap," said Brad, flipping the folder shut.

"Oh, you'll do fine," said Sheila, heeding the endless trill of six phone lines.

"It's not that, really. It's just that Compton doesn't like all this development. He'll flip if he finds out they're building right next to us." Brad watched as Sheila jogged toward her desk, holding her index finger up, disappearing around the carpeted corner. "Hold on, hon," she called. Brad waited a few moments, then slipped down the hallway with the folder tucked under his armpit. He didn't want to see a guy from high school, particularly one who had excellent hair.

He had ten minutes to peruse the paperwork, which was essentially parcel dimensions and diagrams of the area, but he couldn't stop thinking about Compton. Brad quickly dialed 411 and got the hospital number. The usual automated customer service menu was droned into his ear. He hung up and dialed Sheila's extension. "Hey," he said, rushed. "Will you get the hospital for me?" Sheila agreed. "He's fine, Brad, but I'll see if I can get them on the phone." Brad hung up and situated his body in the chair, made himself focus on the documents. The next sheet was a glossy 8 x 10, an aerial view of the entire road. A large red circle encompassed where 210 homes on three-quarter-acre lots would be slapped together. "250K to 425K," it read in small print. "Tennis, pool and nature trail." When Brad read the last part he, too, could feel himself escalating like Compton, sickened by the sprawl. Watson and his cronies called it "stretching prosperity."

"A fucking nature trail," Brad said under his breath. "It's already nature." On the last page, an enlarged mock-up of the Watson Ultra-Convenience Mart beamed seductively from the page. It was to be the biggest yet, but with everything compact so it still felt like an escape from the grocery store to the consumer. The back of each page contained a stamp he'd read before: "Intellectual Property of Watsons Convenience Store, Inc. Authorized Use Only. All Parties in Violation of its Use Shall be Prosecuted Under the Full Statute GA-04c-d3R." Brad shook his head and looked at the brass clock on his desk. He was due in the monstrous Watson office in just a few minutes. He got up and tried not to look at his bald head in the window as he passed.

At Watson Sr.'s office, Brad stood in the doorway. "Come on in, Brad," said the elder Watson, shaking Brad's hand with such force it seemed a socket might pop.

"Hey there," said Toby, smiling like a jack-o'-lantern. He grabbed

Brad's numb hand and pumped it several times, too. Toby's hand was damp, and his strong cologne couldn't cover the smell of nervous sweat. Dean Birdsong remained seated, a thick, tall paper cup of Watsons coffee in his hand. On his lap a stack of papers rested, the top one the aerial view Brad had tried to decipher.

"Sit down, sit down," said Watson Sr., motioning to a plush couch.

"Super excellent!" said Toby, a little lower. The guy might be on speed, Brad thought. On the walls, rows and rows of Watson family pictures hung, including several of Toby's wife, her long blonde hair almost white in the photos, her skin too dark, as she balanced a tiara on her head and kept a bundle of roses from smothering her.

"Hi, Brad," said Commissioner Birdsong, his face neutral, but his lips set firmly; Brad thought he might be hiding some irritation. For the next few minutes Brad and Dean chatted about the high school, the new football coach Brad knew nothing about and how each had opted out of attending his respective ten-year reunion. There was a sadness about Dean Birdsong that Brad had not expected, and Brad wondered where it came from. Finally, Dean became the commissioner once again. "You gentlemen want to let Mr. Orville here in on our problem?"

It was then that Brad spotted Dean's piece. He'd planned not even to look at Dean's hair, knowing it would only throw him into a deep reverie about the dicey game of genetics. But there it was, thick for sure, but something about the bangs, how they seemed too aligned, perfect, struck Brad as artificial, though he wasn't certain. He didn't want to stare—one, because it was rude, but two, because he'd been in Dean's shoes, felt the scrutiny of eyes. Yet something about a guy who'd attained public office wearing a hair system made Brad feel nothing less than happy, even tingly with positivism. He'd seen him only on cable TV, during the Whitchfield County meetings, tapping his gavel and saying yea or nay, voting on sewer lines and rezoning bills, tax-rate mileage and city limit boundaries, and he hadn't been able to get a close look at the man's hair, much less detect a hairpiece.

"The thing is, Brad," said President Watson, "there are people in this county who don't want to embrace prosperity." Toby nodded his head in agreement. If he said "super excellent" one more time, Brad didn't know if he could resist twisting Toby's nose until gristle cracked.

"People in Whitchfield want everything to stay the same," said Watson, a little whiny. "We're part of a great economic boom. This . . . " he motioned with his hands toward the window. Outside, a hazy horizon hung over the metropolis, of which Whitchfield and the eleven surrounding counties orbited like the sun, the New South rising again through pollen and smog. "This is what makes America great. Growth, opportunity, capitalism, all of these things are right here, right now."

"Uh, Mr. Watson," said Dean, "can we move this along? I've got a meeting with the airport administration at two."

Before Watson could respond, Toby jumped in. "What we think would be super excellent, Brad, is if you could help us out on this deal. People in your neck of the woods, they don't want more development. And it would just be great of you if you acted as a Watson ambassador, you know, work the neighborhood, get folks to come on board. That's what would be super of you, Brad."

Brad thought he saw Dean shake his head but couldn't be sure. Watson smiled at his son, and nodded. "Thanks, son," said Watson. "How about you getting us some more coffee?" Toby stood and started to open his mouth, but then thought twice. He walked to the door and left.

"Brad," said Dean, "this is really pretty simple here. We don't want you tromping around your part of the county trying to sign people up."

He itched his head with an index finger, a telltale sign, Brad thought, of a hair system.

"But," interrupted Watson, "it sure wouldn't hurt if you spoke highly of what you know is a great company."

"As you can see," said Dean, ignoring Watson, as he pointed to the sheet with the aerial view, "this new development butts right up against your property."

"That could spell a very large windfall for you boys," said Watson, his eyes flickering; he had a large mole on the bridge of his nose.

"Or," said Dean, "it could simply mean peace of mind. If ever you need more care for your brother, a way to finance a different life, you've got it."

Watson jumped in. "But if you don't help us out then the whole development might get stalled, and . . . "

"Mr. Watson, let's just stick to the facts here. There's no reason to get this process bogged down in speculation."

There was a small pause and Brad saw that Watson seemed miffed for a moment but then forced a wide smile. "You're right," Watson said somewhat stiffly. "Of course you are, Commissioner Birdsong. Brad here is a fine employee of Watsons and I'm happy to have him." He looked like he couldn't think of anything else to say.

"Just think it over, Brad. If you are interested in selling, I could hook you up with a friend who brokers these kinds of things. But I'm sure that's not what you wanted to spend time thinking about today," said Dean, tucking his pen into a notebook.

They all stood and Brad was glad for not having to actually speak much. Watson pumped his arm again with bravado, a twinkle of hatred in his eyes now, but maybe Brad was mistaken about that. "You should come to our church some Sunday, Brad, bring that brother of yours."

Behind Watson, Dean rolled his eyes. Still, Brad felt that Watson's offer had an element of sincerity; God had his lambs, and Watson seemed to believe in helping them find a home.

Down the hallway, Sheila was walking toward Brad.

"Compton's fine. They put four stitches in a cut over his eye." She handed Brad the notes she'd taken. "But when I talked to him on the phone he told me to tell you that no one hurt his peaches." Sheila crinkled her brow, amused. "Why is he so concerned about some peaches?"

nine   Brad drove to Dr. Reggie Banter's office on his way home. The office was in an industrial park, one of the first built ten years ago when the county's expansion was just wishful thinking. The complex now looked dated, reminiscent of the 1990s, with taupe brick and hunter green and mauve address placards, framed with faux brass. Office parks like these dotted the perimeter of the county, most sitting idle, fallen prey to the optimistic view that if they were built, large numbers of employers would come. Still, it didn't stop the county from erecting finer, more modern complexes farther in, ones that did seem to hold high-tech start-ups and brokerage firms that worked with Indian and Chinese outsourcing.

Next to Dr. Banter's office was a different kind of day program. The name was screen-printed on a large rectangular banner: "Happy Valley Enterprises, a program funded by Whitchfield County." Dr. Banter had told Brad on the phone he'd be waiting outside his office. "It's next to a mental retardation facility. I've got red hair."

Dr. Banter stood by a vending machine, his hands in his pockets, a satchel dangling over his shoulder. Brad noticed his hair first, of course, a ponytail no less, and as red as a tomato. The doctor chatted with two older men who Brad thought might have Down syndrome, their russet shocks of hair gelled into shrubs, identical, squat bodies clad in denim walking shorts, tube socks pulled up to their kneecaps, and black orthopedic walking shoes on their feet like boxes. Brad got out of the car and approached the doctor. Dr. Banter introduced himself, then told Brad, "This is Ronald and Donald, twins. They've been on break too long so they can't chat." The two men laughed and didn't seem to care about the jibe.

"You got no hair upstairs," one of the guys said, his stubby teeth exposed, grinning.

"That's not nice, Ronald," said Dr. Banter. "Apologize to Mr. Orville."

"It's okay," said Brad.

"I sorry," said Ronald, snickering. "I've got my granddaddy's hair." He rubbed his hand over the stiff hair and jabbed Brad in the side. "You got a little peter, too," added Ronald, which sent Donald into wheezing laughter.

"Hey," Dr. Banter scolded them, his finger pointing at Ronald. "I said that's not nice."

Brad waved it off, smiling. "It's fine, really."

Banter seemed to ignore Brad.

"I sorry again," said Ronald, but Donald jumped in now.

"Papaw says baldies have teeny dingers!" The two brothers elbowed each other in laughter, giddy and bouncing slightly on the balls of their feet.

Finally a woman's voice beckoned them inside, and Ronald and Donald scooped up their fanny packs from a table, buckled them around their stocky waists, and were gone, clucking and grinning like they'd won the lottery. Brad called after them. "Nice to meet you."

"They need more behavioral instruction," Banter said as they walked to the car. "They are happier than what their situational life experiences should allow." Brad nodded, though he wasn't sure what the doctor was talking about, and as he opened the car door and slid himself inside, he wasn't sure about the doctor himself. Brad felt a shot of misgiving; how was it wrong for someone to be happier than what life allowed? On the drive to the house, Brad filled Banter in on the day's activities. The Paradise Club had taken Compton to the emergency room, where a sedative was ordered and the stitches were sewn. Compton was resting at home with Peaches, the woman he'd married covertly.

"Is the woman in question impaired?" Dr. Banter asked at a stoplight.

"I'm not sure," said Brad, his hand sweaty on the wheel, eyes tired from the day. "She's obviously got something wrong with her. I mean she attends the Paradise Club, and they run programs specifically for people with problems." Brad decided to keep Peaches's kleptomania to himself—why, he didn't know.

"Because if the female is somehow impaired, that is, if she exhibits certain nonsocial traits, or appears to be a threat to herself or others, I could arrange for a 1013."

Brad's stomach turned. "A 1013? What's that?"

"An involuntary committal. It would keep the female away from your brother until she was further into the pregnancy. Then I could ask a friend a favor and get her into a hearing for endangerment of an unborn child. The family law court judge is all for getting people off the streets and into places where they belong. He would be a real ally in this."

Brad glanced at Banter in the passenger seat. His flaming hair looked like a warning, some kind of sign that he'd had a troubled child-hood himself, picked on, and forced to accept names like Carrot Top, Red, and Rusty.

"I don't think that'll be necessary," said Brad, trying to sound much more offhand than when they'd spoken on the phone. Did I cue this guy into thinking I wanted some kind of radical approach?

"You'd be surprised, Mr. Orville. These things can get out of hand quickly. Before you know it your brain-injured brother will have two, three, four kids with this female, and just like that the state's got five new mouths to feed. Better to nip it in the bud now than have to use taxpayer dollars later."

Brad noticed a booger hanging from Banter's nose. "You've got a . . . " said Brad, rubbing his own nostril, then looking back at the road. Banter didn't get it. "You've got a bit of a thing there on your lip," Brad said. Banter caught on and rubbed his mouth and nose vigorously.

"As I was saying, taxpayers deserve to know we're doing all we can to minimize their exposure."

"I don't believe that way, Dr. Banter. And let's get this straight. I'm paying you for counseling and that's all. You got it?" Brad tapped the brakes too hard at the entrance to the driveway, lurching Banter forward in his seat, the red ponytail slapping his cheek. Dusk had started to fall, the sky a pale yellow as bats swirled and dived for insects. "I don't need any political commentary, just some kind of assessment."

"Okay," said Banter, looking out the window. "Have it your way, but for a hundred dollars an hour I'd think you'd want the most bang for your buck." Another booger had appeared. How did this guy get into the business of human service? Brad made a mental note to check the guy's references again. "Just meet them and give me an assessment of their needs, their barriers. Things they can't do on their own. And you might want to use the mirror there," Brad added. "It's back."

Banter yanked down the car mirror. "I've got allergies. I can't help it."

Brad watched as the doctor pulled down the mirror and swiped at his nose, sniffing. Was he making a huge mistake? Brad wondered. Should he just tell the guy to go fuck himself and be done with it? Beside him, the doctor was digging into his pocket for something. Brad pulled the key out of the ignition and stared up at Compton's window, glowing yellow in the night. He thought of Peaches and her tiny hands holding those cigarettes, how vulnerable she was. He thought of the baby on the way, how he or she would need so much, the kind of care and attention he was pretty sure he had no idea how to give. And then there was Compton, Compton with all of his own suffocating needs. Christ, he needed some help. Maybe Banter was an asshole, but at least he was something. Brad took a deep breath. Tough love, he murmured. Banter was sticking some kind of inhaler up his nose. "Allergies," the doctor said stiffly. "Can't let them get the best of you." Brad nodded and bit his lip. "Okay," he said. "Let's go inside."

The house was dark except for Compton's window, where light spilled out onto the large white columns, casting a small area of the porch below in a golden radiance.

"Let me take you up to Compton myself, Dr. Banter. I don't want Comp getting spooked."

The two men walked to the front porch. The door was locked. Brad tried the doorknob again. It wouldn't twist. The humidity was thick, spoiling his dress shirt, mapping his back with sweat. "I don't know what the deal is here. We never lock the door," said Brad.

"Compton," he yelled, stepping off the porch down a few stairs. The light in his brother's bedroom went off.

"Looks like your brother and the female are already in possession of the authority here. That's not a good sign, Mr. Orville." Banter rubbed his chin at a withered patch of goatee.

Brad ignored him. "Compton? Hey, open the door! It's Brad!" All around them the darkness grew, katydids clicking in unison. Across the road, the lights of the heavy machinery flashed on, as they crawled about the red earth, digging and working like dazed fire ants. It was the first time the operators had started working after dusk, which meant that a time line had been crunched, a new schedule was now in full effect, lest the developer lose thousands in "on-time" completion bonuses. Now Compton would have the opportunity to freak out over the excavation, day and night. Just yesterday, Brad had woken up to Compton standing at the end of their drive, beating on a trash can lid with a spatula and shaking a fist. "Go to helluva, stinkers!" he was yelling. Peaches was beside him in a baby blue nightgown, rubbing at the small of her back with one hand, the other raised in a tiny fist. It had been all he could do to calm his brother down.

Brad fiddled with his keys and couldn't find one that worked. He punched in the home phone number on his cell. It rang and rang inside the kitchen. "What the hell," Brad said to himself. He could probably get in through the cellar door, but that would mean facing the dark, wet basement.

"In all likelihood your brother is demonstrating his control over you by this stunt," Banter said. "The only thing to do is leave. Take me home and get yourself a hotel room. That way his obnoxious behavior will have a direct negative consequence."

"Yeah, but what if something is wrong in there? They might need help."

"So what? If they are going to act like children, then treat them like children. There's a whole renewed interest in eugenics these days," said Banter, "precisely because of this kind of situation."

"See," said Brad, shutting his eyes, then opening them. Could this guy be any more of a jerk? "That doesn't make sense, doctor. I wouldn't leave children in a house that is locked and spend the night at a hotel. Either your logic is totally off or you don't know the first thing about taking care of children, and I don't think I want you meeting my brother after all. Please go sit in the car, and when I'm inside and everything is okay I'll take you wherever you want to go."

"No, that's not what I meant. The use of strategic sterilization could be beneficial to local, state, and federal governments as a way to save billions in tax dollars."

"Please," shouted Brad. Then he stopped. "Please," he went on, controlling each word. "Please, and I'll pay your hourly rate plus another hour of travel time if you'd just go sit in the car."

Banter moped off, his shoulders hunched. Brad went to the back of the house, where a mossy smell clung to the steps. The screen door was latched. He walked carefully around the side of the house, the darkness deepening. At a high windowsill, he stretched on his tiptoes and tried to peer inside. Only bleak outlines of the sofa and the entertainment center came into view, the rest of the living room clad in shadow. He leaned against the house and tried to call the home phone again. Nothing. A spider had taken advantage of Brad's preoccupation and crawled onto the back of his neck. Brad swatted at him, then stepped into a cobweb. He rubbed hard at his bare head.

"Shit." He rounded the corner of the house back to the front and stomped up the steps. Maybe Banter was a little right after all. "Compton!

Open the door right now," he commanded. Brad glanced back toward the car.

Peering through the glass on the front door, Brad saw a figure move stealthily from behind a chair to the opposite wall, ducking down, motioning for someone to follow. Brad looked at Banter in the car, but as it was darker he couldn't make anything out now. Another figure started to move from the same spot behind the chair toward the wall. This person was thin and didn't seem to be in any rush. The dragging leg gave it away. Brad heard whispering. Someone said, "Come on, dude. Come on." More murky figures fluttered inside the living room, at least three other people were in the dark house.

"What in the hell is he doing?" Brad said as he quietly glided off the porch and snuck around the side of the house.

Brad heard the back door lock twisting. Someone pushed the door hard, making a cracking sound. Could Compton have brought new "friends" home from the emergency room? Did Peaches have family they were sneaking into the house?

Brad braced his back against the wall of the house just shy of the back door steps. He heard voices; apparently the new friends or whoever they were were now outside.

"Shit," said a young guy's voice. "I thought he was going to nab us for sure."

"Like seriously. Comp, your hair looks great like that. The color is killer!" Now Peaches giggled. Brad was tired, sick of being outside in the heat, and annoyed at this game. He stepped around the corner of the house and came face to face with what seemed to be five people, all of whom jumped and screamed.

There was Compton, sporting a dye job. His hair was caustic

blond, cut short now and spiked. He had a large bandage above his eye. Peaches clung to his side, while the three other people scattered.

"What in the hell are you doing, Compton? For Christ sakes I couldn't get into my own house." Brad looked over Compton's shoulder as the three kids, college age, huddled under the elm.

"It's cool. I just dyed his hair like mine is all," a girl called.

"Get back here," said Brad. They didn't move. "Come on. I'm not calling the cops or anything." The three of them scuttled back to the house. Brad opened the door and ushered them inside.

He poured them all iced tea, remembering that his goal was to get Compton and Peaches to realize how foolish they were acting. Befriending their friends was the way to go.

Around the kitchen table they talked about what had happened up to the point of Brad finding them hiding in his house. "We just thought you'd be pissed is all," said a kid with blue hair. "So we were trying to get out of here without a bunch of shit." The boy's name was Tiny, he informed Brad. He had a pierced nose and a tattoo of a unicorn on his wrist. The girl, older than Tiny, was named Ratchet. She licked her chapped lips a lot and had greasy hair the color of Compton's when it was brown. The other boy, a kid with a line mustache and eye makeup, was Ratchet's cousin, Gordon, Ratchet said. Gordon didn't talk and kept playing with a pack of unopened cigarettes.

"So you all three attend the Paradise Club then?" Brad asked, watching Compton put a fifth packet of sugar into Peaches's iced tea, stirring it with a pencil. Compton turned away, and Brad saw Peaches sneak a handful of sugar packets into her purse.

"Yep," said Ratchet, apparently the talkative one in the bunch. Compton licked the pencil and started to put it back in the glass.

"Compton, why don't you use the spoon I laid out?" Peaches said.

She looked sleepy. Brad examined her midsection, half expecting to see a little bulge, but there was only a splatter of old paint sprawled at the bottom of her black Jack Daniel's T-shirt.

Compton picked up a spoon but kept the pencil immersed in the tea.

"Now, explain to me what happened today," said Brad, turning to Compton. "And why these folks have gotten involved." He was using his best mediation skills, cocking his eyebrows, "listening with his whole torso," as the books said to do, but the truth was he wanted to throw them all out and lock the doors, hide inside the house like they had, and wait for them to leave.

"I'd rather not speak of it, actually," Compton said stiffly, almost with a British accent. He had one pinky cocked and a snooty look on his face. The three kids burst out laughing.

"Man," said Ratchet, turning to Brad, "that's why we love being with your brother. He's got a great sense of humor. He keeps us rolling during break times." Brad was puzzled. She seemed fine—not "impaired" at all—even smart, and besides her greasy hair Ratchet was attractive: slim, yet curvy.

"Yeah," said Gordon, finally speaking. "The day he brought me back to the Club, I thought I was going to bust a nutter."

"Did Compton bring all of you to the day program?" asked Brad, piecing things together, trying to guess in his head what each kid had: mental illness, brain injury, an addiction to glue. Again, Ratchet seemed normal in almost every way.

"Uh-huh," grunted Tiny. "Compton is our peer tutor. We voted him that at the Club. We're studying the eco, uh, the eco . . . " Tiny looked to Compton.

"The ecosystem. Remember, the ecosystem in Whitchfield County is under attack. We've got to do something about it," Compton intoned like their dad Milo might have, professorial yet down to earth. Maybe Compton had inherited their father's knack for organizing and motivating people.

Brad rubbed his head, the skin damp with sweat. He thought to scold them all and warn Compton about dragging people to the program, about getting riled up over something he had no control over, but he stopped himself. Just get some balance back here. Tomorrow I'll find a new psychologist who's sane and everything will work out.

"Yeah, we're starting a group called, um, what is it called?" asked Tiny.

Ratchet spoke up. "No, there's no group, remember. That guy is nuts. He's burnt down houses, you guys." She turned to Brad, "Compton started a group called Eco-Greenies." Ratchet smiled at Brad, as the table erupted in laughter again when Compton pretended to straighten the knot of his imaginary necktie. Peaches yawned.

"Okay," said Brad, clearing the wobbly kitchen table of the glasses of tea. Tiny hadn't touched his. Under the bright light, Compton's hair looked ridiculous. It was nearly chrome colored. His eyebrows now appeared as though they'd been painted on with shoe polish. Peaches had drifted off and was slightly snoring.

"Hey," Ratchet said as Brad dumped the slivers of melted ice from each glass into the ceramic sink.

She stood up. "It's cool that you're fine with Compton and Peaches. I mean, interracial marriage is still not okay down here."

Brad was about to respond, but just then Banter tromped into the kitchen, his red hair mussed on one side; he looked like he had just woken up.

"Are you ever taking me home?" he said, a disgusted look on his face.

"Hello there, fine comrade leprechaun!" said Compton, smiling broadly. Beside him, her head nestled into his shoulder, Peaches hummed a little in her sleep.

Ratchet widened her eyes with curiosity. "Would you like some tea?" she asked.

"What?" Banter said. "No! I just want to go home!" He looked like a child for a moment, ready to stamp his foot with impatience.

Brad felt something like laughter begin to rise in him. It was all so absurd—the red-haired doctor, Tiny with his blue hair, and Compton with his surfer-dude blond. He took a deep breath, let it out. "Sure, doc. Let's go." Brad grabbed his car keys from the counter and pushed Banter toward the front door. He called over his shoulder, "I'll be back in a half hour. Don't lock me out again."

ten It took almost an hour to drive the night-blind doctor home. On the ride, he didn't say much, except for telling Brad that the whole group in the kitchen looked weak in character. Brad had turned the radio up, and for the remainder of the drive the college radio station blared cacophonous new age metal.

When he got back home Brad peeked in on Compton. He was sound asleep, Peaches spooning him, her wooly hair poking out from the blanket. It was hot, but Compton loved to stay warm, and apparently so did Peaches. Brad watched. They didn't even seem to be breathing. After a few seconds it scared him, so he crept inside the room, stepping on a squeaky floorboard. Brad flinched, then tried to remain perfectly still, holding his own breath now.

"Hey," said Compton, sitting up some in the bed, propped on one elbow. His chromatic hair shone in the light slanting in from outside. "You okay, Half Pint?"

Brad stayed frozen. "Why do you call her Jesus?" he finally asked, relaxing some.

"Because she's my savior," said Compton.

"Oh," said Brad. "Compton?"

"I'm still here."

"Things will get better."

"How could they?" Compton smiled and put his hand on his wife's shoulder, looking down at her in quiet slumber. "I just don't know how they could, Brad." Compton sunk back into the bed and was asleep again as Brad tiptoed out, pausing for a moment before he pulled the door shut. Sometimes Brad couldn't square the new Compton with the one he remembered. Before the accident Compton had converted to Catholicism, even though they were raised without religion, nothing to convert from except the love of nature. But he'd done it, Compton told Brad, because of the women. "They're pent up, brother." Compton liked to recite his favorite writers, along with the names of the saints, to anyone who'd listen. He had more dates to attend mass than Brad did for Saturday nights.

As he walked toward the bathroom, Brad tried to connect the learned Compton to the guy who sometimes knotted his shoes rather than tying them. Brad gargled and thought about the way Compton spent his nights before Peaches showed up. During his first few weeks home from the hospital, Compton went on and on about Marilyn Monroe, how she talked with him at night while they were in bed together. When Brad went to check on him one night, Compton was whispering sweet nothings into an empty picture frame. Compton had looked up at Brad and said in a raspy voice, "How about a little privacy here, Half Pint. Me and Marilyn are talking about eloping."

In his bedroom now, Brad logged on to his laptop. Somehow, as the minutes ticked by, without even consciously thinking about it, he went from finding a new psychologist to personal ads. He was now on a matchmaker site, trying not to rush through the sign-up process. He put in his age, hobbies, body type, and his annual salary range. Next a screen asked for more specific information about height, weight, and hair color. In bold lettering, a required text field stated: "For men, please describe the accurate amount of hair you have. 1) full head of hair 2) receding 3) bald [i.e., no discernible bangs].

Brad let his fingertips lightly touch the keys. He contemplated how to answer. It was late now, well past two a.m. His eyes stung as he studied the Web page. In one definitive motion, his index finger hit the number 1. He paid the monthly subscription fee and logged off. It was difficult to sleep, knowing that his profile had been posted and that women ages twenty-five to thirty-five could be reviewing his stats right now. They'd see Brad O., reachable via e-mail (bradO2525@radar. net); made between 50K and 100K a year; had his own home; worked in Whitchfield County—and had a full head of brown hair.

It was morning, rays of lemon light filtering through Brad's bedroom windows. He lay in bed, touching lightly at the hair system he'd attached when he first woke up, almost an hour ago. He'd gone immediately to the matchmaking site, where there was a message from a "Linda T.," and before he knew it they had a date planned for that very evening, at a place called the Spirit of Foods. He'd wear the hairpiece, of course, and after signing off he tried it on before climbing back into bed. It felt better than ever—natural, even—and his thoughts strayed to Linda T. and the night ahead. He pictured slow-dancing with her in this very room, the house ripe with the scent of lilacs, Brad sporting the line mustache of a great lover, Linda's entire body wrought with passion, her heartbeat thumping under her corsage. Her hands would run through his hair and she would coo with delight. He smiled, lost in the fantasy. Then his stomach clenched, and a round of gas from the damn antidepressants escaped his buttocks. "I don't know what's worse," he said to himself, sitting up and throwing off the sheets. "Smelling like a horse or being depressed all day."

From downstairs, Brad could hear Compton singing as he got ready for work. Brad carefully packed away the hair system, making sure to add the vent brush, styling gel, and adhesive tape to his gym bag.

The song Compton sang was wholly made up, something about flowers and the "birdies and bee-bees." When Brad stepped into the kitchen he wasn't shocked to see Compton down on his knee, singing into a spatula. Peaches wore a girlish maternity top, and she looked a little embarrassed. A single peony sat on the table in front of her. Compton boasted a whole snoot full of cologne and deodorant, white pit marks of the stuff rubbed off onto his dark green polo shirt.

"Good morning," said Brad, feeling like a third wheel. All the same, he couldn't stifle a certain giddiness about his plans to meet Linda T. Not even Compton and his irritating silliness could take that away, Brad thought, chewing on a piece of dry toast. Compton sang on: "Today is the day, and is the way for love in May, even if it's Julyyyyyyyyyyyyyyyyyyyyy!"

He seemed to notice Brad, finally, and rose shakily from where he'd knelt. "It's our anniversary," he said, planting a kiss on Peaches's forehead as he tossed the spatula into the sink. Peaches was wrapping utensils into Sarah's old, heavy cloth napkins, and Brad realized that she'd had to have dug them out, washed and ironed them. As her nimble hands rolled the silverware, Brad was impressed. He couldn't remember the last time they'd eaten with a full set of cutlery.

"Your friends are interesting," said Brad.

"My auntie used to work for Ratchet's grandmother and granddaddy," said Peaches.

"True," said Compton. "They were good people, but their grandparents owned slaves," he went on, pouring milk over two bowls of shredded wheat. "Isn't that right, Jesus?"

Brad was struck with how "together" his brother seemed, and wondered if maybe in some way all this romance was healing him, repairing the damaged myelin. Right now, he seemed almost normal, a touch like his old self. Soon, though, he'd probably be back the way he usually was, crying over a candy bar wrapper in the road.

"Uh-huh," said Peaches softly. "They mighta owned one of my kin. Ratchet says they had a plantation farther south. Right around where those wildfires are burning." Peaches gently placed the rolled silverware on the table, glancing toward Brad.

Brad thought for not the first time that she seemed to embody sweetness, with her soft brown skin, her eyes meek and wide. She seemed like a child—a child, Brad reminded himself, who helped herself to the occasional five-finger discount. Even as he watched, amazingly, she pocketed a teaspoon and went right on wrapping the silverware. Brad looked at his brother to see whether he had noticed, but Compton was stabbing at his shredded wheat. Maybe he didn't notice, Brad thought, or maybe he just didn't care.

Brad's mind wandered back to Linda T. as they all sat down. Her profile had read: 36 yr. old female, nursing, average weight, 5' 7, nature, animals, looking for the right guy, brown hair shoulder length, must be churchgoer. Churchgoer. So he'd have to tell a little lie. Not huge, however; after all, he did have Jesus living in his house.

"Brad?" Compton was asking. "Peaches was telling you something."

Brad looked up. They were both staring at him expectantly. "Oh," he said, trying to sound interested. "That's nice. I mean, that Ratchet is your friend and all."

Compton put way too much sugar on Peaches's cereal, added a dash to his. Brad couldn't believe it had already been more than a week that they all had been living under the same roof.

"You guys better hurry up," he said, pointing toward the digital clock on the microwave. "We've got to leave in ten minutes."

Peaches dabbed at her lips with the napkin, as if she were an extremely polite guest, Brad thought. She placed the napkin into her lap and sipped some coffee.

"Nope," said Compton, his mouth full, milk dripping. Beside him, Peaches nodded.

"What do you mean, Compton?" Brad said, his voice rising even though he tried hard to keep it in check.

"Nope, we're withdrawing from the Club. Peaches and I are going to work on the beehives today. And every day after today we're going to slowly, with just the right amount of contenibious labor, get this place back to the grand state it deserves." He smiled, a little bit of cereal falling out. "That reminds me," he added, "I need to use the genital camera. We want to take before and after pictures." Compton paused, as if listening to the sentence inside his head. "I mean digital camera."

Brad felt a fire in his neck, his temper rising. He knew he shouldn't lash out, but he had to get Compton off this track of thinking.

"Oh, I see." He swallowed hard and exhaled a long breath. "But what about your friends from last night? Those kids really need you to teach them, Comp. I mean, they're just kids. They could use someone like you and Peaches to show them how to live, make a smaller footprint on the earth. You've got to keep your ecology group going."

"Got that taken care of, Half Pint," said Compton, standing to take the bowls to the sink. "Ratchet, Tiny, and Gordon are coming over today. We'll work in the hives and cut back some kudzu, then have a quick barbecue, something from the woods, wild mushrooms, a quail if it can be caught, maybe even a few ears of corn." The string of words—lucid and coherent, none of them of his own invention—seemed to tire Compton out and he closed his eyes for a moment.

"Compton, listen to me," said Brad, pushing his chair back as he stood.

"You both need to get in the car now so I can take you to the program. Got it?" He was standing close to his brother, their noses nearly touching. Beside them, Peaches was lighting a cigarette.

Compton smiled and planted a big, wet kiss right on Brad's forehead.

"Put that out," Brad said to Peaches, reaching for the cigarette, mashing it into a saucer with a blue floral pattern. "Don't you know that's bad for the baby?"

"Ah-ha!" exclaimed Compton. "I knew you were thinking about being an uncle, Half Pint!"

Brad bit his lip. The day had barely begun and he was already tired, even with the prospect of a date with Linda T. ahead. His cell phone rang. "Oh, hello. Yes, no, I'm glad you called," Brad said as he edged into the walk-in pantry for privacy. It was Linda T. She had a nice southern drawl, dulcet and kind. Brad inspected the shelves of old canned vegetables their mother had preserved from their teeming garden. All of it needed to be thrown out, the pears and tomatoes, the corn and red beets, but he hadn't been able to toss the stuff. Each one had a label that read: Milo and Sarah Orville, and then the date and what the contents were, all printed in her perfect letters.

"Okay, great. I'm looking forward to it as well. So nice of you to confirm. You have a nice day, too." Brad walked out of the pantry. Compton was telling Peaches how not to get stung by a bee.

"Okay, let's go!" Brad said in his most chipper voice. Sometimes Compton responded to total optimism.

"You go ahead, Half Pint. Give our regards to Broadway." Compton helped Peaches stand. It seemed they were already pretending that she was heavy with child.

"It's going to be just peachy," said Compton, giving his wife a playful little pinch on the rear end. "How about this? We'll only cut needy-weedies around the place. No beehives for Mr. and Mrs. Orvives!"

Brad considered the idea. He had to get to work; he was already late as is. If they only worked on the weeds, kept away from the hives, maybe it wouldn't be so bad. He would give in on this, and then deal with getting them back to Paradise tomorrow. What was so wrong with one day off? he thought. He looked hard at his brother. "Promise?" he said.

"Scoot's honor," said Compton, crossing his heart with his hand; the way he seemed so happy and sincere almost made Brad want to believe him—want to believe that his brother was normal, that he didn't need adult day care, that they were normal. Linda T. was already changing everything, he thought, just like a good woman could.

"All right then," said Brad. "I'm going to call you every two hours to check on you, Compton, so make sure you take the cordless phone with you, wherever you go. It should work."

Compton remained in an official Boy Scout salute.

"But only for today, Compton. Tomorrow you both go to Paradise."

"Absolutely not," his brother replied, saluted hand now at his side. "But we're going to take a nap now, young Orville, if you know what I mean. You have a grand day." Compton flopped a step toward Brad and gave him a quick embrace. "It's all wonderful, Brad. Thank you."

Peaches spoke up. "I'm trying to stop. I mean, I'm going to stop smoking. Thank you for reminding me."

Brad nodded and smiled at her.

Compton and Peaches climbed the stairs slowly, the thud of his heavy leg striking the oak risers. Brad listened as they made their way to Compton's room, their voices muffled, intimate. Brad looked around the kitchen, now empty.

As Brad drove over the bridge and down the wending lane, the excavation was already in full throttle, dust and smoke drifting in masses. Brad looked to his left and saw engineers in orange vests surveying the land right next to their property. Hot pink plastic tape was stretched along the boundary, wrapped around boxwood saplings, entwined in the fencerow Milo had built with hand-hewn lumber from the rear of the property. I better call to check in every hour, Brad thought, as he passed a gaggle of men standing around in hard hats. He thought he saw them laughing.

eleven   Sheila handed him a stack of folders. "You've got to be on a walk-through for the new store in Spalding County. You know how to get there from last time, or should I print off the MapQuest directions again?"

Brad took the folders. "Nope, I remember where it is," he said walking quickly toward his small office. "I'm going to be on a personal call for a while; hold all my calls."

"All right," she said. "Everything okay?" It was times like these that

Brad could imagine that being married to Sheila would have its low points. She had tons of questions about things she didn't know, and although this proved beneficial it could also wear on Brad.

A pot of coffee percolated behind him, the aroma thick in the air. It was cold in the building as the temps outside soared. The power grid had to be bogged down, Brad thought, his neck icy from a vent above his head. "Nope, nothing is wrong. I just want some advice is all." Brad put his hand on the door handle, pausing, trying to mentally balance everything, Sheila's talking, the day's work, Linda T., the worry over Compton and Peaches alone at home.

"Did Comp get his peaches he was so worried about home without bruises?"

Brad thought of just telling Sheila about Peaches and the whole mess, but didn't. "He did. He got his Peaches home without a scratch. And his head will be fine."

"Good," said Sheila. "I'll see you later. I've got two contracts to type for O'Connor. I'll hold your calls, then?"

"Thank you." Brad slipped into his office. His stomach turned, not painfully, but he was a little nauseated. He sat down at his desk and launched the Web browser on his flat screen, clicking past ads for SUVs, shampoo, and the occasional real estate popup. He logged on to Personal Tru-Connections and clicked the Greater Metro tab under Georgia. Linda T.'s profile still didn't have a picture posted, but then again neither did his. The protocol was to ask for a photo to be sent to your personal e-mail if you wanted. Personal Tru-Connections' motto was: "There's more to a mate than what's on the outside." Brad liked this idea, but still, he wanted to see whom he was meeting. And it bothered him that she hadn't asked to see of photo of him. But it also would've bothered him if she had asked to see one, he thought.

He typed in "Linda T." and "nurse" into a search engine, and then back-clicked and added: "Whitchfield County, Georgia." A whole host of images appeared, a ribbon cutting, the new hospital, even a photo of Mr. T. with a woman named Linda from Arkansas, but nothing seemed promising. He logged off and called the law office of Joseph Randall. Brad was put on hold; as he waited he doodled, drawing a woman's face, scratching long ink lines of hair, her face becoming more and more obscured. He tossed the pen on the desk.

Brad sat back and waited. Joseph Randall came on the line and Brad went through his list of questions. The lawyer was polite and succinct and immediately asked for Brad's mailing address, his home phone number.

"You'll have to spend some time on this issue, Mr. Orville. But it's not an impossible situation. I understand these things can be difficult emotionally. Your brother's marriage can be annulled if we prove he is indeed mentally incompetent. That's where you'll need the expert testimony of a friend of mine. I'll have my secretary send Dr. Gibbons your referral. I would suggest getting this under way as quickly as possible. The longer your brother and his wife stay married—that is, without any problems—the harder it will be to proceed with an annulment."

"I had a guy named Dr. Banter set up to see him, but that—"

"Stay as far away as you can from Dr. Banter. He's got an agenda. I'm not entirely sure what it is, but trust me, he could be a real detriment to your brother. I've heard of more than one case where he made things much worse."

Brad hung up the phone. He stood up and stretched, his back achy again; it seemed he was more rife with dull pain than he could ever remember, tired, too, a little groggy, but still, it was a good day. A proper day for a date, a drink, and some stimulating conversation. Brad thought over where he could put on the hair system. The bathroom at the office wasn't private enough, but he didn't want to run in just anywhere. He settled on finding a place on his way back from the inspection near Spalding County.

His mind flashed with the images of Compton and Peaches, the beehives that they swore they'd stay away from, and the surveyors, the cloud of dirty progress billowing at the front of the farm, starting at the side of the property, too. Brad used his cell phone to call. He was surprised when Compton picked it up so quickly. There was a loud sound in the background, but Brad couldn't place it. A blender?

"What are you doing, Comp?" asked Brad.

"Peaches and me are whipping up a fruit fly smoothie. She needs all the vitamins she can get for our little pumpkin."

"Where'd you get the fruit, Comp? We haven't had fresh fruit in the house for months."

"That's all gonna change, too, Half Pint. We need to get back to the earth, eat right, you know, like Mom and Pop. Ratchet brought bananas and pears and some little clementines." Compton broke into a song about his darling Clementine. Brad could hear Peaches laughing.

"Good. Just take it easy there, Compton. You guys just stay inside today and out of the heat. There's no reason to tackle everything at once."

"No can do, bro," said Compton, now slurping from his smoothie. "We're heading outside to weed the fencerow, row, row your boats!" Brad heard the others chattering in the background, laughing. They did seem to like Compton, Peaches, too, but still, they had their problems—more, Brad was certain, than he could imagine.

"But," Brad began, debating whether what he was about to say was wise, "since you're not going back to the day program, you'll have all kinds of time to work the place. Just stay inside and out of the heat. The work will wait." Brad could envision Compton and Peaches having heat strokes, their enthusiasm outweighing common sense; they'd work too hard and pass out by the beehives, and Brad would find them covered in lumpy stings, heads swollen like basketballs. What he'd said to Compton about the day program was a kind of promise, Brad thought, a way of saying he wasn't going to pester them about going back to the Paradise Club. Anyhow, none of that would matter once the new doctor saw Compton, when Compton and Peaches weren't married anymore, and a baby wasn't on the way.

The lawyer had said Peaches was another situation altogether. Brad couldn't raise the issue of her incompetence, and even if he could, the matter would be left up to child protection; a social worker would have to determine what would happen to the baby once it was born. "They usually leave babies with their mothers, Mr. Orville. You'll need to think about what role, if any, your brother will play in the child's life. Unless, that is, you can convince the couple to abort the pregnancy."

The other end of the phone crackled with movement, as if Compton were purposely rubbing corduroy over the mouthpiece.

"Compton," Brad called into the phone, pulling the disagreeable sound from his ear. "Hey, Compton, did you hear what I said?"

"Yes," said Compton. "We're just celebrating here is all. No more Paradise Club! Hot doggies! Peaches is so much fun to hug. Here, she wants to say something to you, Half Pint."

"Compton, no, what I meant was—"

"Hello, Mr. Brad," said a breathy voice. "Thank you. We've outgrown the Club." She breathed into the phone with little scallops of air. "You're a nice man, Brad," she added, before handing the phone back to Compton.

"She's been worried you were going to be a prick about all of this. Not her words, though."

"Compton," said Brad, convinced now that he'd only made things worse. "I've got to go for now, but listen, stay inside today and rest. Everything else we can talk about, okay?"

"Sure thing, Half Pint. We'll just flimflam the day away here and keep it on the down low town." The kitchen erupted with laughter, as Compton continued with his silly riff, elated. When his energy was high, the verbal banter could be nearly as expert as before the accident, but when he was tired or disappointed, or simply bothered because it was a Tuesday, Compton could have trouble stringing together thoughts.

"Good-bye, Compton," Brad said, exhausted, then hung up.

The phone rang.

"Yes," said Brad, bracing himself for some kind of instantaneous calamity. Come quick, Compton has scaled the house and is holding a county engineer hostage with a spatula.

"Brad, Mrs. Watson is here to see you," said Sheila, using her best professional voice, indicating to Brad that the person was right at her desk.

"Who, what do you mean? As in Toby's wife or President Watson's wife?" Brad felt sticky all over, damp and jumpy.

"I'll send Mrs. Watson in right away. She'd like to speak to you." The phone clicked and Brad tried to clear his desk. Sheila called just seconds later.

"It's Toby's wife, Brad," said Sheila, rushing to explain. "She was here doing some flyers about an event to end homelessness. She just wanted to see you. I don't know what for."

Brad hung up in a hurry and took a quick inventory of her possible motives. He'd met the woman only briefly, while she was in the office last spring. They'd shaken hands and Brad felt the air leave his body. She smelled like hyacinth and her hair shone like gold bullion. The other time he'd seen her she had stopped him to ask about Compton. "How's your brother doing, Mr. Orville? I'm sorry to hear that." The beating Compton suffered made the Orvilles minor celebrities in Whitchfield County.

Maybe she knows I overheard Toby setting up a date with another woman while hiding in the stall with a toupee?

A light rap on the door and Julie Watson took over the space before Brad's desk, her long legs crossed in a chair before he could even think straight. He knew he was going through the motions, offering her coffee or bottled water, but he couldn't hear himself saying these things, only felt like some sort of protocol was being followed. He noticed he was making way too many hand gestures. Julie smiled at him. "Why don't you sit down, too, Mr. Orville. I'd like your advice on a matter."

Brad was struck by her formality, the Old South in her accent. He pictured the former Miss Connor under a parasol, saying things like, "I do declare!" and clasping her chest, fanning herself.

"What can I do for you?" Brad asked, hoping his head wasn't as damp and barren as it felt, looming over his face like a bad patch of ground.

"But before I get your thoughts on what interests me, I'd like to know how your brother is doing. I saw him last week, you know, while I was volunteering at the day program, the Paradise Club. He told me you were in the building, but I couldn't find you. The administrator said you left in a hurry. I wanted to say hello."

It unsettled him and made the whole idea of Peaches and Compton much more public than he wished or even conceived of.

"He's fine. Thank you," Brad said, fidgeting with his watch.

"Mr. Orville, I truly wish you weren't so uncomfortable with me," Julie said, a twang of authenticity in her soft voice.

"I guess I'm just a little tired this morning," said Brad. "I apologize if I seem on edge. Really, I appreciate your concern for Compton." Brad swiveled in his chair, as Julie offered a concerned smile. "Now, what can I help you with, Mrs. Watson?"

"Please call me Julie," she said, crinkling her nose. Brad marveled at her body, the way she seemed not to notice how perfect she was: slender, slim waist, with hips that made Brad want to paint her, even though he couldn't even doodle very well.

"As you may know, Mr. Orville, I coordinate the outreach programs at Watsons. For a number of years we've given money, time, and other resources to many causes, mostly to do with homelessness and mental illness." She looked around conspiratorially and pretended to whisper. "It's actually not so much what the Watsons want to do with the money as it is what I feel fortunate to work on. I had an uncle who died on the streets of Charlotte."

"I'm sorry to hear that. And please, call me Brad."

Julie smiled. "Well, I'd like to know, in your opinion, what the Paradise Club needs. I met with the administrator and certainly she has some ideas, but I wanted to know from the viewpoint of a family member."

Brad thought about telling her they could use a staff person whose sole job was to keep attendees from fornicating, but Julie just kept looking at him, no, looking inside him, staring at him woefully, blue eyes wide, lashes dark and thick and lovely.

"I suppose they could use some funds to offer more activities. But I'm really not an expert on this kind of thing. Compton's not gone there long. He's at times not willing to participate."

"Hmmm." Julie made the noise as if she were meditating. Her dress was summery, exposing her tanned shoulders. She stared at Brad. "You know, Brad," she said, now standing, "I sometimes think, when I visit places like the Paradise Club, that they've got the wrong people there. Seems to me everyone has some kind of thing that just isn't right." Julie put her hand on her hip and waited for Brad's response. He didn't have one, so he just looked back at her as if she were on-screen, answering a question posed by a handsome game show host.

"Well, I've taken up enough of your time. This was nice. I do appreciate your input."

Brad walked her to the door and held it open. Even after she left, he could feel the energy there, occupying a space not unlike a ghost, only there wasn't a cold spot, but a warm orb of electricity. Julie had left in her wake a balmy aura, something he thought was wholly feminine. His cell phone rang. It was Compton. "Hey," he said, "just wanted to let you know we're going to use those dandy-lion jobber-snips and get to whapping the weeds." Laughter burst again in the kitchen, like a theater with applause, encouraging an encore.

Compton said, "Don't worry, Half Pint, we'll be careful."

"Why don't you just work inside," said Brad. "The mudroom needs cleaning. There are dead flies in the corner." Brad imagined Compton in some terrible weed-whacking accident, blood everywhere. As it often did, his mind dragged up the image of Compton's head broken open, 350 sutures like blackflies stuck to the shaved skull.

The memory surfaced for Brad often, and as far as he could tell, Compton was haunted by it, too, only not quite as much, especially now with Peaches around. About once a month, though, it all came back to Compton, how awful the attack was. Even though—and he can't remember this, or won't—a good part of the beating was his own fault. Compton had slept with a burly mechanic's wife and the man cracked open his skull, so badly that the docs could see clear through to his brain in the emergency room before they even got him into surgery. During these flashbacks, Brad would just hold his brother and let him cry, a part of him wishing to God he could run away. But Brad knew he couldn't do that. Compton was the only family he had. Lately their common blood seemed more like Compton had been born to Brad, as if the beating had turned them into some kind of inverse family, making Brad the father to a brother's broken son, birthed from himself.

The first weeks out of the hospital, Brad walked Compton all over the farm, pointing and saying "shovel" or "creek," as Compton stared blankly at him before starting to cry. Brad would cut up bananas for his brother and feed him, even read to him. The long-ago betrayal between the two then seemed nearly insignificant, half forgotten. But somewhere, hidden under his potent desire for his brother to heal, Brad still held the idea of Jennifer Hunton as his wife and the fact that Compton had wiped away Brad's marriage as surely as the mechanic had his head.

"Oh, we'll get that mudroomer spic and spammed, too, Half Pint," Compton went on. More laughter. Brad held the phone away from his ear. His heart raced, and he wasn't sure whether he should blame Julie or Compton.

twelve The new site near Spalding County was a mess. The gas pumps arrived with puncture points from a forklift, and the county code inspector reprimanded Brad for wasting his time. To top it off, the franchisee was getting cold feet, asking Brad questions for which he had no answers. "What happens if this joint doesn't take off? Do I get my two hundred thousand dollars back? What if I want to carry soda from another vendor?" The guy was a former pine lumberman, with a long beard. He wore a Pink Floyd T-shirt and dark glasses. He asked Brad, "What if I just want to forget this whole goddamn thing and breed pugs instead?" He wrote down the number of the Franchisee Relations Department for the man, who smirked and tossed the card over his shoulder like a handful of salt. Brad said, "I thought you wanted to talk to someone who could answer your questions."

The franchisee ignored him, lumbered off, and slipped into the area behind the walk-in coolers. Brad could see he was opening a tall-boy of Bud.

Now, Brad pulled the Sentra into the Dawson City Public Library parking lot, yanked the emergency brake, and cut his eyes to the dashboard clock. Two hours. That would give him a full forty-five minutes to make certain the hair system looked good for Linda T. His stomach was aflutter once again with anxiety and expectation. It felt a little like Christmas as a kid.

The librarian gave him a cursory nod and went back to straightening tax forms on a wobbly table. Brad ducked into the restroom and was pleased to see that it was a single toilet. The door locked securely, a deadbolt clicking into place.

Brad washed his bald head, "to remove any particles, be they oil or dirt, that might impede the adhesion of the tape." Next, while he was at it, he washed his face, the antibacterial soap leaving his skin dried out, tight. Slowly, so as not to bend the hair strands and produce a cowlick effect, he brought the hair system out, placed it on his head, and settled the entire piece over the hairless area. It looked good. He turned from side to side, taking in his profile. Brad removed the toupee and placed it back inside the briefcase, careful once again not to muss the hair. He applied the adhesive tape to his head; the double-sided foam strips formed a small chalk outline, as if to indicate where his hair had died.

Brad stooped and lifted the hair system once again from the briefcase. The hair smoothed down nicely. Brad squirted puffs of the fine gel mist over his entire head, making certain not to apply the stuff too closely and risk a matted catastrophe. He used the vent brush to gently sweep specific areas into conformance. The key was not to hurry, or tackle more hair than was prudent. Slowly, he worked his way around the perimeter of his head, stopping only briefly to apply one additional squirt of the gel mist.

There was a little hump in the back that wouldn't quite lie down. Brad brushed it, sprayed it, and finally tried applying pressure, but no matter how he tried the cowlick stuck out like a tumor, a hunchbacked mouse.

"Damn it!" Brad said, his voice sounding desperate in the empty bathroom, an echo in a cave, lost and running out of air. Outside the doors he heard children, their mother scolding them for running. It was getting late.

If he and Linda T. hit it off and decided to have dinner after a drink, he wouldn't be home until eight or nine, which would translate into almost twelve hours of unsupervised time for Compton. But Ratchet would be around, and Brad had sensed in her some degree of maturity; she seemed like a young woman who could excel in college. Brad checked his watch. He should be leaving now, heading toward the Spirit of Foods, which was close to Bowman College. It was 4:30. Brad flushed the toilet to make it sound like he had been doing something other than applying a toupee. When he walked out of the bathroom, the same librarian nodded again. Did she smile this time? Was it mockery or appreciation?

On the drive, Brad called the house, but the phone rang and rang. He tried again and nothing. He phoned Sheila and filled her in on the Spalding site, and asked her whether Compton had called.

"Only once today. He told me he was about to bathe his peaches. Brad, I don't want to pry, but it seems like Comp might need some counseling. Bathing fruit is weird."

Brad almost laughed out loud, but instead said, "I don't think that's what he means, Sheila. You know how he sometimes rearranges language. It's okay." She didn't seem convinced, sighing before they hung up.

As Brad drove his mind drifted; sometimes he'd drive like this and end up way past a turnoff, miles out of his way, and it had only gotten worse lately, his attention to memories more keen than what was happening in the moment. Now he thought about how his brother used to be. Compton was considered a genius, tested over and over in high school, acing his SATs, receiving offers from all over to attend college on a full academic scholarship. Compton never studied and never cared about the attention that rained down on him from his parents and school officials. In the end, he went to Bowman, the same school Brad would graduate from. But the attention didn't stop; every professor Compton had would ask his parents, "What in the hell is your boy doing here?"

Brad wondered what those same tests would show now. Could Compton's genius-level IQ withstand a heavy metal pipe? Did his medulla oblongata still carry the propensity toward deciphering insanely complex math equations?

Brad missed University Drive, took a U-turn, and headed back. He circled the town center and found a florist, where he ordered a bouquet of yellow roses, a half dozen. He knew it was too much, but going without them made him feel unprepared, not as good as he could be.

In the parking lot of the Spirit of Foods, Brad ran his hand along the edges of his hair where the toupee met his real hairline. Everything felt tight, no gaps or security breaches, but that damn spot in the back, it just wouldn't obey.

The parking lot was full of couples coming and going, young ones from the university, gray-haired retirees with their arms around each other's ample waists, but not many his age. Where were they? Home with kids, that's where, Brad thought, making dinner and reading bedtime stories, picking out day cares, and wiping down the kitchen. Couples his age were in the active throes of parenthood, tired and hungry, grabbing their own dinner while sitting on the couch together, falling asleep during a sitcom.

It was past 5:30 now, the agreed-upon time to meet. Could Linda T. be waiting for him in the parking lot, too? Maybe she was lying in wait, trying to determine if she'd actually come in for a drink after seeing him.

Brad decided he couldn't stand waiting any longer. He applied some ChapStick and opened the car door. He went toward the front doors, but no one was there. A potted plant sat beside the entrance, a hibiscus, the pink blooms totally collapsed, gray and hopeless. Brad moved swiftly into the lobby, where a college girl addressed him with a hearty welcome, her eyes, teeth, and hair glittering with metal and specks of makeup.

"How many in your party, sir?" she said, braces exposed, her lips not enough to cover the metal.

"I'm looking for someone. Have you seen . . . " He couldn't describe Linda T. "Um, never mind."

"You can look around if you want," she said, holding tall, rectangular menus, the back plastered with pictures of oozing desserts.

Brad stepped into the bar area and surveyed the seats near the counter, the booths, and square tables. His eyes lit on a woman sitting alone, looking bored. She was tall and beautiful, and the white top she wore strained at the buttons. Brad took a step forward, about to extend his hand in greeting when a man strode past him, almost knocking him over. The guy sat down with the woman and glared at Brad. Five televisions blasted a baseball game. It wasn't at all romantic, Brad thought as he forced the heat from his embarrassment to recede.

He walked back through the dining area, inspecting every woman, but each was with either girlfriends or children or a man. The smell of garlic bread was strong, along with the scent of pine cleaner. Brad nodded to the young hostess and exited. He stood with his hands in his pockets, flowers under his arm, looking around whenever someone approached or a car door slammed. He lightly touched his head, trying to seem as casual as any man with hair. It was difficult to get used to, like having to wear a pot holder or maybe an ankle brace. The sun was slipping down the sky, but the heat wouldn't go with it. To keep from soaking his dress shirt he went back inside. No one was at the hostess station. The restaurant was teeming with people now, clacking plates and tinkling glasses; a live musician began singing. Brad thought the song was from Maroon 5.

Behind him he heard a voice. "Are you Brad?" He turned toward her too quickly, seeming, he thought, like a man who would immediately delve into stalking.

"Yes, hi," he said. The woman was pretty, but plain. She wore an out-of-date long dress in a floral pattern. She carried a purse that reminded Brad of his aunt.

"Hi," she said confidently. "I'm Linda."

"Nice to meet you. I'm Brad." He handed her the roses and she seemed embarrassed. She had to work at it a little while, but before long she managed to sort of tuck the bouquet into her deep purse.

"Thank you," she said, a kindness in her eyes, bordered by a slight reprimand in her downturned mouth.

They walked through the crowd to the bar and found a table. The baseball game was even louder now. When they sat down Brad watched her eyes, which were wide and becoming. Linda didn't seem to look at his hair at all; in fact, she rested her eyes near his mouth, and every so often she flicked her gaze to his hands.

"So," she said. "This is kind of weird. I'm not used to using the personals, but it can be interesting."

"You've done this before then?" asked Brad.

"Oh, you make it sound like a sin," Linda said, sipping ice water, laughing. She was completely at ease. Brad was amazed at her demeanor, the way she seemed utterly without expectation.

"It's not that," said Brad, smiling. "I just meant, have you had any luck with meeting people this way?"

"Yes, I guess you could say that," she said, trying to speak over the sixth inning. "I dated a man for about six months. He lived in Whitchfield County, too, a veterinarian. We enjoyed each other's company, but in the end we weren't a very good match. For one thing, he wasn't interested in doing much more than watching TV, and at times he could be an unintentional bigot. Just not someone I wanted to spend more time with."

Brad didn't know what to say. They ordered a drink, both beers. Brad wished she'd use a glass or ordered a chardonnay. Linda asked several questions, to which Brad could respond only with terse answers.

"Can I ask you something, Brad?" said Linda, politely telling the waitress they didn't need another drink.

"Of course," said Brad, a persistent sense of disappointment lodged in his skull. He knew he was being less than cordial but couldn't change it, work out of the funk.

"Are you looking for someone to date or marry?" she asked. "I don't mean to pry, and certainly it's none of my business, but I get the feeling I'm not what you had in mind, which is okay, we all have preferences, but you seem to be looking for the one." Linda sipped her bottle of beer. Brad noticed how her face seemed settled, lovely even, but that nagging fog in his mind wouldn't move on, clear out.

"I guess," he offered, "I'm just like you, trying to meet someone."

Linda nodded and started to gather her things. "Maybe," she said, "but I see lots of people on a daily basis, most really sick, who don't realize they've wasted time, you know, not worked on it. I can be that way, too, I suppose, but I want to find someone who doesn't have all that romance stuff in their head. Love, yes. Hallmark? I'll pass."

Linda was standing now, offering her hand. Brad shook it, a leaden brick in his chest.

"It was nice to meet you, Brad. Thank you for the drink. I hope things work out for you." Linda took a step away. Brad stood, then sat again.

"Thanks, Linda. You have a pretty smile," he said, the dimwitted comment ringing in his head.

Linda said, "Okay." She patted him on the shoulder and left. Brad sat at the table and felt a tingling under his hair system, something he couldn't get at in public. He had another beer and pretended to be interested in the game on TV.

thirteen   The drive home in the dusk was a welcome respite, like watching a stupid sitcom after a long day, mindless and yet relaxing. Brad turned up the radio and let himself blend into the thump-thump of the speakers. Fields of blinking fireflies seemed to expand and contract. He'd taken the back roads home, following Lick Log Creek, and veering north, past the old Senfort factories that had loomed cotton, along the fence lines that enclosed rolling pastures. Before long, though, he broke into the strips of chaotic development, and the tranquil scenes outside the window turned into enormous aluminum culvert pipes and pallets of shingles, drums of floor sealant, and more of the massive excavating machinery. For the last ten miles to the house this was the scenery: stacks of plywood, manufactured trusses, heaps of earth and foil insulation, permit signs hanging on every other tree.

The images made Brad sullen again. He had thought of removing the hair system the minute he left the the Spirit of Foods parking lot, but a fantasy of Linda T. chasing him down in her car kept it on his head. She'd flash her blinkers until he pulled over, and the two of them would sway in a tight embrace on the Old Hemlock Bridge.

A murky sheet of light hung over the house when he pulled into the drive, the farm sheds hidden in shadows. Brad nosed the Sentra near the pump house and pulled himself from the car. His legs ached; there was that old fatigue again, a virus that felt unavoidable. Looking back toward the driveway, he noticed how neat the grass looked around the orchard; the whitewashed beehive boxes were actually visible forms, no longer ensconced in towering ragweed and whorls of fescue. In comparison to his own unproductive day, the sight of these improvements agitated Brad, sending a message to his brain he knew was unfair. Even brain injured, the asshole is still getting more out of life than me.

Standing by the car, Brad exhaled and stretched. A flash of movement caught him off guard; he jumped involuntarily and gave out a loose scream. A weight, not a significant force, pushed him to the ground. At first, he imagined opening his eyes and taking in the face of Curty, Old Man Tyler's black Lab, but once he turned over onto his back, the gravel poking his spine, Brad saw the thick swab of dyed hair and the slack eye. Compton was on top of him, throttling his neck. It was surprising how much strength he could produce with his arms, but it paled in comparison to the tight clinch hold Compton applied with his legs. All Brad could think of for the count of ten was how someone with a bad leg was able to grapple him with such a pinch, keep him shackled. Brad plied Compton's hands from his neck but he couldn't seem to throw him. He bucked and twisted and thought about a knee to the groin, but it hadn't progressed that far yet.

"You sucking, dildo shit consumer!" yelled Compton, a dollop of spit falling onto Brad's chin.

"Get off of me! Now! Compton, get off!"

"You can kiss my very typical ass. You suck loser!"

Peaches was nowhere in sight, and if Ratchet and the other two were in attendance for the wrestling match, they were hiding in the gloom.

"What the hell is wrong, Compton?" Brad yelled as Compton's hands once again went for his neck, less of a strangle this time. Compton let go and lowered his head, pushing his face hard against Brad's ear, a tactical maneuver meant to ensure eardrum pain. This was how they fought as kids, competitive and sometimes cruel, their sibling rivalry coming out during board games or badminton matches. The next day all would be forgotten, and they'd be walking the farm, looking for a spot for a fort.

"You know what the issue is. You filthy, sealed-off malefactor! I'm gonna sew your ass to your face!"

Brad rolled to one side, effectively giving Compton a partial dismount. But in a dusty blur, pebbles pinging the car, Compton flopped his torso over Brad, landing perpendicular, their bodies now crossed in a T, as if they were performing a floor routine. Compton struggled to get hold of Brad's throat again, trying to push himself parallel, the two of them floundering in the night. In the distance, a dog barked, probably

Curty tuning in to the commotion. A bitter taste entered Brad's mouth, then something salty; in all the ruckus he'd bitten his lip.

"Get off me, Compton! For Christ sakes!" Then Compton's wild and crazed hand managed to grab the hair system. It was as if a large Band-Aid were being peeled from Brad's head. Compton yanked, and ripped it off, the adhesive tape actually making a tearing sound. Brad's eyes widened, and for a moment the two brothers lay motionless near the back tire of the car.

"What was that?" Compton asked, breathing heavily. Brad pushed Compton completely off and thrashed about to finally stand. His dress shirt was untucked, pants edged down, sand stuck to the entrance of his crack. Compton brought the toupee slowly toward his face, as he stretched out on his back.

In the darkness he said, "Holy moly, is this what I think it is, Half Pint?" His anger had slipped away as easily as it had exploded.

"Give me that," Brad said, snatching it from Compton's hand. They both sniffled and gasped for gulps of air.

Brad said through clenched teeth, "Get up, Compton." If a sheriff drove up the lane, the spotlight blinding them, Brad thought he would help cuff his brother, even press charges.

"I can't. I'm kind of stuck." Compton propped himself up but couldn't get the bad leg to bend enough to stand. Brad tucked the hair system into his suit pocket and bent down, jerking Compton up by the armpits, leaned him against the Sentra. In a movie, Brad thought, this is where I'd balance him just before throwing the punch that would knock him out.

Compton forced his eyes to focus. The timed security light clicked on, and Brad instinctively put his hands over his head, as gnats buzzed his ears. An orange crescent moon loomed midway up the sky, the horizon brackish; the area where they stood looked artificial, as if they were on a webcam, blue aquarium light bouncing off everything.

"What is that up there? Is that trepanation tape?" Compton snickered, actually putting his hand over his mouth. In the fuzzy light, he looked like a fifth-grader who'd just played a vigorous game of kickball. Compton used what little energy he had left to pat his pants pockets down, looking for something. He pulled out a wad of single sticks of chewing gum, some of them falling into the dust.

"Want a chew, Half Pint?"

"Fuck you, Compton! You ambush me out here for no good reason and almost strangle me in the process and now you want to fucking chew gum together?" Brad turned to walk toward the house. "You're a fucking head case, you know that?" Then he added, "And by the way, your wife steals."

Compton whimpered. Brad stopped but didn't turn around. Something inside him wanted to be cruel. He thought of Jennifer Hunton. A weight in the pit of his stomach felt as if it might drag him to the center of the earth. A slight breeze came and went; riding along its meager ripples was the scent of a forest fire, acrid and sooty.

"What does the name Jennifer Hunton mean to you, Compton?" Brad asked, his face peppered with tiny stones, stuck to the oil and sweat.

It was quiet now. Humid and still. Compton said, "Huh-uh."

"I think you know perfectly well who she was. Who she is. Why don't you tell me what your nickname was for her, Comp. Huh? Or doesn't that fit into your new innocence? You get to be the best man even when your head's been rearranged, don't you? Is that what it takes, bro? A good fucking cranial beating to understand love?"

Compton was caught in a patch of light. His face strained, the loose eye swimming in his skull as he tried to think.

Brad wished he could eat the words he'd just spoken. He wished, too, that they'd break his brother down. In his head, Brad saw tatters of a beach house, and thick, white towels, Jennifer leaning into Compton's arms.

"Wasn't she the teller at the bank? I think I called her Connie Chung."

Brad bit his lip and held back a snotty heave of emotion that settled in the middle of his face. The odor of the fire didn't need a breeze to carry it now. Brad thought he was even seeing a gauzy haze of smoke.

"Yep," he said, exhaling loudly. When he spoke again his voice was low, almost a whisper. "That's it, Compton. Sure. Connie Chung. That's who Jennifer Hunton was." He walked toward his brother, still slumped against the car, his bad leg bent at a wrong angle. Brad pulled Compton to him, and they walked toward the house.

At the steps Compton said, "Did you see how pretty we made the orchard, Half Pint?" He looked toward it, but the whole expansive knoll was cloaked in night.

"Yep," said Brad, the dead weight of despair lodged inside him. "It looks real nice, Compton," he managed, his throat tighter than when Compton had been choking him.

The door squeaked as Brad rumbled into the house. He flipped on a lamp and spotted the FedEx papers strewn over the table and, in that weird warping of time speeding up that sometimes happens, he saw his name and the lawyer's and realized why Compton had gotten so upset. It was the information on annulments that the lawyer, Joseph Randall, had promised to send.

Behind him, Compton was shuffling in, struggling to get his leg past the screen door. "Why don't we sit for a while on the porch, Comp?" Brad asked. "I'll bring us something to drink."

Compton sniffled in what Brad took to be agreement, and Brad watched as his brother lowered himself into the rocker. In the kitchen he hurriedly stuffed the FedEx papers into a drawer. He stood in the yellow-orange light of the kitchen and blinked back tears, his hand trembling as he poured two glasses of iced tea.

"I'm thirsty," Compton called. "Fire's coming. I can see it."

Brad closed his eyes, willed the tears away. "I know, Compton. I know. I can, too."

fourteen "I want to speak to Mr. Randall, please," said Brad, his nose still sore, tender to the touch. The red marks on his scalp looked like tiny tire tracks; they stung and even itched some.

"I'm sorry, Mr. Randall is in a deposition at the moment. May I take a message?" Brad puckered his lips and tilted his head, a face that could only be interpreted as the expression of a monkey wanting to fight.

"Yes, please do, ma'am," Brad said, exuding a saccharine disdain. "If you would, kindly tell Mr. Randall that due to his prompt FedExing of legal papers to my domicile surrounding my brother's marriage annulment, without my knowledge, vis-à-vis Peaches aka Jesus, I have an utterly bloodied nose."

"What, hon?" said the woman, her drawl like the cartoon character Foghorn Leghorn.

"Oh, let me clarify my statement, miss," Brad said, raising his voice. "Please tell your boss thanks a fucking lot for the common courtesy of warning me so I could keep my brain-injured brother from freaking out to the extent of ambushing me in the night!"

He hung up.

Brad sat down heavily in his chair. That was a mistake, he thought. He wondered whether his own frontal lobe might've been assaulted during the fight with Compton. What he had just ranted at the secretary from the Law Offices of Randall, Climko and Jefferson didn't make a bit of sense.

He got up from his chair and paced around the small office. He thought about calling the colossally ignorant Dr. Banter back, but decided that would be akin to asking the Watsons for help. He knew it wasn't incompetence on Randall's part or even insensitivity. The lawyer had simply tried to rush the papers to him. That was it. But with Compton home all day now, curious and energized, the FedEx packet was ripped open. Still, Brad felt the urge to take it out on something, someone. For the next ten minutes he skulked around the room, sometimes stopping to stare at nothing of consequence, a stack of papers or the blinds; all of it appeared watery, diluted, and forsaken, the office of a man pretending to have a job.

He turned on the small television in his office and watched the news. The forest fires, it turned out, had not been only in the south part of the state. In fact, some of the worst fires were popping up in northern Carters County, too, just below Whitchfield, and all along the counties in the northwestern portion of Georgia. Firefighters from Atlanta had volunteered to assist, and now a grungy firefighter with ash sticking to his tanned face was talking to a reporter.

"It's very difficult out there," he said, wiping his brow. "The fires are steady and hot. We've brought in helicopters with water buckets and that's helping." He motioned behind him, where a line of orange flames danced as benignly as a pit fire for a weenie roast. When the camera zoomed out, however, the screen was overtaken by acres of smoking pine trees, the cloud rising into the sky like a silky tornado, as if whatever had detonated days ago still percolated beneath the bent black trunks, the frizzled and charred forest floor.

"We've got dozen of crews out here, and we're using backhoes, bulldozers, and feller bunchers to help with the fire line." Brad smiled. Feller bunchers. That piece of equipment had to have been named by Compton himself. Brad turned the volume down and slid toward the phone ringing on his desk.

"Hello?"

"Mr. Orville, this is Joseph Randall. I understand I made a very stupid blunder, and I'd like to apologize. I had no idea. I didn't think your brother would be home since he attended the day program you mentioned."

"Did you ever think of asking? Maybe that might be some new technique you could use in your courtroom cross-examinations."

"Well, sir. I sure didn't and that's my fault. Like I said, I'm truly sorry for the altercation it caused."

"How would an attorney put it? Oh, yes. The older sibling of Mr. Brad Orville caused bodily injury with no forethought due to a traumatic brain injury, which prevents him from fully grasping the seriousness of his actions. Move to have the case thrown out on the grounds of insufficient short-term memory." Brad had a headache.

"I guess I shouldn't take that as an acceptance of my apology then. Since you mention the law, are you planning on filing assault and battery charges? It might not be a bad idea, could help your brother understand the seriousness of his actions."

"Yeah, right. I'm going to press charges against my brother," Brad said sarcastically, making a perturbed sound with his lips.

"That's what I thought. And good for you. That's how I'd handle it personally, too."

The lawyer's humble attitude made Brad feel ashamed of himself. He didn't know what to say.

"So, what do you want to do now, Mr. Orville? I can assure you the doctor I mentioned can help. At the very least he can provide a full evaluation of the situation. This time I'll leave the details up to you. Everything will be discreet from here on out. Do you think your brother and his wife would meet with him?"

"Sir, I'd be lucky to get him to throw me a line if I was drowning, that is if he remembers everything accurately from last night." Brad dabbed at his nose with a tissue. Could it be broken?

"Let me give you my cell phone. If I can be of any assistance please don't hesitate to call. I've got an older brother myself, and I guess this case just kind of hits close to home for me."

Brad scratched the number down, ready to get on with the day; he had another inspection to do and a meeting with Commissioner Birdsong to prepare for. The Watsons had asked for a second conference with him. For what, Brad had no idea. He certainly wasn't going to run around the neighborhood getting people to welcome yet another development; besides, there really wasn't anybody left. It didn't make sense.

"Jesus," said Randall as they were about to hang up.

"Huh?" Brad said, confused. He thought he was making a remark about Peaches.

"Oh, it's just the fires. The wind is blowing our direction and the whole parking lot is filled with smoke," the lawyer said, amazed. "Damn fires are a hundred miles from here, and there's all this smoke."

The day crawled along, and although the inspection of the store opening near Bowman went well, Brad couldn't shake the feeling of dread in his entire body. Near the end of the day, he packed up early and left the Watson building.

He didn't want to go home, afraid that Compton would attack him again or, worse, have the place working so well it would make Brad realize how ineffective his own life was in comparison. So he drove around, stopping to buy a cup of coffee whenever a Jiffy Mart appeared. In this way, Brad felt he was exacting a blow onto the Watson convenience store empire, even though he realized how lame his tactic was.

He ended up back at the spot where he used to go and think as a child, where he'd met Preston, the homeless guy. As he parked, he saw that Preston stood in the blazing hot sun, his plastic grocery bags flapping gently in the breeze.

Brad got out of the car, shielding his eyes from the glare.

"We're not open yet. Might wanna come back in 2032. Place should be up and running then," Preston said, his face serene.

"Oh," said Brad, walking toward where Preston stood by the Dumpster, a plastic bag trapped under his walking stick. "I thought maybe y'all might be open by now," said Brad, unsure of why he pretended to sound so homey.

"Nope," Preston said as Brad came closer. "We just like to take things slow 'round here." Preston leaned in toward Brad and squinted. "You're here not too long ago."

"How's the work going today?" asked Brad.

Preston was silent. He speared a plastic sack and lifted the stick to his face, as if to see what it was. He snatched the bag from the pointed tip and shoved it into the breast pocket of his Dickies overalls.

"You hungry?" Brad asked. He put his hand on Preston's elbow. "I was just heading over to Howard's for a sandwich myself. I could use some company." Preston nodded.

"What about my stick?"

"Bring it along. Does it have a name?"

Preston breathed heavily as he climbed into the passenger seat. "That's about the goofiest thing I've ever heard of. Right, her name is Sandra, and we're in a bawdy love affair."

Brad backed up the car and they turned onto the road. "Sorry," he said. "That was stupid to say." They drove awhile in silence, Preston sighing pleasurably at the cold blast of air-conditioning.

"So what's your name again?" asked Preston.

"Brad."

"Okay," said Preston, looking out the window at a stoplight. Several plastic bags skittered across a Piggly Wiggly parking lot. "Fucking things are everywhere," he said.

Brad looked at Preston's dingy profile. Maybe the man was seeing things. "They've got medication for that, you know, seeing things. Hallucinations are common in some mental illnesses."

Preston smiled and pointed at the sacks drifting around a light pole. "I was talking about the bags, man." As Brad parked the car near the front door of Howard's Deli, he realized how long it had been since he'd really laughed.

fifteen Brad flinched when he saw the newly painted beehives. The white boxes with freshly applied tar roofs were a pleasant sight, but unexpected. Each one appeared straighter with the paint job, and the symmetry gave the entire hillock a wispy glint of a hard-scrabbled future. Why then, Brad wondered as he sat in the car, the sun still bright but lowering, did he feel an estrangement, as if he resented the neatly painted beehives as much as Julie and Toby's marriage? The car carried the stale scent of Preston's clothes. Brad breathed in deeply.

Alone in the car, the motor idling, he asked himself out loud: "Do you remember the accident? How it all happened?" It was a question for Compton, of course, and the sound of the words, once spoken, threw Brad into a deeply drawn dream of the whole ugly chain of events. He let his memory answer the question intended for his brother.

Compton had his head broken open with a lead pipe, the kind mechanics use to pry engines out of cars. During the trial, while Compton was still in a coma, the very mechanic who had used the pipe, the same one who admitted to bashing in Compton's head, told the jury why he did it. Brad was sitting in the third row of the courtroom. The mechanic looked at the jury box as if it were one entity, a buddy on a bar stool, empathetic and genteel, warm as liquor.

With glazed eyes he said, "That man was trying to steal my wife. He left me no choice." Brad watched as one juror, a boyish man with a scraggy beard and pocked cheeks, nodded slightly. The other jurors looked at the mechanic with blank but perceptive stares. Brad had warned Compton about his sleeping around, but his brother waved off Brad's warnings, smiling through his casual optimism.

For a few weeks, it turned out, the husband had been following Compton. His wife was a nice woman, Brad thought, when she testified at the trial, almost mousy. Her name was Candice Latterby, and her husband, Carl, the mechanic, was also shy, soft-spoken. Compton had ruined their lives, Carl said under cross-examination.

"And for that I gave him what he deserved," said Carl, who was sentenced to two years in prison for assault with intent to murder. He'd said as much on the stand.

"I would've killed him if my arm hadn't of gotten tired. That may be awful to hear, but it's the goddamn truth." Candice left the courtroom that day, and Brad saw her outside, bent against the wind, the rain smattering her coat, a petite down-filled parka that Brad thought looked like a little girl's; how had a woman so small wreaked such havoc? Brad watched her drive away in a dinky Ford Escort, with an SPCA license plate and rosary beads hanging from the rearview mirror. He stood awhile in the downpour, letting the cold, stinging rain have its way with his neck and head, where it hit then slid quickly onto his face. Her tail-lights shone at a four-way stop, and disappeared, but a reddish flash stayed in Brad's vision, hanging there for days. Brad ran to his Sentra and drove to the hospital to sit with Compton.

There were times when Brad believed more in Carl's cause than in his brother's and thought that maybe he should be paying vigil out-side the gates of the state prison rather than sitting in an uncomfortable chair in the ICU, but he never left Compton's bedside until he woke up almost a full month later.

The sunset was now completely in place, an arrangement of warm sherbet: yellow and orange, lines of pink along a gun-metal horizon, pushing a herd of bruised clouds. The car was instantly hot without the air conditioner. "You must remember. Right? Or I do. And isn't that something? A kind of brotherly memory." Brad clutched the steering wheel so hard it trembled. He could feel the sadness descending, the deep darkness of aged futility.

He jumped when Compton pounded on the window. Brad expected another fight and didn't care, actually wished it would happen. He would lie on his back and let his brother do what he wanted, punch him in the spleen, bust his lip, twist his arm until it cracked. Compton hit the glass again, even as Brad rolled down the window. The second thrust of Comp's hand slipped through air and nearly hit Brad's chin. Peaches stood nearby, wearing a new maternity shirt that swallowed her up. She was glowing.

"Come inside, Brad," said Compton, as excited as he'd been when they made a sailboat out of a rubber tree and it made it downstream through a drawbridge they'd constructed from Popsicle sticks. "Me and Jesus have wonderful news!"

Brad reached for the door handle, struck with a sudden understanding of how he'd live from here on out. It would be ambushes in the night, being met at the end of the day at his car, before he could even get out, the news awful or perfect, and him just part of the stage work, an extra whose one and only line had been cut, leaving him standing there like a fool, wordless but semi-needed, a mere backdrop in their scene.

PART II

. . . .

sixteen "See, Half Pint, the babies can eat scrambled eggs at around eight or nine months. That's what it says in our book. So we're going to order some chickadees at that feed store where we used to go with Dad." Compton paused and looked at the ceiling, bunched up his lips, thinking of the name. "Filmore's," he said, slapping his knee. Brad was surprised he'd gotten it, too. More and more, it seemed Compton could stimulate his memory, call up things that had apparently been long for-gotten. Shards and fragments, little snippets of an old conversation, and the odd made-up words, some of them turning out to be real.

"Like hell you are," Brad said, pouring a glass of old wine from the pantry, noticing how easily Compton had gone from saying "baby" to "babies."

"Watch your language, Brad," Compton told him. "There's a lady in our presence."

Brad slugged back the drink and poured another. "N-O, Compton. The last thing we need around here are chickens. You can buy organic eggs now anyway." Brad poured the rest of the apple wine, so vinegary that it nearly gagged him, into a tall drinking glass. He strode across the room to the refrigerator, pulling the business card he'd gotten from Mrs. Tantum, the director at Paradise, from under a pizza delivery magnet. In the morning, he'd persuade her to help him.

Compton and Peaches were looking through a seed and feed catalog with Ratchet. "I like the Araucanas," Ratchet said, tucking her short mane of hair behind her slim ear. Brad watched them, leaning against the refrigerator, the awful wine buzzing his brain. The three of them around the table made him anxious, as if he'd been left out in some junior high school party game. He watched for a few minutes, unable for some reason to tear his eyes away from the dull glow of Comp's platinum hair, Peaches's caramel skin, and Ratchet's firm butt. Finally he crept upstairs and logged on to a different personal site, one based in Atlanta that promised a real connection. As he signed up and typed in his credit card information, the sonogram picture Peaches had brought up to show him earlier crumpled next to the computer, he heard laughter downstairs, followed by the sound of crowing. It sounded so real, so much like their pet rooster, Charlie—a Red Star that Milo had helped them hatch in a homemade incubator—that Brad looked out the window. It came again, and he realized it was only Compton, goofy as usual.

The next morning Brad sat in a pleather lounge chair at the Paradise Club, waiting for Mrs. Tantum. The black-and-white copies he'd made of the ultrasound picture of Peaches's babies were tucked neatly into a manila folder. People wearing knee-high socks and walking shorts seemed to materialize around him, their chitter-chatter like birds, language yes, but undecipherable, and nearly irritating, some squawks and then more parroting. Maybe this hadn't been the best place for Compton, but it had helped him along, hadn't it? Brad opened his briefcase, touched the online receipt he'd printed out for the new hair system, the one that would have its debut this evening if the overnight-delivery promise held up. He blushed, thinking of what he'd paid for it. He allowed himself to daydream about how the meeting with CryGal207, Crystal, would go.

In his head he reconstructed their instant messages, a flurry of text back and forth the night before. He thought of the easy way they seemed to chat, recalling songs and movies from the early nineties. He'd been tipsy of course, the apple wine settling around his motor controls, fingers typing fluidly.

Brad would call her in the afternoon. He worked at pushing the date with Linda T. out of his mind. He blamed himself, and Linda a little bit, too. He'd come on too strong, and she was less than serious about romance. A pang of regret came over him; he wished he'd started the online dating earlier, and maybe if he had it'd be his babies he was worrying over.

"Mr. Orville," called Mrs. Tantum, finally. "Come on in." Brad stood up, but as he moved toward where she stood in the doorway to her office, a man appeared from around the corner, braking to a sudden stop in front of Brad. The guy wore a parka and very short shorts. He looked Brad up and down and said, lisping, "Mmmm, look what the pussycat drug in."

"Hello, Sammy," Mrs. Tantum said. The man was humpbacked and toothless, but there was a clever, almost rakish style about him, even with the short shorts. Brad's heart sort of tightened at the sight of the guy; he wanted to help him, which was odd, when what he was doing for his own brother might be construed in just the opposite way.

Sammy cackled and reached out, clearly trying to pat Mrs. Tantum on the rear end. She stopped him with a firm hand, having experienced this before. "No, Sammy. No. Now you know that type of behavior earns you five demerits. I'll have to report it to your case manager."

Sammy nodded, eyes gleaming, apparently feeling as if the price paid was worth the goods. He trotted off toward the vending machines.

The administrator smiled at Brad, ignoring Sammy now.

Brad watched for a moment as Sammy leaned against a pole and started to whimper. "Is he okay? He's crying down there," said Brad, pointing at the other end of the hall.

"He'll be fine. Come in, please."

Brad remembered why he was there, his heart balky; nothing seemed like the right thing to do.

"How's Compton?" she asked, sitting slowly behind her desk. "Would you like some coffee?"

"No, thank you," said Brad, lowering himself into a loveseat. "He's fine actually, I mean, I guess." Brad fought the urge to simply wave her off and leave the building.

"And Peaches? Is she doing well? Last time I heard they were living with you."

Brad unlatched his briefcase and brought out the copies of the sonogram pictures.

"Look at this," Brad said, scooting forward to pull himself out of the sagging loveseat, clutching the briefcase to his chest. He handed the folder to her. For several moments she looked it over, squinting, turning the pages left, then right. "This is their sonogram picture, right?" She looked at Brad and removed her glasses.

"Yes, but don't you see? See what's there?"

She put her glasses back on and looked again, scrutinizing the black-and-white fuzziness, the grainy churning masses. "It's lovely, Mr. Orville," she said, exasperated, twisting her glasses from her face. "I'm just not sure what you want me to do."

"No, no," Brad said, climbing out of the loveseat. "See here." He walked around the desk and stood next to her. She gave him a sidelong check, sliding her chair back. "I'm not going to have to call security again, am I?"

Brad forced a smile. "Of course not. But see right there. Can't you see that? A second head?"

"Oh, my," she said.

"Ma'am, " Brad said, "what I'm talking about are twins. Compton and Peaches saw the clinic's doctor yesterday and the ultrasound shows twins." He cocked his head and opened his mouth, standing next to her, frozen, expecting that she could right this wrong. "Twins," Brad said, taking the folder and photos with him and retreating to his seat.

Mrs. Tantum straightened her blouse. "Oh," she said. "I see. Is it your opinion that Compton and Peaches cannot handle two babies?"

Brad shot her a look, his eyes wide open. "What do you think?"

"Well, I can see your point. But again, what can I do to help?"

Brad sat down and tried his best to appear together.

"I need expert testimony to go to court. I'm having a trained psychologist visit Compton and Peaches tomorrow. I would push for an annulment based on cognitive impairments. After that, I'm not sure what the options are for Peaches and the babies." Even when he heard the words leaving his mouth, Brad felt dirty, as if taking action and not doing anything put him in the same place, ill-fated and hopeless. The twins were a puzzle without an answer. Lose either your arm or your leg, but decide right now. Sight or hearing?

Mrs. Tantum nodded. "The options are not good," she said. She laced her fingers together as if in prayer and held her hands over her bosom. "The children might end up in foster care, for one. Or they could find an adoptive home right away. But the thing is, Mr. Orville, couples today do all kinds of research. They want to know who the parents are, their backgrounds, et cetera. DNA tests. I'm afraid even in this situation, where Compton's issue is not developmental, and Peaches's is . . . " She stopped short. "Of course, I can't tell you what her past is like, but all the same, I couldn't begin to offer up what might happen to these babies. There is still a great deal of stigma surrounding many disabilities, even TBI."

"Is that a yes? Will you help me?"

"No," she said flatly.

Brad's face reddened, and he realized that a cold sweat had settled over him. "But why not?" he almost begged.

"Because your brother is his own person. I don't make it my place to order the lives of our participants. Compton's also authentically certain about his feelings for Peaches. Sure, he exhibits some classic signs of post-TBI, but he's getting better. He will always need support, help with some things, but, Mr. Orville, if I helped you I'd be betraying my fundamental beliefs. However, I will assist you and Compton and Peaches in finding whatever it is you need to help raise the children. That is, if you plan on being a part of the family. Are you envisioning your brother and his wife remaining in your home?"

Brad rubbed his head and closed one eyelid. "Ma'am, if they have these babies it will be a mistake," he said, trying not to sound like a preacher. He tried to come across as more stable. "I'm all they have, right? I mean, Peaches doesn't have any family to speak of, correct?"

"I can't tell you that, Mr. Orville," the administrator said, stepping toward the door. "What I can say is I realize this is a difficult situation, one with so many unanswered questions. If I could suggest something?" She opened the door even though Brad remained seated. He stood up reluctantly, briefcase in hand. It felt like it was lined with lead.

"What?" he said. "What would you suggest?" His voice was shrill to his own ears as he slouched toward the door.

"Don't pursue the annulment. Don't pursue trying to find the babies homes, or whatever it is you have in mind in that regard."

Brad started to speak but stopped, as the bell for another class at the Paradise Club rang. "Then what should I do, madam administrator?" Brad cocked his head.

"Get out of the way. If you can't or won't help them. Find another life for yourself. Just get out."

Brad shrugged, his eyes watery; he wanted to grab the woman and have her hold him, maybe sit and talk on a park bench, have her listen to him, really listen. He almost couldn't get the words out. "What do you think I'm trying to do?"

He walked away, imagining how the scene would look if he were on videotape: himself staggering down the hall of ocher and tan walls, blasts of Crayola markers on bulletin boards, the silver drinking fountain, a streamer left over from a birthday, gold and listless. All of it jumped around in his vision, as if he were viewing his recorded exit on a television. The shot was unsteady and blatantly sentimental, overwrought and annoying. Brad could watch no more, so he began to jog.

seventeen Birdsong, the Whitchfiled County commissioner, wore dark sunglasses and a massive black watch on his wrist, leaning against his dull silver Toyota on the Orville property, the harsh sunlight only somewhat diffused by the haze of smoke. The fires were under control, for the most part, but the news anchors kept telling everyone it was only temporary, "unless we get some rain." The thick sweet scent of creosote was condensed in the air, sticky when it finally drifted onto parked cars, their windshields candied, dotted with sap.

Brad steered the Sentra over rutted fallow ground, the yellow weeds brushing the undercarriage. He imagined the sound as a kind of human touch; the way it slowed as he neared Birdsong gave Brad the sensation of being cuddled, which he knew was weird. Birdsong rolled up his sleeves as Brad shoved the car into park.

Brad was relieved to see the front pastures motionless, no sight of Compton, only the upright, perfect beehives standing in a line like sentries, red-winged blackbirds perched like statues on top.

A patch of sweat in the shape of a nearly perfect triangle stuck to Birdsong's chest like a badge. Brad crawled out of the car, his feet tingling.

"Sorry I'm late," said Brad, his face red and gleaming as he walked through the patch of high grass, the dead seed heads clicking together like tiny castanets. "I had another meeting," he said, leaving out that it was at the Paradise Club. "Took me a while to get here." The sun seemed as if it might actually explode, disgorging hot lava across the entire expanse of Whitchfield County. Brad saw it in his head, the red-hot shrapnel finally putting everything to rest, consumed in an instant; it would all just be sucked into a heat so intense it would make you shiver. His head pounded from these thoughts, and for some reason he pictured the sperrylite that Milo, his dad, had helped the boys experiment with as kids; the silvery white powder and crystalline platinum was exactly the color of Compton's hair now.

"Now how is that, Brad? I mean, we're right next to your house," Birdsong said teasingly. He was a good guy; for a moment Brad thought about the fact that he had no friends. People used to give him and Compton a hard time because they spent so much time together, not really needing friends. Ironic, wasn't it, that now they spent nearly all their time together?

"I know, I know," said Brad, reconsidering where his headache was coming from. At least part of it had to be the rancid apple wine from the night before.

"Is Compton going to join us?" asked Commissioner Birdsong, not a trace of condescension in his question.

"Right, if we want a full-blown episode he can." Brad blew his nose and put on his sunglasses. He still wasn't sure why Birdsong wanted him out here, other than that the new development was going to be towering over the farm. Even after six years at Watsons, Brad found it hard to connect the dots; he knew something was slightly bogus, but no more so than any other American enterprise.

"Okay, but he's going to find all this out anyway, right? He's a pretty smart guy—didn't he score a perfect SAT?"

Brad was intrigued to see that Birdsong's hair system looked natural even in the bright sunlight. "Sure, but that was before his head was cracked open like a coconut. He's like a reel-to-reel tape recorder sometimes. The tape just runs out and flips around in a circle." Brad looked to Birdsong, watched him nod.

"Oh. Well, here's the thing, Brad," he said, not wasting time now, lifting his sunglasses off his eyes for a moment, then letting them fall down the bridge of his nose. "Later this week, I'm to introduce a motion in the council meeting to proceed with eminent domain on your property." Birdsong sounded as if he'd just recited something off a teleprompter.

Brad swallowed hard, the sting of a quiet, hot burp backing up in his throat. It tasted awful, like a little nibble of sulfur rock. Damn Mega-Well pills, he thought.

"Why would you do that?" asked Brad, his bald head branded in the heat, sizzling.

"Because that's the job I was elected to do," Birdsong said. "But that doesn't mean I like it. Your property is wanted by many, many constituents. Progress is what it's all about, Brad. They can't get enough of it. Really, that's what people out here are addicted to." Birdsong indicated the county surrounding them by splaying his arms wide. "They shake their heads at drug users on the news in Atlanta, and wag their fingers at crack addicts, but throwing up enormous subdivisions is what they're strung out on. The thing is, it all brings commerce and creates a few jobs. But more importantly, it creates statistics, and numbers. Sound bites are what get people elected." The commissioner let out a huff of amusement. "Besides, it's not like you wouldn't get fair market value, which would be very significant money."

"Well, that's real fucking nice. Doesn't there have to be a court order and all that mess?"

"Uh-huh, sure. I just wanted to give you a heads-up."

"Thanks a lot," said Brad, his head swimming, tipsy and woozy, everything kind of tilted. He squinted his eyes and dipped his head from the dazzling light, but it did no good. In the field next to his home, with Commissioner Birdsong watching, Brad puked into the brittle weeds, a fiery tang of spit trailing down his throat. He upchucked again and bent over, blew out air, a guffaw sound preceded by one long, vociferous string of gas.

"Jesus, are you all right?" said Birdsong, stepping closer, his nose a little crinkled.

"Yeah," said Brad, breathless. He wanted to wail, take the opportunity to really puke, like he and Compton used to at keg parties, barf and cry out as if dying. It was so cathartic. "But I might set the grass on fire."

Birdsong chuckled. "Sounds like it," he said, looking at his watch.

A wall of smoke appeared out of nowhere, whipped up and blew across the red clay of the unearthed subdivision, baking under the gargantuan sun. Birdsong waved dust from his face.

"Are you sure you're okay? What's it from?" The commissioner unlocked his car door, pointing his keys at the hybrid, the chirp crisp and high-pitched.

"I'm fine," said Brad, spitting, hands on his knees. "Just celebrated a little too much last night."

"Really? What was the occasion?" Birdsong asked, more like an amused indictment than anything.

Brad stood up and tilted his head to the clouds. He felt weak, the flu-like feeling at him again, much like when he was first diagnosed with clinical depression.

"Oh, we had a toast to Compton's health is all. He's getting better," said Brad.

"It looks like it," said the commissioner, pointing across the old fence line to the Orville property. In the pasture under the fruit trees, Peaches and Compton were busy flapping a red-and-white checkered blanket, spreading it out on the ground. Brad recognized it immediately as being from their parents' picnic basket, the one with wicker plate holders and a metal canteen wrapped decoratively in jute rope. Six place settings accompanied it, nice heavy silverware with maple insets. It would mean that Compton had to have climbed into the attic and dug around in the head-high boxes covered with cobwebs and the fine powder of bored rafters.

Brad took several steps forward to see better. He watched as Compton floundered toward a patch of dandelions, yellow even in the drought. He stooped down and plucked three flowers with unbalanced effort, one whole side of him thrown into the task, as if he were lopsided because of a strong magnet pulling at his torso.

"Who's the woman with him?" asked Birdsong. Peaches's hair looked like a child's at this distance, soft and shiny, truly ebony against one of the white beehives that sat in the background. She and Compton both wore work clothes, long sleeves in the sweltering heat and the oversize gum boots that were two decades old. Brad couldn't imagine how Compton could walk in them without falling flat on his face.

"That, Mr. Commissioner, is my brother's wife. Her name is Peaches, but we call her Jesus." Brad sucked in air. His voice was cagey and a little high.

"Hmm," said Birdsong, looking as if he may not have believed what he was hearing. He began to walk to his car, sweeping through the high grass like chiffon moving, like the rustle of Jennifer Hunton's bridesmaid's dress at a wedding they all three attended near the beach in Savannah. Brad didn't turn around when Birdsong spoke.

"Brad, I'd appreciate it if you didn't let Watson or anyone else know I gave you a tip on this thing. Okay?"

Brad nodded, still watching his brother and Peaches as they sat on the old flannel blanket, opening root beers and unwrapping sandwiches.

"It's none of my business, Brad, but I don't think Watson will approve of the nuptials here. He's an ass, but powerful. Maybe you should just sell and get out. Move closer into Atlanta." Birdsong's voice sounded a little shaky to Brad, as if the commissioner might be readying for a good yodel. He was right of course. Watson would say that interracial marriages were prohibited by the Bible. "The Lord's words, not mine," he'd say to Brad in his palatial office.

Brad turned around and said, "Is your hair real?"

Birdsong let out a small howl. "Yep," he said, shrugging his shoulders. "It's a weird time to ask it, but yeah, Brad, it's real. I get that a lot, though. You can come give it a tug if you want. I'm not sure it's a real compliment to have your head mistaken for a rug."

Brad didn't smile at all, just simply waved and turned back to watch.

"I'll see you later, Brad," said Birdsong, smiling through his words.

As Birdsong wheeled out of the building site, dust hanging in the air, Compton and Peaches looked up for the first time in Brad's direction. They were surrounded on two sides by development; only the orchard behind them and the house at their backs were left. What would these ten acres be in a hundred years, five hundred? Probably ten subdivisions would have been built and torn down and built again in that amount of time.

He could tell that Compton couldn't recognize him from this distance. To him, maybe Brad looked like a county inspector or a mortgage officer. Brad gave a small wave and watched—not entirely surprised—as his brother lowered his dungarees and bent over, mooning Brad.

"Jesus, Compton," Brad muttered, and then he was seized once more with nausea. He tipped forward and threw up again, the same sting in his throat, coffee-laden and caustic, his rear end popping like something too hot in a microwave. "Damn pills." A pile of red ants scurried toward a dome of powdery clay on the ground in front of him.

He stood up and saw Peaches swatting at Compton's leg, but it was clear she was giggling, the sound wafting above the silence of the machinery shut down for a lunch break. No men were visible at either work site, having piled into trucks and headed to the interstate for fast food.

Compton wiggled his pale ass in Brad's direction. For several moments, no one released their positions: Brad stared, Peaches giggled and swatted at her husband, and Compton's butt swayed back and forth. Then a truck full of construction workers emerged over the hill on the road. A whole gaggle of them sat in the back, the front seat crammed, too. Part of Whitchfield County's Rules of Economic Engagement was to hire as many local residents as possible to build all the offices and homes and retail stores that would fuel the development boom, which meant diversity was all but absent. The truck was loaded down with lots of white men.

Brad watched as the truck slowed to a stop, brakes keening. He shot a glance at Compton, who now had decided to actually part his cheeks some, ramping up the insult he intended to deliver to the man standing in the weeds next door. Brad waved with his arms and yelled. "Compton, get your pants up!"

The driver wore dark sunglasses and a cap with a bill shaped into a compact arc. The man stared at Compton. Peaches tried to hike Compton's pants legs up, but he kept shimmying them back down, reaching for her shoulder for balance. The other men in the back of the truck now stood, Brad saw, more than a few spitting Skoal juice onto the hissing pavement.

"Compton!" Brad motioned toward the road with his head, but it was useless. He was too far away for any subtlety to register. Finally, Brad crawled across the fence, catching his dress pants on a rusty barb. The leg tore, a long black skein now dangling from his calf. Brad stomped toward Compton. Halfway there, Peaches realized it was Brad. She stood up and, with her willowy arms, turned Compton around, which only exposed his hairy pubic area and floppy penis, his skin as white as an undershirt.

"Jesus Christ!" Brad yelled as he sprinted toward them, tripping over the unmowed swirls of virescent Bermuda grass. The driver of the truck honked and whooped and hollered and honked again. The men in the back clapped and whistled.

"What the fuck are you doing, Compton?" Brad hissed.

Peaches was trying to hold a smile, her shoulders shaking a little. "Sorry," Peaches said. "We thought you were someone with the county." As if that would explain it all. She let out a little spasm of laughter. Brad caught the expression in her eyes, a look of intuition he felt he must've missed before.

"What?" asked Compton as Brad yanked his brother's pants up in one violent rush, buckling the belt and shoving in his shirttail, the pants hiked so high they formed a moose knuckle.

"For God sakes. You want to be treated like you're not a goddamn fool, then don't act like one!" Brad's lips were wet with saliva, and his sunglasses had fallen off. Peaches bent to retrieve them from the blanket, which held the scent of aged mothballs.

"No reason to talk to him like that, Brad," Peaches said as she tucked Compton's shirt in the back. She slid the sunglasses into her dungaree pocket.

One of the men hollered, "Oh yeah, baby," a rustic accent twisting the vowels. "Show us that thing!"

It seemed that Compton hadn't heard or wasn't registering what they said, and for that Brad was grateful.

"Y'all got a threesome goin' down, huh?" called the driver, snickering. Brad held Compton by both shoulders and watched as his brother's eyes sparkled with concentration, working their way into a comeback.

"Don't, Compton," said Brad, as if telling a pet to stay put.

Compton shook one arm free from Brad's grip and slowly flipped the truck of men off. He yelled, "Why don't all of y'all just move on. Or are y'all fixin to kiss y'alls heinous anus?"

Brad couldn't help himself and burst out in laughter, which brought a broad toothy smile from Compton. Peaches said in a low voice, "No. Manners now. You two need to watch it." She brushed grass off Compton's pants, and Brad noticed that her tummy was compact and round.

The truck shot into the driveway and sped toward them. Brad felt his pants pocket for his cell and pulled it out, as if he could shoot out the radiator with a Razor phone. Compton stepped in front of Peaches, spreading his thin body over her stomach. The driver of the truck slammed on the brakes and craned his head out of the cab.

"We don't want anything to happen here," said Brad, his heart rate pulsing in his ears.

"That a fact, fuck face?" the driver asked, spitting the brown tobacco juice down the side of the door where a flaky line of it had already baked into the paint. "Why don't you teach this asshole some manners then?" The man looked at Peaches, as if noticing her for the first time. He appeared sheepish then and actually tipped his hat. Brad had never gotten over how random racism was here; if you expected a construction worker like this guy to use the N word, you'd be wrong, but more than once, while listening to coworkers at Watsons during lunch, someone would say, "Ooh, don't go into Atlanta at night, unless you want to be carjacked. They'll kill you for twenty bucks."

"Actually your face reckons a heinous anus," Compton said, smiling.

The driver leaped out of the truck and stomped toward them. Brad held up the phone. "I've got nine-one-one programmed in. You might want to get off of our property before the cops show up." He quickly thought of adding that his brother was brain damaged and that something was wrong with Peaches, too, to play on the guy's sympathy. Just then, at the end of the lane, a FedEx van wheeled into the driveway, its blinker still flashing orange.

The driver man spit on Brad's shoe, a glob of brown juice.

"Thank you. That's real neighborly of you," Brad said.

Compton inhaled deeply and sucked in snot; Brad knew he was about to explode. "No, Comp," Brad said, sounding even to himself like a cliché do-gooder from an outlaw movie.

The FedEx truck came toward them all, tires popping on the hot pavement. Brad realized they'd most likely been saved by the arrival of his $750 hair system, called, appropriately, the Life Changer.

The man spit again, but off to the side. He seemed to deflate some and, just like that, he said to Peaches, "Sorry, ma'am."

"It's okay," said Peaches. "Men will be boys." Beside her, Compton grabbed at her hand, his pants riding high.

The construction worker smiled at Peaches, then stopped for a moment to stare Brad down. All Brad could think of was how thick the guy's hair looked, curling out from beneath the cap, shiny and auburn. The FedEx driver stopped behind the truck and called to them, "I've got a live package here for a Mr. Orville."

eighteen   The bar was cold. Goose bumps formed along Brad's arms. He rolled down his sleeves and took another long drink of the merlot. It was rich and tangy, even a little gamey. Brad imagined anchovies in the casks, blended with just the right amount of grapes, aged until a little whiff of the ocean permeated the distillery.

Crystal had described herself as tall, with long brown hair and contemporary eyeglasses. "I've been told they make me look like Brooke Shields," she had IM'd Brad. She worked as a vet's assistant and was enrolled at the college, taking courses in human resources.

The television above the bar blasted a reality show, apparently an experiment in pitting women in their forties against women in their twenties. Where are the feminists these days? Brad thought. Shouldn't someone be outraged over this? He could hear his mother reciting a letter to the New Era editor, asking for all brave and strong Whitchfield County women to demand that the network drop the show. He gulped down three quick mouthfuls of the wine and ordered another glass.

Sitting in the bar made him think of Compton. Back when they cruised the bars together, talking about books and ideas, getting drunk in the process, they enjoyed messing with social conventions. One of Compton's most successful come-ons (and really, he didn't need much) was to claim that he would most definitely, without a doubt, take his wife's maiden name as his. The three or four women around him, sipping margaritas and nudging their girlfriends, would toast his grand idea, and before long all of them, even Brad, would be out on the dance floor.

He missed that about Compton, but those types of easygoing late nights had all but vanished even before the beating. Brad thought back over the day, which after the fiasco with bare-assed Compton in the field had been uneventful. The FedEx man turned out not to be delivering the Life Changer hair system, as promised by the company, but a batch of chirping day-old chicks.

So he wore the original toupee, the "thing." He was afraid it might be slightly worse for wear after his tussle with Compton nearly a week earlier, but it still fit nicely upon his head, and even the cowlick in the back had tamed. He changed in the bathroom at the public library, from work clothes into a pair of blue jeans and penny loafers, a chambray work shirt with a white T-shirt underneath. He spent some time with the hairpiece, adjusting it, and he thought he looked pretty good. He even splashed on cologne, citrusy and pungent.

It was well after six. Brad looked around the bar and didn't see a soul who looked like Brooke Shields, with or without glasses. He downed another glass of wine, then became concerned that his teeth were maybe turning purple from the wine. He left the flowers on the bar, slipped off the stool, and capered along toward the restroom with a spacious intoxication, his limbs almost negligible.

Brad flashed his teeth, scooped some water from the tap, and gargled. In the mirror the hair system didn't look as good as it had in the library. It was slightly askew, not very noticeable, but still. Brad pressed both palms down hard against the toupee, driving the rough tape into this scalp. He did it again, and again, each time hard enough to give himself sparkly pinpoints at the sides of his vision. He shook his head some, trying to make sure the piece would stay put.

Bon Jovi sang about his hometown over the piped-in music, and Brad's buzz gave him the courage to dance a bit in the mirror. He shimmied to the left, then back to the right, twirling some. He realized he was an awful dancer, but if Crystal wanted to hit the floor after drinks, he had to make sure his toupee would come along for the boogie. He imagined the thing floating into the air above the dance floor, landing at Crystal's feet, a hairy urchin. Brad stopped; he was dizzy. Then, just to make sure he was safe, he bent over from the waist, blood rushing to his head, and purposely jerked up quickly, as if exploding from a pool. Brad surveyed his red face, pleased to see that the hair had in fact stayed put.

When he returned to the bar, his heart rate seemed to have slowed to a dull thumping, and his mind wandered over the irritations of the day: arguing about the baby chickens with Compton; the doctor who was recommended by the lawyer, Randall, had canceled; and now Crystal looked like a no-show. Brad glowered at the clock on the wall, a mirrored Budweiser scene, draft horses clomping through snow. Crystal was nearly an hour late. The flowers were wilted, lying on the bar.

Brad was about to leave when he heard a small bell clanging against the entrance. Brad swiveled on the stool, then stood up. In the doorway a very tall woman stood with one hand on her hip, an exaggerated pout on full lips. She wore her signature eyeglasses, and Brad was surprised to see that in fact she did look something like Brooke Shields. The height had a lot to do with it, but her nose and eyes added to the effect as well. His date was blessed with high model's cheekbones as well. Brad stood and walked toward her, flowers in hand. Crystal smiled, exposing a glorious set of ivory teeth. Just beautiful, Brad thought as he extended a hand.

"Oh, you must be Bradley," said Crystal. Brad detected something in her voice, a hoarse sound that made him think of her work with animals for some reason. Maybe she'd had a rough day, perhaps caring for a poor dog that didn't make it and she'd been crying.

"Hello," said Brad. He handed her the flowers, and immediately she stooped a little to kiss him on the cheek. She smelled wonderful, a combination of face powder and a light perfume, along with a little bit of balsam shampoo. He couldn't help the visions in his head of a wedding with Crystal dressed in a long white dress, baby's breath woven into her straight brown hair, she and Brad taking over the management of the farm, selling off a piece of the land to build Compton and Peaches a place of their own, a nurse coming in daily to help them. Brad would take the lead, order how the improvement of the place would go, shucking off the possibility of an eminent domain case with his newfound confidence. Crystal would have an uncle who was generous, a lawyer who could litigate the hell out of Whitchfield County. The story would end up as a small but touching cog in the twenty-four-hour news cycle, a human interest story that showcased matrimonial love in all its hard-earned splendor. "A couple in Whitchfield County, Georgia, have shown that love and family can win out over local and state government. Today, Mr. and Mrs. Brad Orville, newlyweds . . . "

They moved to a table, Brad leading the way. He stumbled some and wished he'd stopped at one glass of wine. "Brad," said Crystal, her voice husky, even a little gravelly. She swallowed and swallowed again. "Are you okay?" she asked.

Crystal was smiling, those teeth truly like cultured pearls. Her lipstick had been applied perfectly, and her face was flawless, skin so smooth and soft looking that Brad wanted to reach over the table and place his hand on her cheek, propose on the spot, leave nothing to chance. It happened. There were great love stories everywhere of couples falling in love and getting married after just one date.

"I'm sorry," said Brad, anxious not to blow it. "I was just noticing how beautiful you are." Crystal pretended to blush, fanning her face, tucking her head some.

When the waiter approached, a young guy with stringy hair, Brad ordered coffee for them both. "That's exactly what I wanted, hon," said Crystal, taking Brad's hand. Sure, she was at least three inches taller than he, which would put her over six feet tall, but they could work with it. In fact, it would become a family joke, a little something to hang their adorable love on, this gorgeous tall woman with a slightly shorter man. Brad believed Crystal would tell him, "Oh, no, I much prefer you bald," clutching her breast. "My God," she'd say, "you are handsome without hair."

The buzz began to settle off Brad, slipping down his entire body, clearing his head some, and fine-tuning his vision. Crystal sipped the coffee with her pinky out. Maybe she'd attended a girl's school where manners were graded, but still, something about that pinky crooked conspicuously out, almost dangling, seemed odd, as if it were purely artifice, the pinky of a mannequin. Brad tried not to stare as he drank his coffee in gulps. He didn't want coffee breath, so he'd ordered his with mint creamer, which the waiter said they didn't have, so he ended up with hazelnut. Now he peeled the lid off of a third creamer and dumped it in.

"So," said Brad. "Tell me more about yourself. What's your family like? Do they live around here?" Brad hoped he didn't sound too forced. He willed himself to take it slow.

Crystal just smiled and grasped Brad's hand again, squeezing. She had a French manicure, the white tips of her nails so precisely painted they looked as though she'd simply been born with them. Her grip felt strong. Brad eyed their hands together, roughly the same size.

Crystal whispered, "Let's not talk about me. I want to hear all about you, your work and life." Brad thought it was odd that she didn't want to talk—she'd been so chatty over the computer.

"Well," said Brad, feeling, really for the first time in ages, that Crystal's hand on his, the heft of it, the heat, was too much too soon. "As I mentioned on the computer, I'm a regional planner with a company called Watsons. I'd rather be working on a green space project or at least a job where there's not a new convenience store erected every twenty-three days. My parents . . . " he said, pausing, noticing one gnarly knuckle on Crystal's right hand, a large emerald ring trying to cover it. He shifted his eyes away and focused on her exquisite skin. As his buzz began to lift, Brad noticed that Crystal's face took on more of an angular quality, still beautiful, but less softened. "They were professors at Bowman College. They taught classes in economics and sociology, but their work focused on sustainable agriculture in poor countries. They are both deceased."

Crystal nodded, peering at Brad's face with intense admiration. "You're a doll, you know that?" The last word was deeper, as if it had come from the bartender.

Brad's face turned red, and he thought that his unease must be noticeable to the few people milling about, munching nachos and drinking beer. Two women, both wearing sports jerseys, glanced at the table when they passed, elbowing one another as they moved on. He stared at Crystal's hand, which seemed to have grown heavier in his, the knuckle more masculine. The word "that" hung in the air, baritone and gruff.

Brad envisioned tight panty hose and surgical tape, Nair and Nads and body wax, the heavy face powder applied thickly to conceal the strong jaw line. He now noticed the makeup was caked over Crystal's chin, trying to conceal a small but deep dimple.

He removed his hand from under Crystal's. Brad sat up straighter in the booth and looked around.

"Crystal," Brad said discreetly, ducking his head toward his date. "Is it a possibility that you are a man?"

She fluttered her eyes and acted coy. Crystal gave her broad shoulders a teensy shrug. "I'm a woman through and through, Brad."

Calmness washed over Brad, born of a pang of empathy. For this, he was glad, even proud of himself. Other men in this situation would have either stormed out or beaten Crystal up. He tried to gather the words to ease from the date without offending her.

"It's probably not a good idea, Crystal, to let on like you're a woman over the Internet. You could get really hurt doing this," said Brad. He was a fine, liberal-minded man, he told himself, who, while not finding love himself, could sympathize with others for whom love had evaded their grasp.

"You might be surprised what a woman like me can do, hon," said Crystal, doing her best Mae West imitation. She reached across the table and took Brad's hand again.

"I'm sure that's true, but I'm not interested," Brad said, pulling his hand back and placing it in his lap. For a second, Brad thought she was going to cry, then she licked her lips, tilted her head, and said in her regular voice, which truly was Tone Loc's, "How about we just go for a ride and see what happens then."

Brad was ashamed that he now wanted to leave the bar as quickly as his sobered-up legs would carry him. Crystal's voice resonated over the line of booths at the side of the bar, and he feared they'd both end up facedown in the gravel out front, arms twisted behind their backs, knees rammed into their kidneys. "Listen, let's just call tonight a learning experience and leave it at that," said Brad, knowing as soon as he'd said it that it sounded arrogant, like he was telling Crystal she had something to learn.

"Or how about," said Crystal in her man voice, "I just lift my dress and give these fine patrons here a look at my tucked hootie. See if your name holds up well in the papers . . . " She looked around the room and added loudly, "Mr. Orville!"

Brad put his hand on hers now. "What do you want then? So we can both leave here with some dignity?"

Crystal smiled. Brad took it in; she did make a beautiful woman. Her voice turned back to the feminine. "What does anyone want? I'd like some romance, a little tenderness, and armloads of cash."

In the parking lot, the moon fought to shine from behind a herd of dark, slow-moving clouds. It was as hot as it had been during the day. Dry lightning flashed along the black horizon. Brad emptied his wallet, sixty bucks. "That's all I've got," he said, hoping Crystal wouldn't scream rape and bring the police. He saw himself locked up, charged with what would appear to the authorities as a John gone bad.

"It's okay," said Crystal. She seemed embarrassed now, a long, curly strand of spiral perm dangling from her temple. "I shouldn't have said that in there. Really, just keep it. I was just hurt, I guess. I'm sorry." Crystal turned to walk to her car, her slim hips now obvious, not womanly at all, a well-rehearsed switch awkwardly swaying, too timed.

Brad was still holding the three twenties in his hand when Crystal's headlights washed over him, slicing his torso with harsh high beams. She let her window down. "Send me an IM if you get lonely."

nineteen The weekend. Before Peaches showed up, Brad had worried over how to spend the eighteen hours each day with his brother. The time between Friday evening and Monday morning was like a calculus problem to Brad; every answer only seemed to reveal how wrong the question was. Up at six a.m. and in bed at midnight, the two days seemed to hold the infinite minutes before him like one of those insurmountable piles of sand, the ones used to visually depict how many grains it would take to form a line from New York to Los Angeles. They'd go shopping for tube socks at Target, take in a movie at the enormous megaplex, have lunch in the café near Polebrook that took its sweet time making burgers. They'd take dawdling walks along the Pine Valley Trail, Compton moving at glacial speed, Brad propping him up, part of the rehab to get his legs stronger. On those walks Brad spent most of his time consoling Compton; people would stare at them, as Compton bawled, then walk on. When Compton leaned on him, his entire head bobbing, Brad would try to recall the times he'd wanted to harm his brother, pound him just like the mechanic had. But it seemed impossible to conceive of it, as Brad held a hanky for Compton to blow into. Brad would purposefully clatter along the scenic routes in the car, sometimes just looping around, hoping that Compton would doze and the labored conversation be broken. Those first several weeks home from the hospital, it was all Brad could do to stick around. Compton's painfully slow gait, the bewildered look in his eyes, the way it made him appear completely foreign had scared Brad and made him think his brother could die right there in his arms. If Compton started to cry, frustrated, Brad would feel emotion surging, too, his eyes filled with tears as Compton tried to tie his shoes, hands shaking. Brad would kneel before him and tie the shoes himself, telling Compton, "It's okay, Comp. We'll get it," even though he felt they never would.

This Saturday would be wholly different than those that had seemed so laborious and unbroken. The psychologist, a man named Dr. Gibbons, was due at eleven that morning. Brad had told Compton about the visit as straightforwardly as possible, late last night. "He's coming by, Comp, to assess your progress."

"That reminds me," Compton responded. "Let's all play Crambo this weekend." Then he went back to giving Peaches a pedicure. Her dark toes were covered with specks of white, smatterings of the paint they'd used on the beehives.

Now, Brad went through the kitchen to the sink, next to where Ratchet was at the stove, cooking eggs. He drank down a glass of orange juice and poured another. He peered at Ratchet over the rim of the glass. She'd dyed her hair a mahogany brown that was flattering, little strands of it hanging loosely at the base of her neck. She wore a fitted black baby-t with baggy plaid pajama bottoms. "Would you like some eggs?" she asked.

"No, thank you," he said, hearing what he thought was peeping from the pantry. He closed his eyes, a light pounding just behind them. It was going to be a long day.

"Good morning, Half Pint," said Compton, now buttering toast for Peaches.

Brad gulped down the last drop of orange juice, then watched as Compton knocked an entire stick of butter to the floor without noticing. "Jeez, Comp, you're gonna get butter all over this house!" Brad snapped.

Compton ignored him. "Oozy coozy jelly!" he exclaimed, spreading jam on Peaches's toast, who giggled and patted his butt. "Oooh, baby, not in front of the children," Compton said, winking.

"Compton!" Brad said, his voice rising. "Pick up the damn stick of butter before you step in it and fall!" Compton finally noticed the butter at his feet. He started to bend down, but Brad rushed over and scooped it up with a paper towel. He wished the doctor could see these little mishaps, the stovetop fires and clumsy accidents; how could any professional not see the danger the babies would be in?

Again came the peeping sound from the pantry. "Are those baby chickens in this house?" Brad asked as he tossed the butter in the sink. He'd at least thought they'd use one of the small sheds. He coughed. Ratchet smiled and looked to Compton. She'd taken up residence apparently, sleeping on the couch. Why, Brad wasn't sure. The other two kids still stopped by to work and hang out most days, but Ratchet seemed to be attached to Compton and Peaches, not quite nurse-like, closer to an ally, a person with vested interest.

"Oh, Half Pint," said Compton. "Mother nature is a wonderful cray-chure." Ratchet popped her gum and snorted.

Hungover, Brad had forgotten his plan and his vow to keep an even keel; he was cranky, and thinking sluggishly. "Why don't you ever listen to what I tell you, Compton? I specifically told you not to get chickens. There's all kind of care that goes into it. Feed, and water, not to mention the newspapers and cleaning the crap up."

"I'm going to do it," Ratchet said calmly, sitting down at the table after divvying out the scrambled eggs. She chewed on a triangle of toast. Brad sensed that her funk was self-imposed, not clinical. She just seemed too casual with her melancholy, as if it were put-on, or part of a social statement.

"Why? Why are you here, Ratchet? I mean, do you really want to hang around here and waste your youth with . . . " He looked at Peaches, who now had started placing Compton's napkin on his lap. She had the expression of someone awaiting tremendous news, hopeful and glassy, her lips pursed.

"I don't know," said Ratchet. "I just like it here. It's not like there's anything to miss out there, anyhow."

"Really," said Brad. "If you really believe that I feel sorry for you, kid. You can't imagine how much there is to miss, trust me." He wondered whether she might be after some kind of money, and then immediately felt guilty for the thought.

Ratchet smiled at Compton and Peaches as they held hands and prayed a silent prayer. "Amen," said Compton. "Amen," said Peaches.

"Jesus," said Brad.

"Amen and Jesus, too," said Compton. When he became a Catholic, years ago, he told Brad, "It's fascinating watching these people constrict their lives around the notion that a hierarchy put in place to come after their earnings is ordained by God to be considered more deserving than they are. They really believe some humans, those of the clergy, are better than them. How they don't see that as an absolute contradiction of what Jesus taught is a testament to delusion. And entirely impossible to stay away from. I love going to mass, seeing such a strange human entanglement in operation. Fascinating."

The chicks cheeped more loudly. "How many are there?" Brad asked solemnly.

"There's only one Jesus, Half Pint, and she's sitting right here." He kissed Peaches on the forehead and made the sign of the cross.

Brad sighed, his headache building. The image of Brad holding Compton's hand as a child surfaced in spite of Brad's irritation—the two of them walking the farm, bending to inspect snake holes and glimmering pebbles along the bank of the creek, letting go of each other's hands only momentarily, the time it took to pick up a twig, inspect it. Brad shook his head.

Brad sat for a while at the kitchen table, sipping coffee and listening. He reminded himself that the doctor would be at the house in three hours and heaved himself up. At the landing of the stairs he stopped. They were talking about names for the babies.

"I like Kernel," said Compton. "And Peck, too, I'm just guessing they're girls, though. That's what they told us." He had his arm around Peaches, and she was snuggled into him, bright-eyed and smiling. Ratchet laughed. "Or how about Sanders?" She tucked hair behind her ear and blew over her green tea. Brad, incensed, plodded back into the kitchen, his steps jiggling something in the cupboards, most likely a kitchen utensil they hadn't used in years, a sifter or one of those old ceramic rolling pins.

"Are you seriously considering naming the babies those stupid names?" he half shouted. Brad's hand went to the top of his skull involuntarily; he clutched his baldness when he was in deep thought. "That's just wrong. And when did you find out the twins were girls, Compton? Isn't that something I should've been told?"

Peaches peered up at him, a wry smile on her face, some darker brown freckles peppering the bridge of her nose. "We were talking about the baby chickens," she said, trying to allow Brad some dignity; still, she seemed on the verge of laughing. She pointed toward the peeping pantry, a red light glowing under the crack of the door, which meant Compton would've had to have dug the old brooding equipment out when he was up there getting the picnic items for yesterday.

"Half Pint, you see, there's a real and concretorious difference between the human child and the offspring of poultry." Before Compton could launch into another one-liner, the kitchen filled with laughter. Brad padded out of the room and up the stairs.

Before the doctor arrived, he wanted to try once more on the personals Web site. Surely, he surmised, there's a woman in the greater

Atlanta area who wouldn't mind an ordinary date with a normal guy. But before he sat down at the computer, he slipped into Milo's study and used the key to open an antique liquor cabinet. It was made of walnut and was a gift from a German professor who Sarah and Milo had befriended at a summit in Switzerland. The boys were young when it had arrived on a truck, and at first Milo thought it was an incubator he'd ordered, but when the cardboard came off via Compton's pocketknife, and Milo opened the door with the brass key, exposing compact rows of gin, bourbon, and vodka, he realized it wasn't for chickens. Brad and Compton played with the tin tumblers, spinning the matching coasters on pencils, until Sarah made them stop. Milo was proud of the gift and sent the German PhD a whole set of vintage Farmers' Almanacs.

Brad twisted the key and listened for the familiar click. In high school, they'd raided the liquor cabinet more than once, and more than once they'd repaid the impropriety by cutting the front pastures, pushing lawn mowers with no engines.

But it had been years since they'd tampered with it, and up until his death Milo had kept the cabinet stocked with bottles of liquor from all over the world: Argentina, Ethiopia, Ireland, and Greenland. Brad placed his long fingers on each bottle, trying to decide what to have as a morning cap. He remembered that vodka was difficult to smell, so he helped himself to a bottle of Nikolai. The clear glass bottle had a black-and-gold label, with a crest that looked like a two-headed bird. The maroon seal hadn't been broken. As he tiptoed down the hall to his room, the bottle tucked under his arm, he felt like a teenager again.

He stopped to open Compton's door. Peaches had redecorated. The bed was angled and made perfectly, the sheets and blankets crisp and folded down tightly. Some throw pillows from the attic had been added on a divan from the garage. Several of Sarah's fine paintings hung on the wall. Above the bed, two red hens bathing in dirt, sun rays across their wings, wattles a cherry red, fertile and feminine. Another painting of a sunset across the road—where now the heavy machinery cut the earth into three-quarter-acre lots—was placed on the floor leaning against the wall, a copper urn with dried flowers at the side. The painting by his mother was difficult to look at, even caused a physical pain, a sharp stab at his sternum.

He held the bottle of vodka and surveyed the room. It was so homey. At the sight of a complete set of Encyclopedia Britannica, Brad opened the bottle. Downstairs the muffled talk about the chicks and naming them carried on, drifting up the staircase. Brad didn't even look at the seal, just twisted the cap off without any thought. He'd planned on doing it carefully, even saving the seal, but now it fell to the floor. Brad took a strong pull from the bottle. It was peppery and slightly menthol. The liquor widened his eyes and threw his head back. He wasn't an expert on vintage vodka, but this was good stuff, 80 proof, with a hint of pumpkin.

He let the alcohol infuse his body, wending its way through membranes, piercing nuclei, and drowning synapses. Brad spotted the cookbook his mother had published with the college press. She'd given him a copy, signed; Compton, too. But the last time he knew, only his copy had been stored in the attic. Compton had approached the task of keepsakes and family heirlooms like everything else; he saw them as overly sentimental and too much trouble. "What's it going to matter in two hundred years if Compton Horace Orville kept a note from his second-grade teacher?" he'd said.

Brad strode into the bedroom and picked up the book. It'd been cleaned, the cover still covered in an oily film of Pledge. He opened it and flipped to the third page. In her flowery cursive it read: "To Bradley, my baby and my heart. Eat well, and love well. Feeding someone is one of the best ways to show you care about them."

Brad slammed the cover shut. He tucked the cookbook under his arm and stood in the center of the room. His head itched and he feared he was getting a rash from the toupee tape. He took another swig of vodka and looked around again at the furnishings.

Peaches paid attention to small details, like the old tobacco canister that now held newly sharpened pencils, ones with real lead. A macramé throw covered the back of a leather chair that had once been in his father's office at Bowman. An entire ream of newspaper print, still on the roll, sat under a copper platter, the perfect bedside table. It held a porcelain lamp with a black canvas shade, imprinted with white Japanese script.

The room didn't look like the same space from just a month ago. A stack of Compton's pajamas, sorted by top and bottom, sat on a low pine shelf. But by far the most noticeable change was the smell. Before, the room held the scent that Compton had brought with him from the hospital, of illness and pain, the light vinegary waft of hydrogen peroxide undercut with stale chrysanthemums, the olfactory clue that he was different, damaged, and stagnant. That was all gone now, replaced by notes of polish and floral perfume, an undercurrent of turmeric and cloves. Compton had provided Jesus with her own dressing table, a white stand, the top adorned with doilies, the lace finely stitched, more of Sarah's handiwork. Bottles of toilet water lined the back, while makeup brushes and little lipsticks were held in crystal dishes, most of it, Brad thought, most likely pocketed by Peaches.

On a table at Peaches's side of the bed a basket held several pieces of silverware, a handful of lighters, two watches, and Brad's sunglasses. He plucked them from the rest of the loot and turned around. Brad moved to Compton's desk. It was stacked high with his college texts, books by Foucault and Darwin. Ten small, leather-bound chapbooks of Yeats and Wallace Stevens, and other poets Brad didn't recognize, sat in a row. He could imagine Compton reading poetry to Peaches as they lay in bed, the turning of faded pages like the sound of butterfly wings, Compton forgetting he'd started the tub, water flooding down the stairs like white rapids, the babies screaming in soiled diapers.

The next gulp of vodka was numb, no taste, nothing to water his eyes, just a beverage, as plain and benign as tap water. The first days home after leaving the hospital came back again to Brad. He heard Compton stuttering, "You're, you're the one . . . " And again, "You're the one . . . I, you're . . . " Compton had started and stopped this sentence a thousand times as they drove around, hopping from one chain restaurant to another. It was here that Compton let it be known he'd never again in his life consume an entrée. A plump waitress at O'Charley's had brought out a London broil, baked potato, and a side of green beans. When she placed it in front of him, then the same for Brad, Compton took one look at it, smiled, and dumped the entire thing on the floor. His speech was still rough, halting and sometimes garbled, but he said clearly to the waitress and Brad, "I will not acquire the taste for these, these, these . . . full meals." Compton then took a sip of ice water. Brad was astounded. He apologized to the waitress, who had not taken her eyes off Compton. "Is he autistic? Or just an ass?" Brad had gotten down on his knees and helped clean up the mess, his necktie dipping into juices and oil.

The front door opened downstairs. Compton's bedroom window was closed, but Brad could hear Peaches, Compton, and Ratchet standing on the steps, still talking, talking. The room was too damn perfect. Brad looked it over again, eyes falling on all the same bric-a-brac, and then spotting new items, a college plaque commemorating Milo and Sarah's tenure.

Without a moment's hesitation he ripped the covers off the bed and mussed up the throw pillows, tossing them to the floor. He picked up the urn of dried flowers and dumped them on the mattress. He stood back and admired his work. Outside, the sound of a hoe whapping the earth made a perfect metronome for the birds singing in the background.

Brad left the bedroom and sat down at his computer, pouring a juice glass full of vodka. He bit his lip and fidgeted in the chair. Finally, he rose and went back to Compton's room, made the bed, and put all the dried flowers back in the vase. He kept the cookbook—his, after all—to show his next date.

twenty   The sun seemed so much lower in the sky than it should be; it hovered stubbornly, a smattering of dark streaks trailing along the horizon, smog stuck over Atlanta. Brad awoke in a state of disorientation, that kind of confusion where you feel as if you've missed out. It was depressing to know that the world hadn't noticed you were gone. Earlier, before falling asleep, Brad had decided against drinking more vodka. Instead, he sat down and forced himself to read over the folder of information Commissioner Birdsong had supplied him, a report on the development of the tracts around their home. It was tedious material, and all Brad could recall before slipping into a dream about pelicans and their long beaks was something to do with underground cable and the need to reroute the creek. He was still in shorts and a T-shirt now, rubbing his eyes, trying to make sense of the clock, his tongue like an oval pumice stone.

His watch read 1:10 p.m. "Shit!" he said. He jumped out of the bed and darted to the window. Looking out the window he watched Compton, Peaches in tow, providing a guided tour to the doctor, stopping to point out newly planted flowers, the patched fence line. The doctor's face was beaming, as Compton used elaborate hand gestures. The doctor actually put his hand on Compton's back as the two laughed, throwing their heads back. Brad scampered to his closet and rummaged through dirty jeans until he found a suitable pair. He pulled them on and yanked a clean T-shirt over his head. For the sake of time, he opted for a pair of sandals—too casual, he thought, but still, he needed to get out there, not waste time tying a pair of shoes. He noticed that his nails needed clipping; the one on his pinky toe looked like a parrot's beak. Brad rumbled down the stairs, tucking everything in, smelling his breath, rushing to get outside and take control of the doctor's visit, funnel the right information to him.

Ratchet was once again at the stove, and Brad wondered whether she had ever moved. The smell of tangy sauce permeated the kitchen. She looked at him and said, "Sloppy joes. Compton wanted to have lunch with the doctor."

Even in his rush, Brad noticed how ineptly Ratchet chopped a Vidalia onion. "Slice diagonally," he said, preoccupied. He paused at the door. "Compton asked you to make lunch for him? He didn't even act like he was bothered about the doctor coming?" Ratchet was still chopping in her slipshod way and, annoyed, he moved from the door and took the knife from her. He quickly sliced and diced on the counter, tossing the onion into the sauce.

"Don't ask me," Ratchet said, watching him work, apparently not miffed. "When we went shopping this week Comp said he wanted to make today's lunch special." She pointed to a platter of fruit. "They cut all this organic stuff up, too. Kumquats and mango, I think."

The air conditioner was set lower, Brad could feel it, probably also tactical on Compton's part, making sure the doctor was completely comfortable, both physically and mentally, just the right environmental factors that would make for an over-the-top recommendation. Brad stood frozen for a long count.

"What is it?" Ratchet asked, stirring the sauce in the skillet.

"I'm just trying to think," said Brad, still nearly motionless, as if he were listening for some faint structural noise, the house shifting or a beam slowly cracking. Finally, he moved to the pantry and opened an old jar of red-and-white mints, popping one into his mouth. He would at least have fresh breath when meeting the doctor.

Brad went out the back door and looked from side to side. He could see Compton's face through a tangle of privet. At the end of the driveway, across the road, a dull sound hummed, and the whack, whack of roofs going up made Brad feel even further beyond everyone else. The temperature was stifling, and the haze of forest fires hovered just above head high. As he made his way across the bridge, Brad stopped and listened. He could hear their voices. He spit and rubbed his teeth with his tongue, spit again, sucked the mint hard.

They were in the grassy pasture, the grape arbor behind them, as Brad approached. Compton waved. "Well hello, sweet innocence," he said. "I surely thought you'd be sleeping the indolentistic day away, little brother. You might want to meet Dr. Gibbons here, that is if you can get the sleep out of your eyes."

Brad waved back, tromping through the dead grass. He tried not to blush. "I wasn't sleeping," Brad said directly to the doctor as he extended his hand. "It's nice to meet you, doctor."

"Likewise," said Dr. Gibbons.

Brad tried to balance things out. "Compton sometimes gets the order of things turned around, thinking, for instance, activities that are appropriate for the day are actual night specific." Brad continued to shake the doctor's warm hand and added, "I'm sure you see this kind of thing all the time." He thought of adding a wink, but hesitated, and when he finally did wink, Dr. Gibbons was talking.

"Your brother and Peaches here were just showing me around." He didn't have a clipboard like Brad had hoped or a video camera, which could be used in a court of law to provide the basis for an annulment.

The doctor nattered on. "You all have a wonderful place here. Compton was sharing with me how your parents taught at Bowman. Sounds like they were on the forefront of green living. You both must be very proud of having a family home like this with such a heritage."

"Uh-huh, yes. Well, we do love the homestead here," Brad said, moving closer to Compton, who wore a blue button-down and gray slacks for God sakes, and black dress shoes, loafers, no shoestrings to contend with. His hair was now dyed back to brown and combed perfectly, and of course he smelled like a barbershop: shaved, deodorized, and scrubbed. Brad had already noticed the doctor's head: some receding hair, but not bad for a man his age, styled nicely, parted on the side. Dr. Gibbons had to be near retirement, and his salt-and-pepper hairdo made him look the doctor part. If anything, his wasn't even thinning; his hairline just started higher on his forehead. Brad hated it when these guys complained about being bald; theirs was more of a cosmetic flaw, a little blemish, whereas Brad's kind of baldness, severe and blatant, over-rode anything else, his nice teeth, his kind eyes, all the good features swept away, overshadowed by a tall, forsaken forehead.

The doctor squinted at Brad, a kind of bemused smile on his face. Brad went right on full bore with his plan. "Of course, I'm sure you saw when you arrived how dreadful the development is. My brother and I here," Brad put his arm around Compton, who imperceptibly tried to pull away, "we sure do hate all the bulldozers and backhoes, all the topsoil runoff and the diesel exhaust spewing into the beautiful blue sky. Why, even the creek is polluted now. It's just about as bad as it can get in terms of the environment." Compton's mouth was twitching, his head almost in Brad's armpit.

"Well," said the doctor, almost as if he'd already signed up for Compton's side, "there are things that can be done about it. If we begin to believe we are hopeless against larger forces, people, pollution, even God, then we in effect become clinically disassociated, which isn't any way to live." He smiled at Brad as if it were a courtesy.

Compton swallowed hard and successfully wrenched away from Brad's embrace. The late afternoon sun shimmered off the equipment across the road. Compton shuffled his body next to Peaches. He stood up straighter and put his arm behind her back. She stayed tucked at his side as the tour continued. Brad walked a few paces behind, an ember of guilt inside, but a small flame of sibling rivalry firing up. He tried to think of his next move as Compton showed the doctor the bridge and creek.

"The bridge was constructed in the late sixties. Our father helped build it, using nativity wood."

Brad caught the mistake and hopped on it. "Don't you mean native wood, Comp," he said, almost whining. "Not nativity, native wood, timber from these woods."

Compton ignored Brad's comment as he led the group down the small sandy embankment. He struggled to make it creek-side without tumbling. Peaches, looking lovely, rays of sunlight in her soft, glistening hair, held on to her husband.

Once everyone was aligned along the creek, Compton said, "As you can see, Dr. Gibbons, my younger brother is making excusisms. My wife and I have taken on the bulkhood of maintaining the place." Compton let his flittering green eyes dance over his brother's face. Brad looked as if he were about to throw a tantrum, his face red and crinkled into a frown. "You see, Bradley has been in a world of his own lately. It's all we can do to get him excited about life."

"Compton, you're talking some of your gibberish again. Don't you want to impress the doctor, here?" said Brad, talking more loudly, as if his brother were deaf.

The doctor observed the Orvilles' banter with the expression of an archaeologist brushing away dust from a rare femur. Brad felt sweat gathering over his baldness. Two squirrels chattered along the trunk of an oak. The creek smelled of the ocean, fishy and brackish.

Peaches lifted her head and spoke directly to the doctor in a soft, demure voice. "They get carried away sometimes, doctor. They mean no harm, though," she said. Brad started to speak over her, but she raised her voice. "They love each other. Sometimes too much."

Dr. Gibbons beamed. He reached for a small pad in his shirt pocket, clicking an ink pen as if he were a detective. He nodded and said, "Oh, that is a wonderful insight, Peaches. I can tell you are someone who can cut right to the core of an emotional situation." Dr. Gibbons scribbled on the paper, his eyes still on Peaches. Brad thought to mention her klepto habits, but refrained; he'd talk with the doctor about that later, when they had a private, one-on-one chat, Brad relaying how taxing caring for a brain-damaged brother could be, the two of them sharing a brandy, maybe even smoking pipes.

"My wife is absolutely correct, Dr. Gibbons," said Compton. "I do love Bradley very much. It's just that he needs so much of my judicious guidance lately. He's so worried about what he looks like on the outside, he can't see we only get better by working on the inside."

"Now that's enough, Compton," said Brad. He turned to Dr. Gibbons. "Doctor, let's change the subject. Are you aware that all this development," he motioned toward the end of the driveway, "is covertly planned?" The doctor seemed more amused, pulling at the hairs of his mustache, and a part of Brad knew that he should shut up, that all this information about their land and the development was not why the doctor was there, but something inside of him wouldn't shut up. He felt like he was ten years old again, at the dinner table, trying to impress Milo and Sarah with his knowledge of ancient Egypt. Compton had showed him up, of course, able to best him with a seemingly bottomless stream of facts about the pyramids and the pharaohs. Brad remembered how it felt sitting there, staring down at his plate, listening to his parents' clucks of interest and approval as Compton went on. "I know these things because of my work. But what I'm talking about is deceitful really. Large developers like these actually have rules about using bulldozers to push down trees in broad daylight. They won't do it. See," he went on, his voice rising a little, "they have studies that have shown that people like us, ordinary citizens, can't stand the sight of a healthy, full-grown hardwood or pine being murdered. As human beings we've got some type of encoded aversion to seeing a tree killed. So they pay heavy machinery operators more to do the dirty work under the cover of night. Think about it, when's the last time you saw them actually killing the trees on your way to work?"

Finally Brad sputtered to a stop. He was tired now, beaten down, but by whom? He looked at Compton, whose face had sunken some; he seemed less spry, more woozy. Peaches removed a tissue from her blouse and dabbed Compton's brow. For several moments, Dr. Gibbons just stood and watched the brothers, as if it might've been a boxing match. He tucked his pad of paper back into his shirt pocket, nodding, apparently satisfied with his findings.

Compton sucked in a deep breath, and announced, "Please follow us to the house. We've asked our friend to prepare a late lunch." The doctor nodded agreeably, stepping in front of Brad and talking to Peaches and Compton all the way to the house. Brad felt doped, less alert than he wanted to be, as if a part of him were hibernating. As he tagged along, listening to Compton telling Dr. Gibbons about his plan to raise organic chickens, Brad resolved to stop taking the antidepressant pills.

The chicks were quiet under the red light as Compton rattled off their names. Ratchet had cleaned the box, put down fresh newspaper, and dusted them with fragrant cedar chips. The pantry had been cleaned and organized. New shelf liner made of vinyl, boasting printed poppies, stretched along each board. Dr. Gibbons admired a black-and-white chick Compton held in his palm. He handed it to the doctor. "Isn't that something? To hold a little life like that. Breathtanking, taking, I mean."

Peaches and Ratchet set the table, while Brad holed up in his bedroom, getting prepped for lunch, changing into decent clothes and washing his face; he'd be a much better version of himself during the meal, really show Dr. Gibbons which Orville brother needed help. He logged on to his computer and scoured the personals. There was a woman whose bio read: "If you like Pina Colada and getting caught in the . . . " Brad scrolled past it. Another one had a monarch butterfly as her icon. Her hobbies were Mariah Carey songs . . . Brad clicked the arrow to jump to the next page. Beside him, the vodka was open so he took a guzzle as if it were soda.

He clicked on a bio that read: "Gina2468. I like nature, hard work, nice people, families, and fresh foods. My dislikes are conceit, conservatism, ___holes, and TV. I'm growing tired of the dating game, so please only contact me if you are serious about the same interests. And please absolutely no perverts! Photo on request if reciprocated."

Brad clicked on Gina's e-mail and began to compose. He introduced himself by complaining about the 2000 and 2004 elections. He commented on the inane reality-television shows that seemed to make dumb Americans dumber. Before long Brad realized he'd written almost two thousand words, so he edited, taking out the parts about the tastes of organic figs (way too laden with sexual innuendo) and his treatise on the environment. He closed with: "If you're interested in meeting, feel free to e-mail me back, and if not, good luck out there. It sounds like you're a good person, and good things happen to good people." Brad didn't believe that, not really, or, if he did believe that, it had been watered down, coated with the ambiguous notion that good things also seemed to happen to bad people, too.

"P.S. I've attached a photo of myself as well." Brad was ready to send the e-mail but realized he had only a digital picture of himself without hair. He opened the deep desk drawer and pawed around, pushing aside a bundle of Watsons annual reports, sifting through a jumble of pens and pencils, a haphazard stack of rewritable CDs. He'd bought the camera before Compton's beating and had planned on taking a continuing education course on digital photography for two weekends. But the most he'd ever gotten around to shooting was the annual company picnic. He turned it on, surprised that the batteries still worked. The first picture that popped up was Sheila at the picnic, a cone of pink-and-blue cotton candy in her hand, her mouth poised, about to dig in. She was exaggerating of course, hamming it up. Brad stared at the picture, at her rosy lips and creamy skin. Then he heard Ratchet yell from the bottom of the stairs. "Brad, the food is ready!"

He took the hair system from the plastic baggy, raising it in the air like an award. He stood up and crept down the hall with the toupee in his hand. "I'll be right there," he hollered. Then added, "Thank you!" Just in case Dr. Gibbons was grading them on manners.

In the bathroom, Brad put on the hair and adjusted it to look natural, teasing it slightly to give him a more full-bodied look. When he was satisfied, he tiptoed back down the hallway to his room, walking so carefully it felt like he was practicing poise with a textbook balanced on his head.

Back at his desk, he snapped a photo and reviewed it. His face looked too ghostly, so he snapped another. This time his eyes were a demonic red, evil and dilated. Brad sat up straight, held the camera before his face, moving it farther away twice before pushing the button. This time it flashed and he thought the picture would look washed out, but it was fine. Maybe his smile could've been less fake, but people knew how hard it was to take a good picture of yourself, right?

Brad downloaded the pic after sorting through the desk drawers again to find the USB cord. He attached the photo, "Brad-O.jpg," and sent the e-mail. He logged off and walked down the hallway with a sense of accomplishment.

He strolled casually through the darker living room, the kitchen beaming just down the hallway, the smells of baked rolls almost like Sarah's. For a moment, he heard her calling for them. "Come on, Orville gents!" He missed her. He decided to be cordial, vague, and even a little kind during the meal.

As he stepped into the brightly lit kitchen, he saw that Dr. Gibbons was already seated at the table with Compton and Peaches. Ratchet was busy pouring more iced tea into their dripping tumblers. She looked over her shoulder as Brad went to the sink and filled a glass with water. Ratchet did a double take, crinkled her face, and squinted, as if she couldn't quite make out Brad's profile. "Hey, Brad," she said. "Um, do you know that . . . " Ratchet looked to the doctor for help. She was still pouring tea but pointing at Brad's head.

Dr. Gibbons noticed as well, starting some, seated in the chair. The table trembled as Dr. Gibbons cleared his throat, and said, "Oh." Brad looked in their direction blankly. For an instant, he thought he might be pantless or had come down without a shirt on. Compton struggled to get up and clomped toward Brad over the linoleum. He motioned for Brad to stoop. Cupping his hand over his brother's ear, Compton whispered loudly, "I think you've caused a brouhaha with that nutria fur." He stepped back from Brad and raised his eyebrows to indicate where the problem lay.

Brad felt the top of his head and realized the hair system had slipped to the side, nearly dangling over his right ear. He snatched it off and managed to fold the thing in half and tuck it into his back pocket. The doctor chewed on a nip of roll as he nodded toward Brad.

"Come sit down," said Compton, taking Brad by the arm. "Ratchet has made a wonderful meal." Brad felt the awful sting of embarrassment flush over him, but the vodka buzz helped, as did the thought of Gina2468.

They all sat around the table, as Peaches answered questions from the doctor about her unique name, the frequency of twins in her family.

"Yes," she said, patting her lips with a folded paper towel. "My great-grandmother was a twin. Ida and Ada were their names. Their mother was sold into slavery in Columbus, Georgia. Freed when she was thirteen. Ida and Ada lived in Spalding County before many blacks dared to set up there. They never got married. Worked at a shoe factory way up into their seventies. I got pictures of them as old ladies. I've been told I look a lot like Ida. My mother named me Peaches because that's what she was picking when she went into labor." Peaches reached for

Compton's hand. She was teary-eyed now, as the baby chicks cheeped away in the background.

Brad's head was light from the vodka. It was the most he'd heard Peaches say at one time, and what struck him so was how she seemed to speak without taking a breath. The alcohol was kicking in, and he felt a little happy even. He said, without thinking, "Sounds like your family was really wonderful, Peaches. You'll make a great mother." It seemed to Brad that they all stopped chewing and stared at him, and really, he couldn't blame them.

twenty-one

He went to sleep and woke up sweaty midway through the night. There was nothing to do but check the computer. Gina had not e-mailed him back and he rechecked the e-mail he'd sent, looking for misspellings or missteps, a word or phrase that might make her think he was desperate. Brad read it aloud to himself, the desk lamp on low, moths and other winged insects fluttering outside his window, futilely trying to break through, pulling instinctively toward the burnished light inside.

Brad clicked on the jpg of himself, zooming in on the hairline until the area looked like the frayed hem of a throw rug. Of course, he tried to tell himself, she wouldn't zoom in on his face. Who would? Over and over Brad checked his in box, and again and again the blasted "0 new messages" glared at him from above the mailbox icon. When he finally did wear himself out, the bottle of vodka was gone. That wasn't a problem, though, he told himself. If you drink it over the space of an entire day, spreading the drinks out, you weren't really drinking because the buzz came and went, never actually building into a full drunk, kind of like a motor idling, taking off, idling again. Brad fell into a drunken, fitful sleep, before waking again two hours later.

The house was quiet when Brad crept downstairs at dawn. Ratchet was on the fold-out couch downstairs, and Peaches and Compton were snuggled in their bed. Outside, silver light hovered in crooked lines along the horizon. Brad watched out his long window at the development. They'd put in the first cement curbs and blacktopped entry streets. Against the red mounds of earth, the whitish curbs and ebony pavement looked progressive, like a still photo from the '50s. Brad sipped a cup of coffee spiked with whiskey. To feel better about drinking so early, he'd gone quietly past Ratchet on the couch and made a pot of coffee as silently as he could, putting a heavy hand towel over the Krups, muffling the percolation. On his way back through the living room, Brad stopped to watch the girl sleep. She had on the same pair of flannel bottoms and tight T-shirt he'd seen her in before, but now her flat stomach was exposed, the belly button staring directly at Brad, bare and verging on risqué because the p.j. bottoms had inched down some.

Brad set his cup of coffee on the round magazine table, stacked high with National Geographics, and moved toward her. She looked cold, hugging herself loosely across the chest. Brad reached down and pulled the blanket over her legs, up past her midriff and to her chin, tucking it in some. He stood back and watched how she had not even moved, eyelids like hulls, thin and nearly translucent. She was completely asleep, not a sound coming from her. Ratchet's face was serene, and it occurred to Brad how easily she occupied the space, a pocket of femininity lying softly on the couch. He moved away and went back to his bedroom.

At his desk he once again checked e-mail, obsessed over the photo he'd sent, and finally searched the Internet for the bottle of whiskey he was drinking.

Brad found a Web site that valued old booze, found the Connemara, and clicked on the icon above its description. "$89.99," it read, over a hundred bucks after shipping. While he was at it, Brad thought he'd check out the others in the cabinet and locate the value of each of his father's unopened bottles. It was mindless, something to do to feel like he was doing something. Milo wasn't a big drinker, not after the boys were born; there were stories of him being able to hold his liquor, relayed by more than a few foreign visitors, but apparently he'd lost the taste for it, which explained the inventory that outlived him. It was an odd thing, finding pieces of trivia about his parents like this; once Brad had moved back into the house with Compton it seemed there were weekly opportunities. He'd sat up late reading their postcards and diaries, stacks of the stuff that gleaned surprises, things Brad had never known about their parents. Milo's penchant for everything organic flourished after the boys had arrived, he learned; Sarah painted in watercolors rather than oil because the boys often made messes otherwise, stains that couldn't be removed. And they both turned down chances to work abroad while Compton and Brad were in grade school.

Brad went through stacks of the letters and notebooks right after Compton got out of the hospital, when Compton spent most of the time sleeping. Every now and then Brad would find him, his thick hair standing on end, sitting on the porch, looking wistfully toward the orchards, and Compton would say again, "You're the one. . . . You're the one I did that thing to."

Now, Brad carried an armload of the bottles to his desk. The Dumbarton Vintage 1964 Clan Denny Single Grain was worth $400, the Web site said. The bottle was clear, with a label that seemed more suited for wine. Brad found it hard to believe it was forty-three years old. Next was a 1977 Ferrand cognac. One site listed it as worth $1,225 if the box was in moderate shape.

Brad picked up a photo of his parents and placed it next to the computer screen. He poured a touch of the Clan Denny into his empty coffee mug and sipped it.

Brad let the morning distract him, watching out the window as a lone jackrabbit munched at the roots of yellowed crabgrass. A slow, tranquil buzz settled over him, and he felt the need to work on his appearance, really test things out with his hair.

Brad put on the toupee again, working on it in the bathroom, then walking back to his room. He crawled on the bed and lay perfectly still for a moment, staring at a water stain on the ceiling, wondering if the hairpiece would stay put if he ever in his life had sex again. He rolled over, then back again, squirming into the comforter as if he were a centerfold. He sat up and bounced in the bed, shook his head. Brad took hold of a pillow and pretended to kiss it, turning his head left to right, mashing his face into the soft cushion. How would he stop a lover from trying to run her fingers through it? He couldn't remember a time, back when he still had hair, that a woman had actually done such a thing, but still. Brad ran his own fingers through the crown without much trouble, but when he started at the front where his fake hairline began, his fingers snagged on the underweaving. He thought of his mother's sewing machine, the needle stuck, the material ripping as it bunched up. He'd be sure to gently take a lover's hand and put it to his heart if she tried to caress his scalp; it would be cheesy and overdone, but at least she wouldn't end up fiddling with the piece, screaming when it loosened and stuck to her long nails, flipping it against the wall like a rat. Brad writhed some more on the bed, even feigned a bucking orgasm before he returned to the computer and sat down.

It didn't matter if Gina had responded or not, he told himself, as he kept hitting the back button, returning to his e-mail. The screen stalled, bogged down with graphics and too many open windows. Down the hallway, Compton's squeaky bedroom door opened, then closed slowly, the sound like an old man's Pontiac. They'd be downstairs milling about again, another day spent right in front of him, Ratchet in her same clothes, cooking and tending to the chicks, while Compton and Peaches played lovey-dovey, retiling the entire house or ordering a herd of beefalos. Brad waited for the e-mail window to open, a count of at least one hundred. Finally, it appeared, a jumble of html code and partially amalgamated advertisements. The connection was screwed up, slow and dastardly, but it was clear, a big fat zero over the in-box icon.

Brad crawled back in bed with the bottle of Clan Denny and shucked off his shirt. It was hot in his room, but the clicking ceiling fan helped. He took a long pull from the bottle, and then drifted off into a fitful dream of Jennifer Hunton, images of lapping water, the lake almost green, placid from the pier, the few boats bobbing along the distant horizon, everything turning turquoise and amber, Compton and Jennifer laughing so hard he could spot their fillings, a dull silver gleam, tongues as red as berries. Brad dreamed on and on, the same images flittering through his head. Memory was not only Compton's enemy.

"You're the one I did that thing to." That was the sound track to the movie that betrayed him.

twenty-two   Brad's workweek started with two major problems. The first was his bitter hangover. The second was the franchisee near the Spalding County line—the same man who had asked Brad if he could give the whole damn thing back—who didn't follow up on his second inspection of the gas pumps. Without the inspection from the city his opening would be delayed. Toby Watson came into Brad's office without knocking.

"You need to get over to sector six. One of the franchisees there is about to fuck things up. Why didn't you hold his hand and walk him through the fuel island inspection?" Toby was not feeling very super excellent this morning.

"Because that's clearly a duty of the franchisee. It's spelled out in their licensing agreement. Additionally, I've never been instructed to do so." Brad could tell that Toby's brain was about to implode. He wasn't cut out to handle the day-to-day managerial tasks of the company, and anybody watching him would conclude he was better suited for the role of company mascot. Brad's stomach tightened, and he wished he hadn't opted for a tube of coconut crunch donut gems on the way to work; they'd tasted even more like Play-Doh than he remembered, and their filmy residue still played along his teeth.

"Hey," said Toby, "I don't want to hear any talk about things not getting done. That's not how Watsons works." He'd molded so much gel into his hair it looked like his head had been dipped in glue. Toby's biceps bulged through a short-sleeve short, and they were tanned like the rest of his body, sprayed on, Brad assumed.

"All I was saying, Toby, is that we've never taken over parts of the franchisee requirements. Are we sure this guy even wants to open? When I was there he seemed fairly tentative about it."

Toby wrinkled his massive brow. "What do you mean?"

"I mean the franchisee, what's his name, Dirks, or something like that. He doesn't seem all that committed."

Toby rubbed his strong chin, stared at the floor. "Yeah, he might be tentativeless," said Toby. Brad suppressed a smile; he had plenty of experience with made-up words.

"Besides, that's not really my area of expertise. Shouldn't the guys in the Franchisee Relations Department handle working Dirks through his concerns?"

"No," Toby said almost shyly, surprising Brad with timidity; he seemed like a little boy held after class. "My dad wants me to take care of all the stuff in sector six. Everything from public relations to inspections, and this crap with Dirks," he said, frazzled. "Shit!" Toby added, punching the air with his fist.

Brad had never gotten used to the company's new schematic grid, the naming of each portion of the county by sectors. It sounded like something from Star Trek, a show he and Compton used to watch religiously, as Milo explained how impossible the science was behind the episodes.

"Well, I'm sure you'll do just fine, Toby," said Brad, a cramp in his stomach.

"That's easy for you to say, I mean, you're good at what you do." Toby popped his shoulders and looked down at his feet.

Brad thought for a moment, trying to decide how to get him out of his office so he could see if Gina had responded and take a swig from the bottle in his top drawer. "Just go talk to Dirks. The city permit isn't that tough. How could it be? They build everywhere out there. And your family name is enough to get you a meeting. Plus, if you're that worried, take Julie along. She's good with people."

Toby eyed him from under the meaty, small forehead. "Yeah, I guess. It's just that . . ." He stalled, then drew a breath. "Never mind, Orville," he said. "I'll give you a ring if I need you to take care of anything."

"Okay," said Brad, the vacant, rattling sensation of his upset stomach taking most of his attention. His hangover was bitter and stolid.

"Super excellent," Toby said flatly, strutting impotently toward the door. The heavy stink of too much CK cologne hung in the air. The phone rang and Brad picked it up, irritated. Ratchet told him to come home, she needed help. "Hurry," she said.

Brad pulled the car into the driveway. Water was draining down along the gravel, little streams of runoff trickling toward the creek, squirming under the leaves from last fall. It was strange to see amid the drought, like witnessing a block of Neapolitan ice cream in the sandy desert. He quickly got out of the car and ran to the back door. It was open, and as he rushed in Ratchet met him.

"It's okay now," she said. "I'm sorry I called you away from work like that. He was just inconsolable for about a half hour." She'd showered and washed her hair, glints of red shining through. She smelled like soap, cheeks pink.

"What happened?" asked Brad, pulling a chair out from the kitchen table.

"I'm not sure," Ratchet said. "One minute he was trying to pump out the basement and the next thing we knew he was sobbing uncontrollably. I thought it might have something to do with his emotional center, snapping or something, but then he just stopped." Brad felt something like anger and impatience at the girl, and tried to quell it. He was worn down by lack of sleep and booze, though, and couldn't stop himself.

"What's wrong with you?" he half-hollered. Brad stared at Ratchet, who was now using an S.O.S. pad to scrub a skillet at the sink, the bluish-gray foam creeping from between her clenched fingers. The central air blew cool at Brad's feet, but silvery beads of sweat encircled Ratchet's hairline.

"No, it wasn't me, Brad. It was Compton. He had a little meltdown, but it's fine now."

"You know what I mean," said Brad, the tops of his ears red. "You know very well. If you're thinking there's money for the taking you can get that right out of your head. Everything's in my name, no matter what he's told you." Brad was lying; the house and the property were still deeded under both Compton and Brad Orville. "And even if it weren't, you'd have to be crazy to think I'd let him fork over our family's inheritance to you." He sneered. "What kind of name is Ratchet anyway?"

He thought she'd break down into blubbery tears, but she put the skillet down and wiped her hands on a towel and sat down at the table, each task she performed making Brad less and less sure of his assumptions, until she looked him directly in the eye with pity.

"I've got ADD," she said. "And bipolar disorder. I don't want a dime of your money, which would be nothing compared to my family's. We're the Spencers, as in Spencers Pecan Rolls? Annual net sales of three-point-five million a year. And Ratchet is a nickname I was given as a child. My favorite toy was a plastic tool set." She stood back up and went to the sink, flipped on the faucet, steam filling the space before her, rising up toward the ceiling.

"Then why are you here, Ratchet Spencer? Shouldn't you be off in Jamaica somewhere sipping the drinks of spoiled brats and partying on yachts with the rich and famous, instead of nursing two nut jobs who have no chance of ever being full-time, real parents?"

She threw the S.O.S. pad into the sink with a slimy whap and stormed past him to the front door. She called over her shoulder, "If you even care, Compton and Peaches are upstairs. He became upset when he found a box of things in the basement. I put it in the pantry next to the chicks."

Brad heard the door close. Alone, he picked at his cuticles and listened to the house purr in silence, interrupted every few seconds by the chirping of week-old chickens. He sat heavily into a kitchen chair, his elbows hard against the table. The phone rang, and rang again, but he didn't budge. He got up, finally, and walked slowly into the living room, feeling as if he were being watched by an audience, an actor on some rickety set, lines forgotten. The smell of the moldy basement had eased. At the long windows he watched as Ratchet raked pine needles from between the fruit trees. No fewer than ten sprinklers had been set up, and the sunlight made tiny rainbows in the mist. She disappeared behind a row of beehives, and even though Brad waited for some time, staring out the window, Ratchet didn't come back into view. He lingered at the window, then finally crept back to the kitchen.

Brad opened the pantry as if a rabid dog had been quarantined there. The pantry was hot and smelled of allspice and the slurry of vinegar and pickled cucumbers. The red light to keep the chicks warm cast an eerie, haunted-house glow on everything. He spotted the box right away, a little damp, but otherwise unharmed. Early on he'd moved the valuable stuff to the top of the shelves in the basement, promising himself he'd have the basement dampness looked at soon.

He pulled back the cardboard and found packets of photos, all still in the twenty-four-hour envelopes, the negative strips falling out, spooky in their sepia and ghostly tones. One packet was completely opened, obviously the one that Compton had been looking at. The entire roll was of the weekend at the reservoir. It'd been over a decade since it had happened, and Brad's hands still trembled as he sorted through them. There was one with all three of them. Jennifer was in the middle, and Brad and Compton had their arms around her. A strong whiff of SPF 20 was right there with him in the pantry; the smell of sawdust and chicken litter didn't have a chance.

Brad went through them all. He was amazed at how easily he could reconstruct the days over the long weekend. In one photo, Brad and

Compton wore dark sunglasses on a deck, a broad sunset behind them, the water like a dark brown pane of glass. The story ended with a picture of them all on the last night. They'd been in the kitchen of the little cabin they'd rented, cooking fresh fish, chopping garlic, and plucking rosemary from the stem, the three nursing glasses of wine, an entire case of Heinekens emptied on the counter. It was after midnight, and they were famished, having spent the day drinking, first on the beach, then at a bar, shooting pool and throwing darts. Brad wanted to cook, to impress his fiancée with his skills. Jennifer was wearing a miniskirt, her hair tantalizingly long, down past her waist. Compton held up a trout to the camera, acting as if he were kissing it. Jennifer was laughing, head thrown back, arms open wide, a pink tank top vibrant against her berried skin. After dinner they'd gone swimming, drinking more. When they got back to the cabin, they shucked off their swimsuits on the deck and went to bed. It was well past three in the morning.

Jennifer claimed later that in the middle of the night her stomach hurt. Brad had watched as she crawled out of bed, clad only in an oversize T-shirt. He was exhausted, sunburned, and drifting in and out of sleep. Finally, he rose and went to check on her. She wasn't in the bathroom or the kitchen. Brad rubbed his eyes as he slid open the glass door leading to the deck. Hoary light shone from a full moon and onto the slats, their swimming suits dripping on the railing, the trickle like a ticking clock.

He became frightened then, worried that something had happened to her, and he ran down the hall to the room Compton was staying in. When he tossed open the door, Brad half expected that he would find his brother with the waitress who had been hitting on him two nights before at a roadhouse they'd gone to. The light in the room was murky, a shade partially open. Compton jumped up, nearly throwing the girl into the wall. Brad was stunned, having seen that hair, that unmistak-able hair. Jennifer's sultry mane flowed around her head and whipped back again, as she wrapped a sheet around herself, huddled against the wall as if he were a murderer, not a fiancé.

The rest, Brad running down the beach, not stopping until almost daylight, his walking into a little town called Riley and hitching back to Whitchfield County, the days that followed, Compton calling and call-ing, Jennifer Hunton's long letter telling him she was so sorry it hurt—all of that was a blur marred by random images of a rented boat, drunken sunsets viewed from a bar, weeks of loneliness, hate, and self-hate. Then, finally, taking the job at Watsons, a job he knew he would despise, a job Brad also knew Compton would see as a desire to give up, settle for any-thing. It wasn't much revenge, but maybe it'd hurt Compton to have to sit by and watch as Brad's life turned into something unrecognizable.

Two months later, Compton said, "Don't take that job, Brad. Don't punish yourself. You'll hate it. You didn't do anything wrong." They were standing outside the duplex Brad had moved into. He threw Compton against the wall, raised his fist, his whole arm quivering with tension.

"If you ever loved me as a brother, you'll never mention any of it again. Do you understand that?"

Compton nodded his head, as if the fist were indeed a gun and he was afraid it would go off. Brad turned to leave and drive to the week-long orientation Watsons gave all new managers. "I'll see you later," he'd muttered to Compton, barely able to breathe.

For the entire drive to Orlando, Brad talked himself through it, forced himself to suck it up. True love was different than this. He'd start again and find someone who would be loyal, all the while checking his thin hair at stoplights, at the truck stops along the way. A real job would help him grow up, put away some money.

When Brad returned from Orlando, having sat through one motivational franchise speech after another until they all seemed like football fight songs, he picked up the phone to call Compton, but put it back down slowly. For six months he did the same thing, almost dialing the number. Then, one night he finally made the call and asked Compton to come over. They went to a bar and grill called Smiley's and ate pasta and steak and drank Dutch beer, carefully avoiding any talk about the past. Near the end of the night, Compton told Brad about his new radio advertising job. "It's not bad really. I can make my own schedule and drive from town to town. The sales area is spread over ten counties." Brad didn't say it, but something about Compton's own diminished dreams did seem to quell some of the anger; it was comforting to know neither of them would lead the lives they'd hoped for, the lives that Sarah and Milo believed they'd lead.

After they paid the bill and stood in the parking lot, Compton said, "I'm going to mass next weekend. Want to come along?"

"Why?" said Brad, passing a little bottle of Jack Daniel's to his brother, dusk settling around them.

"Something to do, I suppose. Can't hurt."

Brad drank the last of the whiskey. "You go. Tell me how it is. Dad would shit if he knew you were gracing the walls of a church with your presence." They laughed and honked their car horns at each other as they sped out of the gravel parking lot in different directions. After that evening, which Brad had come to label the night they moved on, things were tenuous but cordial. But it was always there. Brad would wake from a dream of that night in the cabin and be so filled with disgust and hate and betrayal that he wanted to pound Compton until his nose was squashed.

And then the sheriff called about Compton being assaulted by the mechanic, and for a moment he wasn't completely sure if he hadn't done it himself—somehow sleepwalked through a brutal attack on his own brother. On the drive to the emergency room he even examined his knuckles for cuts or a shard of tooth.

Now, standing with the photographs in his sweaty hands, Brad realized that the pictures had reminded Compton of the betrayal. He'd not wanted to forgive Compton back then, and now it seemed too easy; if Compton asked now, with his memory of it only partially intact, Brad wouldn't be able to throw him against the wall, hurt him, punch him in the head. What kind of person would beat up his brain-injured brother? One good thing about Compton's beating had been that the memory of Jennifer Hunton was gone, at least for one of them. That idea had comforted Brad at times; maybe if it had been erased from Compton's memory, Brad could forget it, too. But now, Compton was on to it. Brad sighed and closed his eyes. Don't bring it up, he said to himself. Stay clear of him and he'll forget all about it.

The chicks had quieted down. Brad shoved the packet of photos into his sport coat and stood for a moment looking at the little heap of feathers breathing. Their eyelids were like tiny bruised circles. Brad heard steps creaking above him, labored footfalls making their way down the stairs. It couldn't be anyone but Compton. Brad switched off the light, then realized the chicks would die without the warmth, so he pulled the chain and in doing so startled them from their sleep. They scurried to all four corners of the box, their little feet on the newspaper sounding like leaves tumbling over a sidewalk.

Brad peeked out of the pantry door and saw that the coast was clear. He rushed through the kitchen to the back door and across the driveway to his car. As he drove down the lane, Ratchet was still raking in the full sun. Brad kept his eyes clearly set before him, never looking to the side; he could catch glimpses of movement, though, and the flaring sunlight dancing over the hood. At the end of the driveway, he wished he'd had time to fetch a bottle of Milo's liquor before heading back to work.

twenty-three   "No, it's not like that. If they're evaluated on the basis of the help she provides, I think that hardly shows an independence, do you?" Brad sat back in his chair, the new hair system on his desk, the packaging strewn over his bed. There was half a Butterfinger candy bar sitting near the hair system; he picked it up and shoved the whole thing into his mouth. The workday at Watsons had gone relatively quickly, and now he took a long pull from a bottle of cognac. FedEx had finally delivered the luxurious piece in the morning while Brad was at work; he was surprised Compton hadn't ripped open the package. The hair system had been shipped in a thick glass container, silica packets lining the bottom. A stamp read: "Kept in a humidor after manufacture. Please allow 12 hours for your new hair to return to room temperature."

"Mr. Orville, this isn't something I arrived at easily," said Dr. Gibbons, his voice low on the other end of the phone line. Brad fought the urge to holler at him to speak up. "Compton and Peaches are absolutely impacted by their impairments, especially your brother, but by what I saw they manage most of the major life skill areas well. Yes, they will have to depend on some live-in help, and that will change dramatically I realize when the babies are born, but I cannot in good faith write a report that will help with an annulment."

"So you're going to let my brother drop twins down the stairs?" asked Brad, knowing full well that wasn't the case. He sipped the cognac. To his count, there were ten bottles of good stuff left in the cabinet.

"Oh, I think that's a gross overstatement of your brother's limitations, Mr. Orville. How about we schedule a one-on-one session for you and I to simply . . . " the doctor went on, but Brad hung up, the phone settled back in its base with a small clatter. He poured another drink, this time just a smidgeon more.

He logged on to the Watsons e-mail account and found seven messages from Sheila, all about the same thing.

from: Sheila.T.Morris@watsons.com
to: Brad.L.Orville@watsons.com
sub: Meeting!
Brad, Where were you? Two of the developers needed to see you.
I left two messages on your phone and text-messaged you too. Big
Watson is pretty mad. Call me right away!

It didn't matter now. It was well after nine at night. He'd deal with it all tomorrow. Surely he could schmooze a couple of corporate lackeys. After all, they only wanted to go over the specs, just a meeting so they could bill their time, really. After another swallow of the cognac, Brad logged on to Personal Tru-Connections.

No queries on his account, not even a bit of activity. He emptied the remainder of the cognac in the glass and tilted it back. He checked his radar.com mail account and found a response from Gina.

"Hi, Brad, short notice here, but can you meet for a late dinner tonight?"

Brad typed back instantly, "Sure. Where?" He moved from behind the desk to his closet and chose a pair of dry-cleaned, smooth-front khakis and a knit short-sleeve shirt, tan and light blue. It would be too warm for it, but he had always liked how the shirt made his chest look, firm and broad. Pulling on the pants, he hopped on one leg back to the computer. Gina had written back: "Great. Let's meet at the Greenwood Tavern around 10. It's right next to the TJ Maxx on Jimmy Lee Smith Parkway."

Brad thought twice about it and shucked off the clothes, showered, and shaved, applying just a splash of cologne, something from his college days; the bottle was cracked and dusty, one of those personal items that just never gets thrown out. "Let's sponge down and spiff up!" That's what Milo had always told the boys to do before a night out at the college theater or after they'd pretended to pan for gold in the stream, marl caked to their forearms, the smell of algae in their hair. The hot steam always took him back to those days, but those memories had been displaced (like everything) with the images of Compton needing to be bathed. For the first two months, Brad helped him into the shower, instructing his brother all the way. It was embarrassing, watching Compton try to lather up, dropping the soap over and over, stooping without a trace of inhibition. Once, Compton had said, "What's this?" He was soaping up his tumescent penis, a thick patch of hair dripping suds. Compton held on to it, his eyes searching Brad's face for an answer.

"That's what got you here," said Brad, only half joking.

"Like a belly button you mean?" asked Compton.

"Not quite," said Brad.

And just like that, Compton began bawling.

Brad was so ashamed that he resorted to singing an old Irish song, just to get Compton to smile again. The tune had just popped into Brad's head, and before he realized it, a pattern had developed and he was crooning "Lish Young Buy-a-Broom" every night at bath time. The song was about a man meeting a young woman on the street selling brooms, a romantic story that ended with her leaving for Germany. The singing went on for almost two weeks before Brad started seeing the therapist, the one who told him he was trying to meet his own emotional needs for a child and family through Compton. From then on, until Compton met Peaches, Brad would set up an old clock radio outside the bathroom door and blast classic rock. Compton loved it.

Every once in a while, after his bath, he'd come into Brad's room wrapped in a towel and relay a bit of a memory that had come back. "One time we ate so many fudge pops you threw up chocolate milk," or "Did we skinny-dip with a large woman from Amsterdam in the creek thing out there?" And later, "Didn't she dance with me in the water? I think I touched her nipple."

In the bathroom, Brad opened the glass case. The hair system smelled woodsy. As instructed, Brad had kept it at the right temperature, as the hair "learned" to lie just right, but it hadn't been twelve hours, more like five, thought Brad, but he couldn't help himself. To meet Gina without his best hairdo felt like leaving the house without his wallet. Brad had signed up for the six-month plan, which allowed a new system delivered discreetly to his residence twice a month. All told, his monthly fee of $800 plus the necessary grooming kits would cost more than $5,000, a figure that would normally twist Brad's insides like a vacuum hose, but it would be billed in installments, and the world's finest aged liquors seemed to help with his reticence about nearly everything.

Besides, it was worth it. The Premium Human Hair Systems (PHHS) Web site claimed that its product was created and tailored using the real thing. The trans-base is very light, thin, comfortable, with an invisible natural hair line, and a scalloped and French front lace along with a super ultra thin polymer base, and bleached hair knots makes this system look like you were born with great hair. Made of 100%

European human hair, and the finest remy hair and kanekalon fiber. For everyday styling, this is the best quality hairpiece available.

Brad peeled off the backing from the surgical-grade adhesive tape, already sewn right into the hair. The piece felt more substantial, less coarse than the other. As he placed it on his head, it even felt more real, comfortable, and natural, even if he couldn't shake the image of how the company came to possess real human hair. PHHS claimed the hair system could be worn continuously for a solid two weeks. A little vial of solvent, which guaranteed a pain-free removal of the epoxy tape, came with the grooming kit.

He stood back from the mirror. The hair gleamed under the light like Compton's; in fact, the hair system made Brad look more like his brother than back when they were eighteen and twenty-two. That was the time when people, strangers, would comment on their close looks. Then, as Brad careened into baldness, it stopped. Occasionally someone might mention their similar eyes or the way they said a certain phrase, but that was it.

He redressed and didn't care if they heard him leaving, didn't even mind if they saw the hair system. He bumped into Ratchet in the hallway. She had on a sundress and her hair in a short ponytail.

"Hot date?" she asked, as if they hadn't quarreled earlier. Brad was surprised to see her wearing heels, something floral floating from her skin. Past her, the door to Compton's room was closed and he could hear Italian opera music playing. Ratchet didn't even flinch; her eyes never even went to his head. Brad wished they would.

"Uh, no, I've got to go meet someone for work," Brad said, his buzz slowing his words some.

"Oh, I see. She must be very demanding calling you away in the evening." Ratchet raised her eyebrows and popped her lips.

Brad gave her a courteous smile. "Work is work. But I should be asking you where you're off to. You look nice." He pointed at her shoes for some reason.

"We're going to mass tonight. St. Luke's off the square. Compton and Peaches invited me."

"Huh," said Brad, something inside of him wanting to get out of there and also wanting to understand. "So you're Catholic?"

"Nope, but I sure like the building. It's a gorgeous church. Roman Doric. I've gone there before. One of my best friends was married there." The bedroom door opened and Compton flipped on the hallway light. Brad and Ratchet turned toward him.

Compton, exuberant, hurtled toward Brad wearing a broad grin, his wild eye floating energetically inside that crumpled face, as if it could lift off and orbit the room. "You're coming to church, too? That's a splendiferous idea." Compton was shaking Ratchet's hand, as if she were somehow responsible for Brad's conversion. Brad felt a bit dizzy and had an urge to race out of the house to Gina. "I've got to go," he said, brushing Compton off, much like they'd both done with their great-aunt Ester on Sarah's side of the family; she always seemed to want to kiss them for too long.

Brad pushed past Ratchet and Compton, only to come face to face with a dolled-up Peaches. She wore orange-ish lipstick and a black dress that could've fit a twelve-year-old. Her hair was fluffed and it glistened with something that smelled like olive oil. Her little pouch of a stomach stuck out over her thin legs, a pair of white flats on her feet. Brad recognized the brooch on her dress, a copper palm tree with enamel flowers and faux pearls. Either Peaches had helped herself to Sarah's jewelry box or Compton had gifted it to her.

"You smell nice, Brad," she said. He ducked his head and galumphed down the stairs, taking them two at a time.

Compton called after him, "See you later when I bring Jesus back from church, bucko." The laughter that followed sounded like a real family's.

Brad burst out the front door as if there'd been no oxygen inside the house, dragging his drunken legs like Compton. He flopped into the Sentra and touched at his new hair. It felt somehow heavier than the other toupee, almost burdensome. Brad took a quick glance in the rear-view mirror and started the car. The headlights in the darkness seemed to swim a little. He squeezed his eyes shut tight and opened them, then shook his head. A little buzz, that was all, he told himself. He'd driven plenty of times with a buzz on. He'd be fine. He grappled in the glove compartment and finally found a box of tic tacs. He flipped open the top and shook a bunch onto his tongue. They were orange-mint and he gagged a little as he sucked on them.

As Brad passed the Tyler place, a single light burned in the shed, and Brad thought how Old Man Tyler hadn't stopped by to visit in nearly a month. Back when Milo and Sarah were alive, Mr. Tyler would be invited over for a Sunday night meal, and he'd sometimes bring Kyle. Brad stared at the light burning in the barn, as some shadowy movements meandered inside, a black drawn-out figure swaying with strain against the wall. Brad sped off, talking to himself, practicing what he'd say to Gina.

He had trouble keeping the front wheels from swerving over the line. He rolled down the window and let the humid air rush in. Only by speeding up did he feel more awake, the air conditioner on full blast. He took turns too quickly and squealed tires, and at stop signs he only let the car slow some, never making a complete halt.

When he was halfway there, about ten miles away from home, he came to a traffic light. Bright floodlights blasted the land at all four points, revealing tractors and backhoes and something Brad thought might be a crane, but he couldn't quite focus. It took a while, but Brad finally realized where he was. The intersection had been put in only a few months before, and the whole area now looked haphazard and treacherous, as if the earth was indeed flat and falling off was just a matter of losing one's point of reference. Where trees had once connected him to the geography, Brad now found the vast, cleared space absolutely disorienting. He drove on, wary, careful not to swerve, checking in the rearview mirror for cops. He was relieved to see the strip mall where he was to meet Gina.

The parking lot of the TJ Maxx shopping center, called the Avenues at Whitchfield, was jam-packed.

Brad opened the Greenwood Tavern door, letting another couple out, and walked inside. A huge whiff of greasy food and stale air shot up his nose. He wondered whether the smells would infiltrate his hair system, working their way into the roots. Brad looked around, and then walked in farther, past the hostess who didn't acknowledge him. He was starting to feel the dying swirl of a buzz, stomach empty, everything taking longer to do, his hearing muted.

A wave of exhaustion hit him, and Brad turned to go back outside, his dull hope ebbing. He had his hand on the door when he heard the rapid clip-clop of a woman in heels behind him. A hand was on his shoulder, turning him around.

"Brad?" said a long-haired blonde woman. She had wide eyes, blue, and jangling jewelry on her wrists. She wore a pair of tight jeans and a sleeveless blouse, the buttons open to her sternum, exposing a pushed-up bosom. Brad blinked, and realized that he'd been expecting another train wreck, a date that would end shortly after it had begun, maybe with a woman who, after they talked awhile, would end up saying, "You know, I think we're cousins," or "I'm just now getting over the time I did for manslaughter and want to get back into dating."

Gina smiled, her teeth perfect, a dusky shade of lipstick over her plump lips.

"Yes," said Brad. "And you're Gina?" She gave him a kiss on the cheek, and Brad couldn't help himself from wanting to rush her under a bright light to make sure she wasn't another man.

"Come on," she said. "Let's get out of here."

"Don't you have a purse or something?" Brad looked past her, toward a loud bar area with flashing lights.

"Nope, I left it in the car. This was just a meeting point. I hate places like these. The air alone could give you a skin condition," she said with a laugh, a kind of raspy giggle really.

Brad thought of his lonely, fading buzz, his need to medicate his nervousness. "Can't we get a drink, though?" he said, pointing to the bar.

"Sure, but I've got a bottle in the car. Come on." She moved past him and pushed the doors open. Her Personal Tru-Connections profile didn't seem to match the woman. She had the air of someone about to leave the country for a few years, carefree and more than slightly in a rush, her habits connected to another culture already, as if convention and time were always negotiable.

As she crossed the parking lot, Gina didn't wait for Brad to catch up and never turned around to see whether he was following her. He watched as she opened the door of a convertible BMW. Once she was behind the wheel she tooted the horn. "Come on. Let's go for a drive."

She had music playing before he could even sit down, something from the late '80s, maybe Tears for Fears, he couldn't tell. The car was spotless and obviously brand-new. The entire dash was alight with a

GPS screen and a sound system, the buttons glowing a surreal blue. Some kind of strong perfume hung around the interior of the car, making Brad both aroused and sick to his stomach. His craving for carbs flared up again, and his mouth watered at the thought of another package of waxy donut gems. Heavy trans fats, thought Brad, the drug of choice for the mildly depressed.

Gina gave him a sideways glance, a sedate curl to her lip. "You wanna drive?" she asked, and for a moment Brad thought he'd say yes, but she was already backing up, too fast, too jerky. Being beside this stranger was exotic; her strong perfume, the perfectly cleaned car, uncluttered except for a rose-colored Buddha stuck to the plush dash, all of it made him feel like a risk taker.

"Could we put the top up, you think?" he asked.

Gina sat erect behind the wheel, large silver hoop earrings swaying against her long neck. "Why?" she asked. "You're cold?" Brad nodded. "I can't believe you're cold," she said again, pushing at a button on the dash. The black vinyl top rose slowly from the rear of the car. As it eased down out of the dark night sky, Brad sat up some. He rubbed his arms and could now hear the music more clearly, no outside noises to contend with. It was Don Henley's "The Last Worthless Evening." Brad wondered whether Gina listened to this with every man she picked up, the CD always cued and ready. Still, it was haunting, the lyrical melody and words about alienation at the hands of romantic collapse. It occurred to Brad that it had been years since he'd heard the song. How was that possible? He thought of that singular notion as they cruised an overpass, the car ripe with Gina's perfume. You could go forever without hearing a song, after listening to it over and over; it just disappeared. Now, it seemed to linger inside the car, holding its tune as they careened to nowhere, the song like a person breathing.

"You wanna open that," said Gina, handing him a bottle in a brown bag. "It's not great, but it'll do." She tossed her hair over her shoulder. "Don't worry," she said as Brad removed the bottle from the paper sack, a fifth of Jim Beam. "I'm not a serial killer."

He tipped the bottle back without offering Gina the first pull, then handed it to her. They stopped at a railroad crossing at the Oak Ferry intersection. Train cars rattled slowly by, the clacking tracks like the music from a bass guitar, dull and spaced out, cadenced to the beat of an ailing heart. Gina handed the bottle back. "Really, I'm not going to hurt you."

"Shoot," said Brad. "I was hoping this would be a complete massacre. I could use that right about now."

Gina smiled and caressed the back of his head, her fingers tantalizing at the nape of his neck. "Okay," she said, reaching inside her purse. She took out two doobies from a pack of Kools. "Let's make a mess of it then." The train inched to a stop, the graffiti in focus now. An orange juice logo was plastered over with beautiful graphics, a moonscape that looked textured. "Look at that," said Brad. And they did, silently, as if standing before a canvas in an art museum. For the first time in a long while, Brad Orville sat with a woman and didn't say a thing.

twenty-four Watsons staff milled about the company's auditorium. Cold air, piped in via huge ductwork, gave the place a meat-locker feel. Brad sat next to Sheila, gulping as much black coffee as he could.

"So, how is everything?" Sheila asked, tapping her foot. She glanced at Brad's hair and cut her eyes toward the stage, like she'd spotted roadkill and couldn't bear to see it. Brad had a blistering look on his face, as if he'd wanted someone to punch him just to see if the expression would hold up. He'd worn the same look before, especially in the months after

Compton's hospital stay, but even then it was more contained, less reckless. Brad told Sheila too loudly that he was getting another cup of coffee. He was aware how she was watching him, worried he might do something awful, like piss on the floor or offer to tutor Toby to his face. He felt her eyes following him as he shook President Watson's hand like he was a senator on his way up the aisle. Watson was on his way to the stage, doing his Man of the People stint. Brad pumped his arm, and said too loudly, "Great, just great. Happy to be here and be a part of the Watson Family." Brad threw his head back and chortled, hoping Sheila would see. When he glanced back at her, she'd turned away. The lights dimmed, and Toby Keith music idled in the background.

Brad fumbled in the dark to pour another large cup full of coffee. He hadn't slept at all and walked about in a stupor, Gina's perfume on his lips. Even under the bitter coffee it was there, like a little reminder of their night. He walked back to where he thought he'd been sitting and licked his lips as he searched the seats for Sheila. It was almost pitch dark in the auditorium as the board members took their seats on stage.

"Sheila," Brad said in a talking voice, too loud. "Sheila," he said louder. She raised her arm and waved it in the air, hanging her head. Brad meandered toward her, his vision palpitating. He squeezed past two men who worked in accounting, both of them now playing with their BlackBerrys.

"Geez, why don't you just hide next time," Brad said, again too loud.

"Sit down," hissed Sheila, pulling him into the seat. She leaned into him and said into his ear, "You smell like pot, perfume, and booze. You better watch out or Watson will have you escorted out of here."

Brad slurped the coffee. He parroted her whisper. "I doubt that. I'm family."

"What?" said Sheila, backing away from Brad's stale breath. "Are you still drunk?"

"I'm sure of it. But we Watsons take care of our own," he said, a sly, woozy look on his unshaven face.

Sheila shook her head. "Get away from me. You're acting like an ass."

"What's wrong, Sheil, you jealous I'm finally out there?" Brad slugged back the cup of coffee, a sixteen-ounce Watson "Bright and Early!"

She grabbed his arm and pulled him into her, pinching him. He could feel her heat. She rasped into his ear. "Who's taking care of Compton, Brad?" She pushed him back and raised her eyebrows, then yanked him to her again. "I haven't heard from him for two weeks. When I called two different women answered. Are you even watching out for him now, or is it just yourself?"

Brad made a kissing sound at Sheila's face.

"I'm moving!" she said just as the stage went dimmer and the spot-lights came on, illuminating the men and women of the Watsons board of directors. Sheila pressed past the accountants and settled in an empty area away from everyone. Brad sat up straighter in the chair, pulling himself into a respectable posture. He didn't look at Sheila again.

The board meeting was held every two months, and most of the time President Watson talked about stores opening, their diversified portfolios, and the future of the Watsons franchise. Sometimes, after the newspaper had spotlighted some new Watson family purchase, a lakeside home or an addition to their office suites, President Watson would bring in a franchisee to talk about his success, using a Power-Point to show early-morning customers lined up to get their gas and Vanilla Latte Espressos.

Brad sat in the dark auditorium, numb all the way through. He'd told Toby and President Watson, finally, yes. He'd agreed to their request and was told it would be announced this morning at the meeting, followed by a Watson Family lunch. Brad watched as Julie sashayed across the stage and sat down next to Toby. She looked distracted, sort of ruffled, her blouse billowing, the seat of her pants so tight the black material appeared like a neoprene scuba-diving suit.

The call had come only hours ago, while Gina and Brad were sitting, nude, in a rickety lounge chair in their room at the Heart Themes Hotel. They'd rented the cabana room, which really looked like a screened-in porch with green indoor-outdoor carpeting that made Brad's feet itch. The hot tub in the room was the shape of a coconut, the outside covered in something approximating a coconut husk, a kind of brown, woven fuzz that shed onto the carpet.

"It looks like a testicle," Gina said as she stripped off her blouse and jeans, standing in the full light before Brad. "Come on, let's get in." She unclasped her bra and shimmied out of her underwear, while Brad tried to clear his head. The joint, followed by another, followed by groping at the train tracks, had created a fullness in his head that felt like a cottony blitz; he thought of the time he'd been knocked out cold by Compton for playing with his Erector Set. He had that same woolly mind-set, coming to, fading out.

"I'll look the other way. But you shouldn't be shy, Brad. I can tell by your build you're a thirty-two-inch waist, right? I can tell," she said as she smoked a cigarette, cupping the ashes. Brad thought he recalled her saying she hated smoking in her personals ad.

He undressed quickly, cold air from the a.c. on his skin. After the hot tub, Gina actually escorted him to bed. Brad was about to pass out when he felt her touching him, putting on the condom like a nurse and then straddling him, working slowly, her nails digging into his chest. Brad was relieved when she came. "I'm done, are you, or do you want me to keep moving?" she asked as Brad tried to catch his breath.

The tips of her hair brushed her nipples. Brad put his hands on her waist and thrust, feeling her lovely hip bones under fleshy padding. He said a little silent prayer that the new piece would stay put; his scalp prickled as he slowed down his movements. Afterward, she said, "That was nice. I came twice," her words like a rhyme. For two hours they dozed in and out and drank from a new bottle of vodka.

The sun had just risen when Watson called. Brad answered the cell phone without looking at who it was. "You got a lawyer, son?" President Watson asked after a few minutes of back and forth, during which Brad finally agreed to sell his place. Watson convinced him it was for the best, the best for Brad, the best for his brother, the best for the community, but in the end, Brad knew he'd agreed to the sale as his last-ditch effort to prove to himself that he was still in control. Even inebriated he was aware of his spite. Gina was sleeping, her legs kind of spread. Brad gently pushed one long leg back in place so that she moved onto her side.

"President Watson? Yeah, um, I don't have his number, though, uh, let me see." Brad tried to remember how to pull up the recent calls list without hanging up on Watson. "I'll get it to you at the board meeting."

"Fine, son. But for now, keep this quiet. We'll announce it all formally later this morning."

"Super excellent," Toby said in the background, the speakerphone crackling.

Brad found the lawyer's number, and although he wanted to just lie back down he phoned Randall himself.

"Good morning," beamed Joseph Randall.

"This is Brad Orville. I'm sorry to call so early."

"Think nothing of it. I'm out walking the dog." Brad could hear panting and the jingle of a leash. How simple life could be. A routine, something that felt familiar and homey; it seemed everywhere he looked this was happening—in checkout lines where a couple helped each other load groceries, at the Watsons picnics when families worked together to win a stupid sack race—hell, it was even happening in his own house, Peaches and Compton feeding each other cheese on Triscuits. The lawyer had to have a wife and kids; he probably even had a golden retriever. The dog's name would be Duke or something more collegiate, perhaps Connor.

"No, Tanner, no," Randall said as the dog barked in the background. "Sorry, Brad, he's spotted a squirrel. Black Labs love them." Close, thought Brad.

"What can I do for you? I'm sorry Dr. Gibbons's report wasn't more helpful. But I suppose it's good to know your brother is quite intact, able to live a good life?"

"Yeah, I suppose," said Brad. "This is about something else. I've just given a verbal approval to my employer to have them buy our property. It was under eminent domain anyway, and the price seems fair enough. His attorney will be calling you, if that's oshay." Brad coughed, "I mean, okay."

Randall was quiet, even his dog seemed to quit panting. Brad could tell Randall had stopped walking.

"Where are you, Mr. Orville?"

"Uh, I'm at home. I just wanted to give you a heads-up."

"Do you have a check with you?"

"No, actually, I . . . I'm at a friend's."

"Okay. Listen, I'm going to call you back in ten minutes. You're going to give me your credit card information."

"Why?" asked Brad, growing weary. Gina moved beside him. She looked cold so Brad got up slowly, found a blanket, and spread it over her.

"Because you're drunk, and you've just agreed verbally to a contract. That's not prudent. We need to establish our attorney-client privilege."

"No, it's fine. I don't want to fight."

"Then do it for me. Or your brother, or whomever it is you're with right now. Just let me run your information and set up a file. I'm going to come to you. Tell me where you are. The address."

Brad's head hurt, his mind swirling. "Okay, you're gonna love this." He told him about the hotel.

"Of course, I know it. I worked divorce cases for fifteen years back in the mid-eighties right through the nineties. More than a couple nights I staked out that hotel. It used to be a favorite spot of adulterers."

Less than an hour later Randall showed up at the door. Brad had pulled on his clothes, and he blinked as Randall took him by the arm and led him outside, guiding him to sit inside a Lincoln Navigator and sign forms. "Here, blow into this," Randall said, placing a Breathalyzer in front of Brad's mouth.

"Is this necessary? I mean I'm just selling the place after all, not testifying before Congress."

"Fine. And this may be something that you'll never want to pursue, but all the same, breathe into this for posterity's sake. If we had to, we could argue you agreed to the contract under duress." Randall wriggled the Breathalyzer until Brad finally blew into it. "Again," said Randall. "One more."

Brad opened the door of the SUV and puked into the parking lot. "Sorry," said Brad, stepping over his own vomit.

"Pretty impressive, Mr. Orville," Randall said, looking at the digital readout. "Just a tad over one-point-four."

Brad swayed, holding on to the door. "I'm just trying to get rid of a cold."

Randall laughed. "Well, as your attorney I'd advise calling in sick or taking a cab. The last thing you need or anyone else for that matter is a DUI."

"Will do," said Brad.

"Not that it's any of my business, but what are you trying to accomplish here?" Randall asked, filing all the forms away, placing the Breathalyzer into a baggie. He looked like a realtor, not a rich lawyer, a clipboard resting on his leg, an Atlanta Braves cap pulled down too far.

Brad shrugged his shoulders. "You ever feel like the life you're leading isn't your own? That you're only here to work and never ever find anything else?" he asked, his eyes welling up with shiny tears.

"Well, that's tough to say, but I suppose a person could do worse. You've got a hot piece of property to sell, and your brother is better off than what most people in his condition are."

Brad nodded, the hair system now tingling his head. Randall had not said anything about it, and Brad couldn't tell if that was out of pity or lack of attention.

Brad leaned over and puked again, his hacking like a dying person's. Randall said, "I'll call you a cab myself."

Sitting in the auditorium just a few hours later, Brad thought he might puke again. Up on the stage, President Watson fiddled with papers at the podium and Julie and Toby sat side by side without speaking. Brad tried to look in the direction of Sheila, but in the darkness he couldn't find her. A pang of guilt rose inside him, but he swatted it away. Watson had given him an off-the-record deal, too, one that would get him a sizable raise and allow him some control over how the land was developed. "The way I figure it, son, your place is going one way or another. With what we're willing to pay for it, plus your salary increase, you'll be able to care for your brother real good."

The sound system popped and sizzled a little, then President Watson cleared his throat. "I'd like to call this board session to order, folks, so if you would kindly take your seats."

Brad wanted another cup of coffee, something else to lift the tiers of fog from his head. A cigarette would be nice. He shifted in the chair, legs going to sleep, and wished he had a drink.

"This is a special day for us, folks. Please, if everyone could take their seats, we'll get started so we can finish. The company is providing a lunch when the board comes out of executive session."

Some techies fixed the microphone and blasted the screen behind President Watson with the company logo, a "W" encircled with a filigreed wreath and a small set of stars just outside the holly, two at the top and at each side, one underneath, larger.

"I say today is special for a number of reasons," said Watson, his perfectly tailored suit iridescent in the spotlights. "First, it'll be thirty years next week that my father and I started a little grocery store over near the Spalding County line. Yep, that's right. What is now called store number one was the first place we did business.

"Today, we've got more than one hundred stores around the greater metro area, nearly all of them franchises, owned and operated by some of this country's hardest-working entrepreneurs!" President Watson shoved his fist into the air like a football coach. Brad thought he saw two board members roll their eyes.

The image on the large screen changed slowly, an even bigger Watsons logo emerging from ghostly whiteness, blending slowly into focus. A shot of the new prototype store beamed toward the crowd. An aisle stocked with colorful foodstuffs in similar packaging was blown up on the screen and zoomed in, first one level, then a deeper view.

"Welcome to the new era of Watsons own proprietary food label!" announced President Watson. "In today's hyperactive lifestyle, people don't want to spend time in a big grocery store. They want to dash in, dash out, and put off today what they can always buy tomorrow. That's where we come in. It's not enough to provide our consumer with the regular food products of yesteryear. They want snazzy packaging, high-falutin names, and mix-and-match capacity. Right?" Watson cupped his hand to his ear to get the crowd to chant in unison.

"Right!" came roaring back at him, Toby leading the charge.

"So today we mark not only thirty years of honest, wholesome, American hard work, we also celebrate the new age of Watsons. The twenty stores that are still operated by the company will be franchised, and we'll build fifteen new stores every two months, all of which will carry the new food line. And all will be franchised!" He took a deep breath and patted his forehead with a folded napkin.

"Who will run the food line, you ask?" Watson motioned for Toby to come forward. "Ladies and gentlemen, please meet Watsons' new vice president of specialty foods, Mr. Toby Watson!"

The president stood back and let Toby approach the mike. They both were still clapping as Toby said simply, "Thank you, everyone!" Even his father seemed dismayed as Toby went right back to his seat next to Julie and sat, a wounded expression over his features, as if he'd been told he was ugly and there was nothing he could do about it. Brad watched Toby. Some people had everything—hair, looks, a wife, an easy life—and still they didn't want it. All he wanted now was Gina, a bottle of something drinkable, and the firm hope of annihilation.

"Thank you, Toby. That was simple and straightforward, folks. That's what Watsons has always been about."

For the next twenty minutes, different officers presented information about sales forecasts, franchisee relations, and the company's new health benefits that cost more and paid less, all of it packaged with PowerPoint slides that beamed American flag graphics and, of course, differing versions of the Watsons logo. Brad drifted off and dreamed of Jim Jones, the cult, and the syrupy drink of eternity. He woke with a start. Brad had heard his name, but he couldn't figure out why it was being called over a loudspeaker.

Someone was elbowing Brad, which brought him fully out of the dream. His mouth felt hollow and scorched. "I think they would like for you to approach the stage, Mr. Orville," said an accountant, his lap full of handouts; Brad's own pile was strewn over the sloping floor at his feet.

He stood up and tucked in his dress shirt as he walked. He'd been on this stage a few times, mostly during staff meetings when the progress of a certain new store was off schedule, but as he plodded up the steps the light seemed much brighter, like the lights in a surgery amphitheater. He staggered, and then righted himself, only to return to a wobbly pace. Your brother's gait, his gait, gait, gait . . .

Brad finally stood next to President Watson. Somehow he could feel Sheila's stare, her wicked disapproval. It fired him up, and suddenly he felt composed, completely at ease because he was taking on a role, acting the dutiful employee. He actually put his arm behind Watson's back. The hairpiece seemed to attract the hotness from the bright lights, and Brad felt as if the damn thing was now a heating pad.

"Folks, the last bit of announcement today is a promotion. Most of you know Brad Orville. He's been with us ten years, and his parents were teachers at our fine college. He's being given the opportunity to take on the environmental design for all of our new stores. Today's consumer wants its corporate citizens to belly up to the table. Let's give Brad a round of Watsons congratulations." The crowd clapped, but it wasn't unlike the pitiful appreciation people show after a drunken uncle makes a toast. President Watson offered Brad the microphone, and as he stepped back Watson gave Brad's head a squinted inspection, as if he'd spotted a rodent in the corner of his home.

"Thank you," said Brad, the lights making it nearly impossible to see even the front row. "I'm pleased to take on this new responsibility," said Brad, something sentimental rising in his chest. "I guess I should thank someone who is here today." With that, people became uncomfortable; it wasn't an awards ceremony.

Brad strained to find Sheila, squinting into the darkness. "Sheila," Brad said into the microphone. "Sheila?" And he would've gone on, but the screen behind him went to black, and then surged again with the message: "Lunch is served in the main lobby. Today's choices are Watsons Braised Roast Beef, Roasted Chicken or Dill Chicken Salad. Sodas, desserts and an assortment of samples from the New Food Line are available." The lights over the audience ebbed on, brightening the space.

People in the auditorium scattered and filed out through the back doors. Watson slapped Brad on the back as the mike went dead. Brad thought he could finally see Sheila out there, her face bunched in disgust.

twenty-five It was well past ten p.m., the same day. Ratchet stood outside the front door, smoking. "She wants to talk to you," she said to Brad, pointing to the house. Mosquitoes buzzed his ears as he stomped inside.

"Brad," said Peaches, pulling out a kitchen chair. "Will you please sit down so we can talk?" She was so small in her long nightgown, a Tweety Bird on the front, that he thought she might have questions about homework.

Brad shuffled to the refrigerator and yanked it open. "Not tonight. I've still got work to do and it's late."

Peaches let out a sigh. "It will only take a minute. I've got a favor to ask of you."

Brad turned around and leaned on the fridge, his necktie loose, and his feet hurting. The scene in the auditorium—just that morning—seemed like years ago. His head throbbed and the only thing that would help, he knew, was dead silence and a long pull of something cold. How long had it been since he had a drink? He thought back, the effort making his neck pinch. He'd found the opportunity to take a quick few drinks in the parking lot earlier in the day, when everyone else was busy sampling Watsons' Apple and Gorgonzola Pita Wraps. A dense blanket of smoke hung over the cars. When Brad returned to the building, everyone had been talking about the forest fires, how much more intense they'd grown, something about wind direction and how brittle and dry the crunchy forest floor had become in the drought.

He sighed. It seemed that Peaches wanted him to respond. "Fine, but I'll stand if you don't mind." He considered the way Peaches was sitting, her slim legs crossed, looking at Brad with one of the softest expressions he'd ever seen, serene and timeless, as if she knew exactly how everything would go from this point right up until the time of her death. He knew Sarah would have loved Peaches immediately, Milo, too, and it was a testament to his self-loathing that he couldn't do the same right now and sit down with the mother of his nieces or nephews or both.

"Okay," she said, her forehead crinkling with concentration, trying to get out what she wanted to say. "Compton feels bad about something and he wants to talk to you. He won't tell me what it is. He doesn't think he can remember it all that good. He said he needs you for that."

Brad took three rapid drinks from a longneck, his eyes red. He thought about what the staff at the Paradise Club had said, that she'd come a long way. He imagined a jail stint. She'd warmed up even more over the past month, talking about her family, smiling at him, helping Ratchet do laundry. But there had to be something; how else could she have been admitted into the Paradise Club?

"He's probably just having one of his memory lapses. I wouldn't worry about it. That's what his doctor is for, Peaches," said Brad. He guzzled the rest of the beer.

She rose from the table and shuffled in her slippers past Brad, stopping for just a moment, staring straight ahead. "All he wants is to be forgiven for something. All he wants is for you to be happy for him."

Brad ripped the fridge open and twisted open another beer. "Yeah, well, Peaches, the best I can tell, nobody gets forgiveness. Besides, he's got nothing to be forgiven for." Brad tossed the beer cap in the sink. When he turned back, Peaches was gone. He could hear her small feet scratching the stairs as she made her way up to her husband. Ratchet came in from outside, her face calm, a little sunburn on her shoulders.

When Brad slipped into the pantry for something to mix with Milo's booze upstairs he saw that the chicks were all nuzzled into a pile. He was surprised how much they'd grown in just a few days. Most all had tiny tail feathers sprouting from their rear ends, and some of their fuzziness had vanished. Brad searched the pantry shelves for anything that would work. Once, long ago, Milo had kept one whole shelf stocked with grenadine, ginger ale, and cocktail mixes, but they'd been used up years before. He spotted a large can of pineapple juice, its spiraled top freckled with rust, and grabbed it before it could disappear, too. A sack of brown sugar sat on the shelf in front of his face. He opened it and sniffed, put a glob in his mouth. If his stomach could handle it, he'd eat the entire bag, his craving for carbs nearly as much as for the booze. He twisted the bag shut and put it back on the shelf, the inside of his mouth sticky. He felt the top of his head, pushed down on the piece, then walked out of the pantry into the dimly lit kitchen. Ratchet had started to shut the lights off for the evening, and only the short fluorescent tube over the sink sputtered. She turned from closing a cabinet door and saw Brad, the old can clutched to his chest.

"Aren't they cute?"

"Who?" asked Brad, noticing Ratchet's backside as she bent to pick a tracked-in pine needle from the wooden floor.

"The chickens, silly. They're so fun to watch. We've named them all," she said, pointing toward the pantry. "They're listed on the clipboard behind the door." She moved with such deliberateness, straightening up the kitchen, that Brad believed she knew the house he lived in, the people, too, much better than he did.

She ran the clunky disposal; it sounded like a charm bracelet had fallen into it. Brad grabbed another beer and waited for some quiet.

"So where are your burglar friends? Did they decide the Orville Memory Loss Farm was just a little too much reality for them?"

"Man, you must be losing it yourself. They were here yesterday. You even told them hello." Brad couldn't remember even though he tried; in this way he realized he and Compton were truly alike. The booze was his mechanic with a lead pipe.

"Oh, yes, I just : . . I had forgotten," he said, swilling the beer inside his mouth. He leaned again against the refrigerator and checked his cell phone. Nothing. He hoped the message he'd left Gina would make her want to see him again. Earlier that morning, when he left to go to the Watsons' board meeting, she was still sleeping. Brad left her a note, but while he was riding in the taxi to work he was afraid that he'd rambled; maybe she couldn't even read his sloppy handwriting.

"So," said Ratchet. "We're planning on working on the fencing this week. Are you okay with that? We'll need money for paint, brushes, too."

Brad half-nodded, feeling the beer hit his brain like a warm blanket. He stared at Ratchet's chest, unable to look away. "You know," he said, thinking he was pulling off a vintage Compton come-on as he strode around the island and sat on a stool, the cuff of his trousers soiled with something yellow, "maybe we should take a bottle of Milo's best out under the stars. We could spread a blanket, even play a little strip poker."

"Gross," said Ratchet, backing up. "I think you should go to bed, Brad."

He heard himself in his head then, lascivious and ugly. Brad stood up and picked up the ancient can of pineapple juice. "There's an account at the Ace Hardware. They'll let you charge the stuff for the fence." Brad started to slink out of the kitchen toward the foot of the stairs in the living room.

He felt shame thick in the room. What had he been thinking? He wouldn't blame the girl if she slapped him one.

But when Ratchet spoke, her voice was soft. "Did you see Compton yet? All he's talked about for the last two days is apologizing to you for something bad he did." Brad turned and watched as she dried a cup and placed it in the cabinet with a clink.

"He's brain damaged, Ratchet, that's all. He's mistaken."

Ratchet mumbled something.

"What was that?" he said.

"I said aren't we all." Ratchet closed the cabinet door and added, "By the way, you've got a visitor upstairs."

Brad stood still and sniffed; the wind must've changed course because he could definitely smell smoke now.

twenty-six
Brad smelled marijuana smoke. He opened his bedroom door. Someone was sitting at his desk. The room was shrouded in murk, the computer screen saver pulsing, offering strange shadows.

A figure came into focus as Brad's eyes adjusted to the dark. Long legs propped up on the desk, Gina spoke, her voice husky.

"Hey there, mister," she said. She sounded tipsy.

"How did you get in here?" asked Brad, pulling the side chair away from the desk, squinting at her. He could see now that she wore a trench coat, the collar of which made her appear like a vampire in the shadows.

"Wow, I knew you were drunk last night, but yikes. You told me to come over? Sent a text this morning with the address? Any of that ring a bell?"

"Oh, sure," Brad said, although he wasn't. Her words were ringing some kind of vague bell—"love to see you again" punched hurriedly into his phone at some point during the day. He cleared his throat. "I just meant, how'd you get past my posse?"

"Your brother actually showed me upstairs. Told me Half Pint would be right with me," said Gina laughing. She paused. "His thumb looks pretty bad."

Brad flinched. "What's wrong with it?" he asked, sucking in his stomach, hoping his breath was good.

"Looks jammed, black and blue. The girl was icing it."

Brad was distracted now; he hadn't wanted to expose Gina to all of this, or had he? After all, he had apparently invited her, sending the address in a drunken text message.

Gina pulled her legs from the desk in what was supposed to be a seductive maneuver, but she misjudged the lip of the desk and both legs fell abruptly toward the hard floor, the heel on her right foot hitting so hard she yelped.

"Are you okay?" asked Brad, moving around the desk toward Gina.

She pulled her knees to her chest and sighed. "I'm fine," her voice a little tired. "I'll be even better once you carry me to your bed."

Brad moved his fingertips up the side of his face, acting as if he were itching his beard stubble, but it was a sneaky way to check on the piece. He pushed his fingers above his ear and was glad to feel the hair system in place. Sometimes, he'd forgot if he had it on or not. And lately, in dreams, he'd be wearing a large fro, or a pageboy cut, and sometimes even a bouffant, stacked so high above his head he'd fall over in front of a line of faceless but perfect women.

"You want a drink first?" Brad asked. As much as he had wanted Gina to reappear, now her presence was overwhelming.

"That smoke outside is so thick," Gina said, looking vaguely to the window. Then she answered Brad, "Yes, I'd love a drink."

Brad poured two drinking glasses half full of whatever liquor he'd snagged from Milo's den and worried that the glasses were dirty, or at least sticky from previous nights.

"The fires, they're closer now," Brad said. He handed Gina a glass.

"I heard the forest near the interstate is about to go up, too. They're worried about the ridge. They're dumping that red stuff on it from planes." Gina took a gulp and another. In the dark, Brad thought she looked like someone dressed for Halloween, the shadows playing contortions over her features, exaggerating her eyebrows. He hadn't noticed it before, but now he could feel Gina's desperation, sense it like an animal—her fear, the costumish coat covering up something more than just her naked body. Brad swallowed the liquor, his tongue on fire.

She stood up slowly and drank the rest of her glass of liquor, downing it quietly. She let the coat drop to the floor.

Gina walked around the desk. Her heels tapped the floor, a sound Brad was glad to hear, relieved that something other than the two of them occupied the room. The smoke went from a leafy aroma to something more burnt, singed, the smell of scorched hair.

As Gina pressed her body against his, she said, "Mmmm, you going to take me to bed or not, Mr. Orville?" She ground her pelvis into Brad's midsection, stirring him, even through all the booze and depression and the world burning up outside.

Gina stood, legs set apart, as Brad stood, too, kissing her mouth hard, walking her backward, his hand between her legs. She bit his lip and fell back onto the bed. Brad smelled his own staleness on the comforter as he helped Gina undress him. For some time, they writhed and bucked, never fully committing to any one position. Sweat gathered on Brad's back and chest; he worried it would loosen the piece, so he visualized the center of his own head, pictured the hair system tightly secured, willed it to stay put, his eyes squeezed tight.

"Brad?" said Gina, now motionless underneath him; suddenly her skin felt cold, clammy. Brad could feel her pointy chin rested on his shoulder, staring at something behind him, near the doorway.

Brad rolled off as she pointed in the direction of a figure in the darkness, a scratching sound like nails on wood as the figure inched forward.

"Compton!" Brad sat up straight, pulled the covers to his chest. "Compton," Brad said lower, "go back to your room now. Peaches needs you. Go on back now." Compton stopped at the foot of the bed. "Compton just turn around and go back to your wife." Wife, thought Brad. He didn't know why, but it hurt to say it. Right in the center of him—a hurt that burned.

Compton slurped, and the sound in the darkness was like a clogged sink, a gurgle.

"What's wrong, Comp?" Brad squinted at his brother.

Gina moved her right leg so that it tangled around Brad's, her thigh muscle squeezing and releasing. "Is he okay?" she murmured.

"Yeah," Brad started. "It's just that . . . "

"I'd like to apologize, Half Pint," interrupted Compton, stammering, his fists clenched at his sides.

"No need to, Comp. It's all forgotten, bro," Brad said, and it occurred to him he and Gina knew so little about each other. The last thing he wanted her to hear was an apology from his lame brother for stealing his fiancée.

Compton shook his head as if he were shaking out his hair after a shower. "Uh-huh, yes I do, Brad. Yep." Compton's eyes glimmered wet like a seal's. He stood up straighter and pulled his bad leg closer to the other.

"Look, Comp, you may not have noticed and all, but I'm entertaining a lady myself tonight." Brad motioned to Gina. She smiled and waved at Compton like she was making a hand puppet. He didn't even seem to see her at all.

He slurped again, and snorted a forced laugh. "I'm seriously counterfeital here, Half Pint. I'm needing to correct the bogus karmageddon we've gotten into."

"It's okay," said Gina. "What are you trying to tell us, Comp?" she asked, sitting up, covering herself. Brad frowned. To tell us, Comp, her voice low and maternal. Like she knew him, like there was some kind of intimacy brewing here that he wasn't sure he was comfortable with. Brad surveyed the side of her face, lovely in the dark, flawless. When what you want shows up quicker than you'd imagined, it's almost too late.

"Who is that?" Compton asked Brad. "Who's that next to you?"

"A friend, Compton. That's what I was trying to tell you." Brad's stomach cramped. Compton edged along the end of the bed, trying to get around to Brad's side, smiling as he moved half-foot by half-foot.

"Go on back to bed, Compton, and we'll talk in the morning," Brad said firmly.

Compton rounded the corner post and made a quick succession of abbreviated jerks toward Brad's headboard, stumbling. Brad caught his brother before he fell headlong into the bed.

"Sorry, Half Pint," said Compton, his voice ragged.

"You okay?" Gina asked. She sat up straight and the sheet slipped, exposing her breast.

Brad saw that Compton had noticed and was now staring. "Jesus, Gina," he snapped, pulling the sheet back up. "Watch it, okay?"

Gina raised her eyebrows. "Sorry, Mr. Touchy." She smiled a lazy grin and lay back down.

Brad turned back to Compton. "Let me see your thumb, Comp. I heard you hurt it."

"It's not important," Compton said. "We've got more sincerity problems to discuss."

Brad took a deep breath. "Then go back to your room now, Compton. We'll talk in the morning." He stood up and guided his brother to the door. From down the hall, they could hear Peaches snoring, awfully loud for such a small body, Brad thought. "Come on," Brad said, pointing to the door, aware of how much it sounded like he was talking to a dog. "Go to your room."

Compton reached a hand toward his brother, patted his arm. It was clear to Brad that Compton was stuck, hung up in a kind of loop, snagged on splintery recollection.

"I wanted to tell you, Brad, that I am sorry. I'm sorry I did that thing to you . . . "

Brad cut him off, pushing him to the hall. "Back to bed, Compton. Now."

"Half Pint, let me finish," Compton protested.

At the door to Compton and Peaches's bedroom, Brad steered his brother inside. Compton stood confused again; he was never worse than when his sleep was incomplete, and Brad was grateful, for once, for his brother's lack of clarity. He said slowly, "Just go back to your wife, Compton." Brad pointed to where the tiny Peaches lay in the bed, a plastic cap over her head protecting several little white bows tied to her tufts of hair.

Compton looked at Peaches, then up at his brother. "I think, sir, that you hate me," he said. They stood there, Compton hanging his head and Brad somehow unable to let go of his brother's arm. Outside, light smoke that Brad thought must be rolling its way from the fires drifted in foggy scallops under the beam of the security light. Beside him, he felt Compton move away, then watched as he crawled into bed, finally, snuggling in beside Peaches.

He went to the hall and shut the door quietly behind him. Darkness was all he wanted, but as he stood in the still house, grasping the doorknob, Gina crept lightly down the hall, completely nude. Brad rushed toward her, ushering her back to his room.

"Is he okay?" she asked, sounding worn out, maybe skittish now, too.

Brad said, "Uh-huh," focusing on getting her back to the bedroom and covered up.

Back in the bed, Gina talked about a movie she'd seen where two lovers died in a freak car accident, but then were alive on another plane of existence, together and much more romantic. The movie sounded awful, and Brad knew her talking about it would thankfully put him to sleep.

In the very early morning hours, around four a.m., they seemed to wake up at the same time, kissing and fondling each other. The sex was quick and tame, lonely, too. Brad lay awake for a long time, the smoke smell from outside so rich it seemed like camping out. He wasn't sure what time it was when he opened his eyes again, the dawn trying to materialize, and found Compton standing in the doorway. Brad stared toward him in the unlit room, trying to breathe quietly, hoping if he stayed perfectly still his brother would go away. He must've dozed off, because when he next awoke, with a terrible headache, Gina was gone but Compton was still in the doorway. "Sorry," Compton mumbled, "sorry for that . . ."

twenty-seven It was still early, cockcrow light spilling through a torn shade in the kitchen. Brad stirred a cup of instant coffee, the mug chipped. He stared at the gouge, rough like the edge of a busted tooth. It was good to get back to some kind of routine, a little bit of sanity. The house was quiet, and although he had three strong drinks of vodka before going to bed, his head was relatively clear. Two days had passed since Gina was at the house. Brad had managed to avoid Compton as if he were sidestepping a bully after school, careful not to take the same route, prudently steering clear of common areas and basically hiding whenever he saw him.

Outside, the haze from the fires was there, but it moved quickly along, eddying among the spindly pines, resting briefly at the trunks of the larger hardwoods. The Allhorn's Tomato thermometer tacked to a utility pole by the drive had already risen to ninety-one degrees, and the fires were said to be unpredictable; one minute they were calm, directional, and the next, the current changed and they roared back, dangerous and capable of burning down homes, leaving clotted black plastic and smoldering TV sets.

Brad sat down at the table and sipped the coffee. He'd have to see Sheila today, make amends, apologize. He wasn't looking forward to it, but she'd welcome him back. They'd been friends too long; besides Brad had a new job to do, and he had requested Sheila as his primary assistant, which would give him a reason to submit a pay increase for her. He read the paper, looking foolishly for a mention of the sale of the farm or his promotion, but all there was were stories about the drought, the ongoing war, and something about a visit to Whitchfield County by automakers scouting a site for a manufacturing plant—two hundred measly jobs, most of them probably for corporate lackeys.

Compton came in, and out of the corner of his eye Brad could see his hair slicked back from a shower.

Brad moved the newspaper closer to his face, hoping to look too engrossed to approach. He heard the scuff of Compton's slippered foot on the wood, then a chair pulled out from the table, scraping along the pine planks, wood that hadn't been polished since their mother died. There were gouges and scratches, scrapes and rasps, all markings of a family in full function. Sometimes, when he was his most depressed, back when they'd just moved in and Compton was still mostly crying, Brad would stare at the kitchen floor and try to imagine whose shoe had made which mark. Always, the prettiest defects, the long, winsome chafes, ones barely visible to most, those he'd attribute to his mother, and again he'd see his parents dancing, a heel writing their love into the grain of the wood.

Brad was afraid of Compton now. With two days between their last encounter, and Compton well rested, Brad feared that his brother would drag the memory up from all those years ago and make a proper apology, and despite the fact that Brad didn't want to, he'd be forced to accept it. And Compton would win, again. Brad whipped his newspaper like a bedsheet, folding it in half, a movement he knew was his father's. The hair system jiggled some with the effort. He told himself he'd check it on the way to work.

"Oh, hello, Comp," he said as if he'd just noticed him, the old anxiety building in the pit of his stomach. The doctor had told him that stopping the MegaWell pills could be difficult; he could expect sweaty dreams, stomach upset, difficulty concentrating, and even a bit of good, old-fashioned mania, which he thought he could use right about now to focus on the new job. Brad hadn't taken his prescription for nearly a month, the booze taking its place. Depression, anxiety, sadness—those labels the doctor had thought fit Brad, all of them were just as useless as the pills. Brad sipped the bitter coffee, still trying to appear nonchalant.

Compton smiled and crossed his hands on the table. Brad tried to focus on a story in the paper about a Whitchfield County kid who'd scored a perfect SAT, just like Compton. She was on her way to Brown and loved biology; she wanted to cure AIDS before she was thirty.

Across the table Compton sat, and Brad glanced at his hands. His brother's nails were perfectly manicured, and Brad noticed a glint of gold dancing from his brother's intertwined fingers. A wedding band, something he hadn't noticed before. Brad pulled his eyes back to the picture of the girl in the paper, forcing a smile in her cap and gown.

"Did you all get wedding bands then?" Brad asked, unable to not ask the question but still looking at his paper.

Compton laughed, a loud hoot.

Brad peered from around the newspaper. "What?" Brad asked, irritated. "What's so funny?"

"You're funny, Half Pint," Compton said, shaking his head.

"What?" Brad asked again.

"Acting like you didn't give us the rings," said Compton.

Brad stiffened. There were some blackouts, which he'd accepted, but a sweat came over him thinking through why or how or even if he'd given rings to Compton and Peaches. Was he making himself as forgetful as Compton as a way to compensate? That's what the therapist would tell him. Brad kept up the game. "I did, huh? That doesn't sound like something I'd do, Comp."

Compton snorted with laughter again, shaking his head so strongly that Brad heard a pop, a crack of the neck. Brad stood up and went to the sink, dumping his coffee down the drain.

"You gave them to us wrapped in that silvery bullet paper, Half

Pint." Compton rubbed his smooth chin. "That paper, you know, like a softie mirror?"

Brad gathered his things for work—his briefcase from the counter and a water bottle from the fridge—and started for the door. His back twinged, and a dull headache emerged above his ears. Outside, a car door slammed. Brad looked through the gap in the battered shade.

"Your help is here, Comp," he said. "It's Ratchet. Looks like she's got that Roth guy with her again. The other two, too." Ratchet and some other people Brad half recognized were coming to the door, one of them using a walker, and Brad somehow remembered that his name was Roth. They must be friends from the Paradise Club, Brad thought. "I guess you're all set, then. I'll be at work if you need me." Brad made sure to make his voice sound like his father's, positive and purposefully loud and clear.

"Wait for the hurt to subsidionate," Compton said, reaching out to Brad just as Peaches came in, smiling at Compton. Compton couldn't remember to take a Q-Tip out of his ear, but he'd already laid out Peaches's prenatal vitamins in a neat row on the counter. He did it every night, and it was a task Brad tried to ignore, feeling envy and endearment all at once.

"Gotta go, bro," said Brad, his skin feeling as if a layer of water sloshed just underneath, heavy and full and disgusting. Still, he tried to sound chipper, even tipping a nonexistent hat to Ratchet and her friends as they bumbled into the house, the old guy's walker screeching like an ironing board. Brad had an indistinct memory of meeting Roth but couldn't be sure. "Hello there," Brad said, and the man gave him a watery smile back. A woman was with him, buxom, older but pretty.

Out on the road Brad checked his hair. The thing had gotten nappy, twisted, and slightly oily looking. He put his hand to the back of his head and pressed down firmly, holding it there as he drove, hoping to flatten the upturned lip, the telltale sign that a piece was affixed. The glue had hardened, and he wondered whether the thing could ever be removed. He drove past Old Man Tyler's place, and the house looked more run-down than Brad had ever seen it, and he slowed down to get a better look. Cans and barrels were stacked head-high near the shed. Kyle Tyler was coming out of the barn, and Brad thought he might have had a black eye. His mullet didn't move at all as he walked to the trunk of Old Man Tyler's beautiful Caprice and looked around, almost furtively. He put his hand on the trunk as if to open it, then apparently changed his mind, instead lumbering across the gravel bylane to disappear back inside the barn.

Brad realized he'd slowed the car to a stop, and he gunned the motor, the tires spitting out melted tar. He drove with one hand and mashed his hair down with the other.

twenty-eight Sheila had asked for and received a transfer to a Watsons satellite office inside the perimeter. She was packing up her desk when Brad sat down in her chair.

"Oh, come on. I'm sorry, Sheila. I know I was an ass, but . . . " He paused and whispered at her. "I was going to put in a request so that you'd be assigned to me. I could get you a ten percent raise." He looked around and thought he saw Toby drinking from the water fountain, but it was a woman with the same haircut.

"You know," Sheila said, tossing a key ring of USBs and a stapler into a box, "I can smell the booze on your breath, Brad." She actually pinched her nose, which made him chortle, but Sheila didn't even look in his direction. Over the years, they'd taken pokes at each other, but this time it was different.

"Do you even know how Compton is doing? Are you aware of anyone else but yourself these days?" Sheila wrapped newspaper around two mugs and a commemorative Watsons candy dish from the celebration of opening their one hundredth store. She tucked the wrapped items into a shoe box and set to emptying her file cabinet.

Brad couldn't find a way to respond. For a few moments, he just watched Sheila busy herself shoving papers into an empty paper ream box.

"Forget it," she said, now looking at Brad straight on for the first time. "Just get out of my sight." She let her eyes glance at his head.

"Don't be that way, Sheila, come on," said Brad, getting up from the chair and pushing his hands into his pockets. He could smell smoke coming off his clothes. He took Sheila by the wrist. She wrenched her arm away, then moved right up into his face.

"Don't touch me, Brad," she said between her teeth, her eyes wild and so close that Brad could see two tiny clumps of mascara at the corner of her right eye. She pointed her finger in his face. He looked around, over her head, to see if anyone was nearby.

"I've only tried to help you, but I guess that's not what you want anymore. You're becoming just like them, and you know it. So fine, but I'll tell you this. That thing you're wearing on your head is the least of your problems." Sheila started to say more, but stopped, straightened her skirt, and pulled her sweater on. It was almost 100 degrees out and she was cold.

"Go on," said Brad, a spiteful tone in his voice, as if he'd swallowed a gulp of fuel and his tongue would ignite it. A drink would fix all this, he thought. Not make it go away—he wasn't that far gone, he thought to himself, not like those alcoholics you saw on TV who wanted to off themselves—but just take the edge off. That was all. Was that too much to ask for?

Sheila acted as if he weren't there. She sharpened a pencil, for some reason, an act that stirred in Brad a flash of pity.

"Just tell me why you're so mad at me," he said.

Sheila moved slowly to pick up the biggest box. She held it in her arms as she turned away. "Brad, you're not going to get me to tell you something you already know. That's sick. You're drunk and lonely and hating everything you can find. But really," she said, lowering her voice, almost begging Brad to figure it out, "you're just using a situation to act out something you should've done in high school or college. Women, real women, are better than you can imagine." Sheila tossed her hair out of her eyes. "There isn't any secret. And that's it. Quit pretending. Stop drinking. And throw that awful thing away." Her face was flush and she had tears in her eyes.

Brad thought about it a moment. A surge of indignation rippled through him, and before he knew it, before he could stop himself, he was coming on to her. "Whoa, lady! That kind of assertiveness really gets my cock hard, Sheil." Brad sauntered toward her. "How about we slip off to the copier room and bang out a few two-sided duplicates."

And then Sheila did something that was the last thing Brad would've expected. She lunged for his head and grabbed a hank of his hair in her tight pink fist. Brad moved back, like a dog trying to loosen its collar, planting his feet and rearing his head, but Sheila wouldn't let go. The sound of someone screaming "owwww!" nearly deafened Brad, and then he realized the nasally whine was coming from him.

"Stop it! Now quit!" Brad demanded.

Sheila yanked some more, and finally let go, a look of surprise on her face, clearly intrigued by how effective the glue was. She stood there for a moment trying to figure it out. Brad was bent over, but before he could inspect the damage, the stinging burn on his scalp like a wasp bite, he heard a small slam and the cubicle was empty. Brad shakily straightened up, realizing he was alone. The smell of booze and wet adhesive tape was ripe in his nostrils. The hair system had been on for two weeks straight, Brad realized, and he'd failed to follow the instructions, allowing water to get trapped underneath, between his scalp and the piece. And now Sheila had made things even worse.

A few moments passed as Brad tried to get his bearings, and then he heard heels clicking from outside, coming toward where he stood. He touched at the hair. Brad's skull felt lopsided, and a thick, dark tangle hung at the side of his right eye, the hair system wildly undone but still firmly stuck. It was a mess, and he had to get it straightened out before anyone saw. He danced around the space, trying in vain to find something to cover his head. There was nothing, he saw—Sheila had taken it all—so he made a grab at the doorknob, thinking he might escape before whoever belonged to those heels showed up, but it wouldn't budge under his hand. Somehow, Sheila had locked the thing from the outside. "Shit!" Brad swore under his breath. He closed his eyes and pictured a long, tall glass of something, anything. Something he could drink forever.

The heels outside clicked louder, and then Julie Watson's face was at the window in the door. "Well, Mr. Orville," she said, "I believe you're in a fix." She popped her hand on her hip.

Brad stood facing the locked door, looking at where the door hit the floor, anywhere but at Julie's face with its amused smile. He focused on the wood grain, a pattern that looked as if a wayward ghost had lain dormant inside the tree for years, even through the planing and sanding, and was just now about to materialize, drift from the door's interior and draw even more attention to him.

"Please, go away," murmured Brad, the top of his head afire.

"Okay," Julie said quietly. "I was just putting some flyers out for the company prayer circle. The governor is calling for the whole state to pray for rain." She placed a stack of them on the receptionist counter behind her. "Are you okay in there, Mr. Orville?"

Brad didn't move. His legs ached and the hairpiece seemed to be dying right on top of his head, curling into a floppy pelt.

"Yes. Thank you. I'll be fine," said Brad, still unable to look up.

"I'll leave you be then," Julie said, whatever it was in her voice that could've been pity making Brad feel even worse. She went back down the hall, and Brad listened as her heel clicks died off.

Brad slowly looked up. A few accountants milled around, butt cheeks clenched tight. Two junior accountants walked right past him, discussing a spreadsheet that tallied all the sick days accrued in the metro-area franchises. One guy, bucktoothed and sporting a semi–Dutch boy do, seemed like he was about to tumble over with sheer bliss as he told the other guy how they could set up an entire report document and link it inside a PowerPoint presentation.

Brad jiggled at the doorknob again, and this time it gave under his turn. He scuttled down the hall, one hand still on his hair as if it were a hat in high winds, and slipped inside his office. He yanked open the desk drawer and found his hand mirror. He glanced at his reflection—a mess, just as he'd thought, the hairpiece dangling over one ear. His heart was pounding, and for the first time since he'd quit taking the pills something felt wrong, medically wrong, as if his heart might explode if he didn't get some relief.

Brad laid the mirror aside and rummaged through the drawer. He'd stashed a whole bottle of Milo's vintage cognac, a bottle of Rouyer & Guillet. He set it on the desk so carefully that even he realized it was a precaution more fitting a loaded gun or a powder keg. He had no idea how old or rare or how much the bottle was worth, but he imagined it was significant on all counts. The dull green foil over the cork felt more like melted wax as he picked it off, only to realize he didn't have a corkscrew. But with a letter opener he managed to harpoon the cork, twisting it back and forth until it busted up and pieces of it floated in the 80-proof alcohol.

Brad didn't wait to find a glass; he clutched the bottle like it was a microphone and tilted it back. The liquid tasted like smoke, but then again, everything had started to take on the flavor and smell of smoke. Brad paused, his eyes watering, but he didn't remove the bottle from his lips. He sucked in a deep breath, then took another long swig, then another, until his body cooled and the jittery movements in his hands subsided.

He let the half-empty bottle dangle at his side as he walked to the window. Outside, the parking lot seemed to glint from every square inch of glass and chrome on the vehicles sitting there, the dashboards protected by silver window shades. Brad watched as people from other offices walked gingerly across the hot pavement. Two women carried umbrellas, protecting themselves from the sun. The smoke hung like stratus clouds, low and stretched out. He took another swig from the bottle, the woodsy taste bitter on his tongue, slightly sugary, too.

Brad had another full drink in his dry mouth when he spotted Sheila loading her car. He pressed himself against the window as if she might just look up and see him and notice the regret on his pale face. "Up here," he muttered. "Look up here." He squashed his whole body against the glass, surely appearing from the other side as if he'd been splattered on a windshield.

Sheila stooped to pick up a box, then tossed a scarf into the back seat, along with something Brad couldn't make out. He rushed back to his desk and dialed her cell phone number. He ran back to the window, listening to the ring trilling in his ear. Sheila was about to get into her Mazda. She stopped and reached inside her purse, pulling her cell phone out, flipping it open. She pushed her sunglasses up. The sun seemed like it was about to ignite her hair; it glinted like flint, as black crows hopped lethargically from a wire and flapped down toward a tiny puddle of air-conditioning condensation. They were parched; Brad noticed Sheila looking in their direction, pausing, apparently thinking about answering the phone.

One of the birds was so weak it collapsed into the water, flailing its wings before going completely still. If you did the math, Brad mused, nature was dying all the time. Every second held a million bereavements.

Sheila shoved the phone back inside her purse, never taking her eyes from the dying bird. Brad was shocked at how she didn't go help, just watched as the others flew away, leaving the one facedown, dead. If he'd been asked by someone six months earlier just how exactly he believed Sheila would act in this very scenario, he would've gone on and on about how she'd provide mouth-to-mouth, keeping the bird in a towel under her desk. Of course, the bird was already dead; wouldn't that mean Sheila would be keeping a dead bird under her desk? Brad's head hurt just thinking about it.

He drank the rest of the bottle down.

PART III

· · · · · · · · · · · · ·

twenty-nine Old Man Tyler sat on an ATV at the end of the Orville lane. Brad slowed down and flicked the turn signal. It was late, almost turning dark, and the old guy looked like a cowboy on some kind of squat and boxy animal, a hippo perhaps.

The construction crews were still at it, and as Brad waved to Old Man Tyler and turned into the driveway, a single beam of light from a bulldozer flashed over Old Man Tyler's face, and Brad was startled. His face was so wrinkly he looked like a shrunken apple, his collar turned up, as if it were twenty degrees outside instead of eighty.

Brad opened the car door and stepped out. Bats looped erratically in the umber sky, backlit by the construction work. Old Man Tyler sat perfectly still on the ATV, and it appeared that he'd crawled onto it and died, arrested right at the end of Brad's lane, a statue erected: "Whitchfield County Man Seated on Conveyance."

"Hey there," Brad said hesitantly, thinking he wouldn't be surprised if Tyler just tilted to the side and fell onto the ground. Brad walked toward him, staggering a little. He stopped a moment to gather himself. When had he finished that cognac? Hours ago, he thought. "A long, long time," he muttered. "Long enough." He shook his head as if to clear it. He remembered a time when he and Compton were just kids and Old Man Tyler took them quail hunting. Brad hated it, sickened by the dull thud of the birds falling from the sky. He cried, while Compton simply wouldn't shoot, and Kyle ran around pointing his finger at Brad, hollering, "Cry baby! Cry baby!" Old Man Tyler swatted his son on the ass and told him to hush. The day ended roughly, with Compton and Brad walking back across the road and down through the ditch mallow, where two beavers had dammed the creek. They sat there a long time, until Brad's eyes weren't red anymore. Compton told him, "That Kyle's gonna end up killing Mr. Tyler one day."

"You okay?" Brad asked as he walked slowly to the ATV, concentrating on not stumbling. In front of him Tyler was still. Finally, Old Man Tyler moved; he swung a leg over the seat so he was angled side-saddle. In the nightfall he lit a cigarette; Brad tried to remember the last time he saw anyone use a match.

Tyler cupped his hand around his mouth and sucked in air, shaking the fire out of the match, opening his mouth, and sticking it on his tongue. Brad thought he heard the sizzle.

"Can't be too damn careful, young Orville, with a hundred-year drought like it is." The old man tucked the match behind his ear, took a long, slow drag from the cigarette, and blew smoke above his head. A few stars peeked out from the hazy low sky, bluish and dirty.

"Is something wrong, Mr. Tyler?" Brad asked, acutely aware that he was slurring slightly. "Did Compton walk down your way again?" Brad had to pee and the sensation burned in his midsection, made his gut feel even emptier.

"Naw, nothing like that, son."

Brad turned to look up the lane toward the house. Compton's light was on, and Brad could see a few people mingling near the kitchen window, though he couldn't make out who they were.

"Oh, good then," said Brad. "I better get to the house." He turned to walk back to his car, but Old Man Tyler spoke up.

"I just thought I'd give you the news before the signs went up." He removed the cigarette and admired it, the ember tip glowing like a coil. For a moment, it seemed like the old man had forgotten what he'd just said.

"They flat out offered me more than I could even count, Brad." The machinery across the road went silent. Somewhere way off, farther out into the country, a car revved down a gravel road. Brad had always been amazed at the sounds out here, how even now, at nighttime, it was like twenty years ago, deadly quiet, so silent that a car like that on the pebbly back road sounded like a little piece of music, compact and pure, as lonely and sad as any fiddle ditty. But then a backhoe fired up.

"Well, I guess when it comes to that, the money, you need to do what you think is right." Brad felt phony saying it, and like a traitor, too, since he hadn't even thought about visiting the Tylers to let them know he'd signed a contract on the Orville place.

"Hmmm," said Tyler.

Brad felt a little sick. Could alcohol, he wondered, fill you up inside, so much that it replaced your blood? The burning sensation inside grew stronger and he realized that he couldn't wait. "Hang on a sec," he said. He stepped into the shadows and unzipped his pants, finally able to pee. He finished and turned back to Tyler. He felt immensely better.

"I tell ya what," said Tyler, climbing off the ATV with more agility than a man of nearly eighty should have. He opened the toolbox on the back and pulled out a bottle. "Let's have us a drink to toast old times, what ya say?" He twisted off the top and handed it to Brad. "Why don't you do the honors?"

"Here's to fortune and health," said Brad, kind of choked up. It had snuck up on him, thinking of Old Man Tyler's place bulldozed over and the seventy-five acres turned into a subdivision called Mild Mannered Oaks or Sunset's Sunny Side. Brad tipped the bottle. He handed it back.

"I don't care much for money, but I'll sure as hell toast one to health," said Tyler, his lips smacking at the opening. For a while they drank and passed the bottle back and forth, and before long the old man had also become sentimental. It was very dark now, the only light coming from the floodlights across the road. The old man looked, yet again, like a cutout of some folk artist's rendition of "the people of Whitchfield County, before the suburban sprawl."

Finally, Tyler crawled back onto the ATV like it might be a horse, actually patting it on the side. Car lights came at them, and a Chevy roared by, pebbles from the shoulder pinging off the chassis. Old Man Tyler flipped the car off.

Clutching the bottle like a baby, Tyler sniffed, then hung his head slightly, as if in reverence. "I suppose you've got enough of your daddy in ya to stick this out. He was a strange man to me, honestly. We were close to the same age, but he lived more like a fella twenty years younger." Old Man Tyler spoke over his shoulder to Brad. "You think you'll ever sell?" The question sounded as if it had been posed by a boy on a playground, tempting another—If you do it, I'll do it. But there was a trace of melancholy in it, too.

Brad's eyesight shifted, swarmed, and whorled until the darkness felt as solid as the black wheels on the ATV. He stammered, "I guess not. I've got Compton to think about, and this place is one big memory, Mr. Tyler. Our parents loved it. I just can't see selling it." Brad felt the force of his lie fill up his mouth, cramming it so full he thought a handkerchief was shoved inside. Old Man Tyler steadied himself on the ATV, turning a key and flipping a switch. The headlights came on. In the trees behind them a hoot owl gave a deathly whoop.

Old Man Tyler gunned it and sped around in a circle, then another, spitting dead grass and dust in Brad's direction. It seemed the old guy might just keep going round and round until he passed out from dizziness. But in one jerky blast the ATV shot across the road and into the ditch, the headlights casting yellow cannons along the clay banks.

Brad watched as Old Man Tyler flew down the road and into his lane. The headlights beamed on the Tylers' shed, and from where he stood, Brad could make out the shed door shutting quickly, Kyle disappearing from view. The ATV idled for a while, then went silent.

Brad's back ached. He sat down in the grass, twenty yards away from the beehives. He stared up at the night sky and blinked so much it felt to him as if a seizure had taken hold. The drinks with Old Man Tyler, he realized, had put him near blacking out. He tried to count the hours of sleep he'd had in the past week, and the number of bottles he'd emptied, but the number just kept fading into darkness, an impossible calculus question. The heat of the day had left him sticky, and the hairpiece on his head felt slightly damp when he touched it. He let his face fall into the grass, particles of dry weeds stuck to his cheek. The soil below his wracked body felt explosive, as if the core of the earth was about to boil over, seethe, and keep burning. Brad tasted the stinging bile of vomit in the back of his mouth, but he breathed through it.

He rolled over so he could see the house. He watched it for a while, thinking of Gina, how he would try harder, take her on a formal date, dinner and dancing, and maybe even tell her about his hair system, go au naturel, nothing to hide. The lights in Compton and Peaches's room flickered, then went out. A small lamp was on in the living room, and Brad surmised that Ratchet was lying on the couch, reading, smelling like toothpaste. Then that light went out, too. Brad closed his eyes, just for a moment, and in the next a sheriff's deputy was standing above him in the glaring morning sunlight.

thirty The heat was like a wall. Brad sat up, legs sprawled like a child about to play "roll the ball," his shirttail crumpled and stained with red clay dust. Across the road, the equipment was silent for the first morning since very early spring. The quiet was strange, no diesel engines to mask the subtle sounds of nature. The sheriff's deputy squinted down at Brad, wearing the expression of a man who wanted nothing more than to be somewhere else.

"Why don't you stand up, sir?"

Brad tucked his legs to his chest and tried to rock enough to stand, then rolled to his side and got on all fours, and finally with a grunt stood up. He watched as his necktie fell to the parched earth.

"Do you live here, sir?" asked the deputy. He seemed to already know, his voice bored and not all that interested. Brad noticed for the first time that the cruiser behind his car was flashing red and blue, silently.

"Yes, I do. I guess I should explain," said Brad, pointing toward his car, the door wide open. Even he could see several bottles glinting in the sun, and he hoped that the cop would think they were just old-timey relics; maybe he wasn't accustomed to seeing booze from 1921.

"Sir, can I see your driver's license, please?" The deputy turned down the feedback on his radio, which was attached to his shoulder by a Velcro clip.

Brad patted his pants and shirt pocket, then looked down at the spot where he'd passed out, but it wasn't there. He had to urinate so badly it felt as if he would burst some vital organ if he didn't piss right that second. "I guess I'll need to look in the car, or I could go to the house and get my passport." The deputy shook his head no and said something in a low voice into a walkie-talkie, turning it up some. A voice rattled on about the fires, how they were spreading. Brad thought he heard that some houses had been burned.

"Don't move from this spot," the deputy said as he walked to his cruiser. Brad kind of pranced in place, his bladder burning now. A small amount of urine trickled out when he breathed. The sun was hot on the top of his head, and he realized that the hairpiece must've slipped askew again. He pushed it up and took a step toward the cruiser.

"Sir," the cop bellowed, "stay where you are like I told you!"

Brad froze and put his hands in the air. "Officer, I've got to urinate. If I don't I think I'll wet myself." It all sounded so asinine to Brad, and when the officer ignored his comment, he let his raised arms fall to his side. Another patrol car pulled into the drive, the siren making harsh chirps.

The two deputies convened, talking and pointing toward Brad. A flash of fear caught in Brad's gut and rushed to his heart, the beating in his temples so strong it felt like an artery might rip open. What if he'd hit someone on his way home? The thought tossed his empty stomach and he stooped over and began to vomit, puking up only air, the hairpiece flipping forward and bouncing a little with each heave, involuntary spurts of pee wetting his boxers. It only vaguely occurred to him how often he seemed to be throwing up.

The second deputy shook his head and eased back inside his cruiser, flooring the engine in a wild U-turn and speeding down the road. Brad's eyes watered and his throat burned. He looked up, hands on his knees, and pushed the piece loosely into place again. If he'd done anything awful, he thought, the other deputy wouldn't have taken off.

The first deputy approached. He handed Brad a rag. "I'll need to see your ID." Brad wiped his mouth and spit, nodded his head yes. "Can I go use the toilet? I can't think of anything right now." The cop twisted his mouth in a frown, then pointed to the stand of pine scrub near the beehives. "Hurry," he said.

After he'd zipped up, Brad moved feebly through the grove of trees, noticing as he walked how good the place looked: the well-kept pine straw bunched around the trees, the fence line cleared and straightened. It all reminded him of his parents, the way they seemed to be able to keep the farm tidy and stimulating without even trying. Clearly, Ratchet, Peaches, and Compton, along with some of the people Brad had apparently met but forgotten, like that old man, Roth, had been hard at work. The fence was painted and the fruit trees had been watered, restaked, and mulched. He stared up through the trees, the tops swaying, wayward pine needles floating down dreamily.

"Hey," called the deputy. "Get over here." Brad had been simply standing, and it seemed for a moment as if the deputy were calling from somewhere very far away; his voice seemed to be behind a heavy curtain or underneath a blanket. Brad stepped in the direction of the officer. His thoughts were muddled and dark, and for the briefest of moments he saw himself storming the deputy, provoking a shooting. Brad could feel the bullet pierce his chest, tearing through flesh and bone and exiting his back, leaving a charred snake hole, a portal to someplace better.

"Sir," said the officer, getting less and less patient, "get over here now." Brad weaved toward the patrol car and stood too close to the cop.

"Take a step back and tell me your name."

Brad wobbled backward. "Brad Orville. I live here with my brother."

The deputy wrote in his small notebook. "Sure looks like there are enough cars up there," he said, pointing toward the house. Brad turned and looked, too. Four cars and a pickup were parked beside the house.

"Why are you out here in the heat sleeping, Mr. Orville?"

"I guess I had too much to drink, to be honest. It won't happen again."

The cop flipped the notebook shut. He hitched up his pants and said, "Why don't you tell me how you know a Gina Fairwell, Mr. Orville."

Brad sniffed. "What? Is she okay?"

"I asked you a question, Mr. Orville."

The door to the house slapped shut. Both the deputy and Brad looked up and saw a group of people climbing into their cars. Compton wasn't with them, but the guy with the walker—Roth—and others were getting in a van. A barely perceptible memory of meeting them, of talking with them with Ratchet, entered Brad's head. There'd been a discussion around the Paradise Club, something about distant kin, but none of it made sense now.

"I know Gina, sir. I guess you could say we've been dating." Brad heard his own words and felt the need to clarify, the drunkard's desire to specify exactly what things were. "I mean, what we've been to each other is in question. She doesn't love me, I'm sure. The thing is, we've just not had enough quality alone time together to know if we're compatible, I would say."

The deputy cut him off. "I don't need to know your Dr. Phil feelings about the woman, sir. Just tell me the last time you saw her."

"I saw her a few days ago. She was here." Brad glanced up at the house again and saw Compton dragging toward the vehicles. He was dressed up, wearing a tie, Peaches behind him, her stomach swollen, wearing a white maternity top.

"And why was she here?" The officer looked up, too, as a caravan of vehicles started down the lane.

"Well, uh," Brad started, watching as the cars first crawled over the bridge and then snaked slowly toward him. Something was going on, and Brad had the deep sense it would spill over into the conversation with the deputy. "We stayed in," Brad said finally.

"Mr. Orville, I'm afraid we're going to have to continue this conversation at the county jail."

Brad seemed almost not to hear, watching as the van pulled up in front of him. Compton worked hard to get out, and with Ratchet's help he walked right up to Brad.

"Half Pint," said Compton, his hair smelling of Prell, "this is an intervening proposition." He licked the spit from the corner of his mouth. "I mean it's an intervention." Compton's hair was longer, and it occurred to Brad that things had kept on growing around him, the babies inside Peaches's round stomach, Compton's hair, the number of people hanging out at the house, even Ratchet's recovery; she seemed so healthy, a quirk of a smile on her face, that she appeared taller. Her hair was clean, really clean, and cut so that it hung in straight, glossy strands around her face. Outside, the earth was as dry and unforgiving as bedrock, but inside the house things had blossomed, flourished even.

The deputy gave Compton an intense and wary gaze.

"That's my brother, officer. He's got a brain injury," said Brad.

"Uh-huh," grunted the cop, taking Brad by the arm.

Brad spoke to Ratchet over his shoulder. "This is just a little misunderstanding. Nothing to worry about." She nodded, looking as though she was sorry, either for his potential arrest or for the need for an intervention.

Compton rushed after them, his bad leg cutting a trough in the sandy dirt. "What's this?" he said. Ratchet tried to put a hand on his shoulder, but Compton bucked it off. "Where are you planning to tear-gate, Half Pint? We have an intervention to do on him."

The deputy didn't seem to be listening as he scrawled something on a pad of paper.

Brad spoke slowly. "Go back to the house, Comp. I've got to go into town for a little bit. You can tell me all about my intervention when I get back."

His brother's words seemed to cool Compton off, and he held out his arms to Brad. "Give me a hug before you go."

Brad was too tired and too worried to refuse. He looked at the deputy, who gave a curt nod. Brad stepped forward and wrapped his arms around Compton's small frame. Brad was surprised; it felt good to embrace Compton, really good.

"Come on," said the deputy.

Brad crawled into the back of the cruiser. "Am I being charged with anything?" he asked as they U-turned and hit the road with an abrupt chirp.

"Not yet."

Brad waved to Ratchet and Compton. They disappeared quickly as the deputy sped down the road. A full blast of air-conditioning hit Brad in the chest. The cop removed his hat, placing it on the passenger's seat. Brad leaned forward to speak through the hole in the thick Plexiglas. "Is she okay? Gina? Can you at least tell me that?"

The deputy didn't answer, and instead turned up the radio. A classic rock station crackled with "Gold Dust Woman" by Fleetwood Mac. Brad pushed back in the seat and watched the pavement in front of the car speeding toward them, the yellow lines whipping under the nose of the car. Thick patches of forest fire smoke filled the valleys in the road, and when the car blasted through it Brad had to hold his breath.

thirty-one Brad sat in the freezing sheriff's office, head swimming, his stomach playing whimsy with another round of vomiting. The scanner on the desk behind him echoed with the fuzzy commands of dispatchers and bleeped with sudden channel changes, but he was able to gather that a part of Whitchfield County, way out almost to Hannah Swamp, was being evacuated. The blazes had broken past a line of counterfires and the planes dropping retardant hadn't helped much. If the fires raged over the interstate, the heart of the county would be in jeopardy.

The deputy sat a can of Diet Coke on his desk, wiping the top clean with a napkin. He acted as if Brad wasn't there as he rummaged through paperwork. Brad thought he might've even forgotten about him. The desk phone rang but the deputy didn't pick it up. He squinted at the papers in his hands, the hairy knuckles rough, gray calluses like buttons, his hands somewhat twisted; maybe something genetic, Brad thought.

He didn't look up when he spoke at Brad. "Your friend is in a holding cell. You wanna try again, tell me your involvement with her, or should I whip out the Breathalyzer and book you for public intox?"

Brad fidgeted, moving one numb leg over the other, then uncrossing them again. The hairpiece kept sidling toward his left ear, inching downward. Brad pushed it up again. "I wish I knew what you were talking about, officer. Like I said, we've been seeing one another, that's all." Brad was relieved Gina wasn't hurt or dead, murdered.

"How long have you known her?"

"I guess, well, I don't really know... "

"You've been dating and you don't know how long you've known her?" The deputy ground his teeth and rubbed his wedding band as if it itched his malformed fingers.

"Okay, let's see," Brad said, trying to calculate the weeks that had slipped past. Nothing registered. "It would be about a month," he lied.

The deputy eased back in his swivel chair, the legs creaking. "Gina Fairwell is an alias. Did you know that?"

Brad had never known her last name, and he was embarrassed to say it. "No, I didn't."

The deputy nodded. "Her real name is Sharon Constine. She's being booked now." The deputy seemed tired and frazzled. He looked directly at Brad, staring at him until Brad asked, "What is it?"

"Your parents taught me at the college."

"Oh." Brad didn't know what to say. It was hard to picture this guy seated in one of his mother's classes, scribbling into a spiral as she spoke. He itched at his ear and finally spoke. "What is she being booked on? About?"

"Theft by taking, bounced checks. She bought one of those new big houses in the Walnut Bridge Forest subdivision and then lost her job. The housing market tanking didn't help, but two of my cousins couldn't pay their mortgage either and they didn't steal to cover it." The cop let the air hiss from his mouth. "Are you sure she didn't find you?"

"What do you mean?" Brad asked, his rigid hangover dwindling into an overall malaise.

The deputy leaned forward, elbows on the desk. "It appears to me, Mr. Orville, that you're not all that involved with Ms. Constine. So maybe this won't hurt too much, but she's got about ten of you. She's racked up credit card charges from at least two men and has borrowed money from others into the thousands of dollars. You might want to check with your bank."

"Oh." Brad felt as if he'd been hit. He could feel his face go hot and red. "Am I free to go?" he asked, trying to sound nonchalant.

The deputy ignored him, leaning back again, leather cracking. He pushed a black-and-white photo of Gina across the desk, a mug shot. "This your lady, Mr. Orville?"

Brad picked up the picture. In it, he thought, she looked good, kind of like a celebrity outlaw, hair thick and wild, her eyes wide, even a nice dip of cleavage.

"Hard to say, officer," said Brad, feeling protective. "A lot of women look like this one," he added, pushing the photo back across the desk.

The deputy leaned forward and reached into the desk drawer, smiling sarcastically. "Let me get the booking form out for Mr. Orville, since you can't seem to place the woman."

Brad watched as the deputy began filling out the form; he knew it was most likely a bluff, but still, a night in jail wouldn't help anyone. The cop noticed Brad fidgeting. "You wanna have another gander?"

Brad shook his head no. "I guess it could be her. I mean, it's hard to tell in black-and-white." Brad shrugged his shoulders.

The cop smiled some, put the form back. "Well, I wouldn't fret over it. It's not like you've turned her in."

Brad asked again, "Am I free to go?"

"Help yourself," he said, pointing to the phone.

Brad had to wait awhile, and then finally Ratchet pulled up with Compton and Peaches in a van; Brad had no idea who owned it. He climbed in and sprawled himself on the middle seat. Peaches sat up front with Ratchet. Compton sat behind Brad, his bad leg propped up on the bench seat. Compton's face was cleanly shaven, and he smelled as fresh as ever, doused in cologne. Brad thought of how awful he must have looked, maybe even smelled. He ran a hand over his whiskery face.

"Half Pint," said Compton, tapping Brad on the shoulder. "I want to apologize for this thing I did to you."

Brad stared right into his brother's eyes and dared him to try. "Jesus, Comp. Let it go, will you?" Brad stared out the window, and Compton followed his gaze, watching as men worked at yet another subdivision development, piles of ripped-down trees stacked like corpses around the machinery. "Open the window, Ratchet," he asked, excited. "And slow down."

Compton's window went down and he hollered, "You can kizzle with your mouth open my delicious lily-snow buttocks!" Everyone laughed but Brad, who glowered in his seat beside his brother. Compton wanted to moon them, he said, and started to work at his pants to get them down, but Peaches got him to stop, laughing as she scolded.

Finally Compton sat back in his seat, a crooked smile on his face. "That felt goodly good," he said, and Peaches turned around in her seat and gave his knee a little pat.

Compton turned to Brad. "Half Pint, you really do need to stop drinking. We'll intervene on you again if you don't."

thirty-two The employees gathered around a huge plasma TV in the courtyard of the Watsons building. A digital marquee beamed over the gated entrance, alternating between displaying the American flag and the Watsons stock price. Brad stood under the marquee, which now flashed: "Governor's Rainfall Prayer Circle to start in 5 minutes!" He'd been in the bathroom drinking from a bottle of cheap merlot. Before that, it'd been a bottle of chardonnay. All told, Brad had sat in the last stall for more than an hour, guzzling wine he brought with him to work in a gym bag. Milo's stash was depleted, his hardwood desk littered with torn-off seals and sideways bottles. In the stall Brad had worked and reworked the hair system, applying more adhesive tape to the edges, where, no matter what he did, the hair popped up randomly, giving him the look of a slightly startled man. Now he feasted on two bear claws, the cinnamon and sugar sickening him with each bite, but he wolfed them down anyway.

Brad thought of his body full of liquid, how his brain was, right at that moment, sopping in the fumy juices of wine, while all around him, and down at the Capitol, too, the world was turning to fire, drying up, mother nature putting the squeeze on faith and science, too. It pleased him somehow, in a drunken sort of way.

Watson Sr. took the stage. The Freedom Cove, the name given to the courtyard by Watson himself, was actually monstrous; it could easily hold five hundred of the Watsons corporate staff and even those who'd come from the outlying branches. Security guards manned the two entrances with handheld metal detectors, waving the wands around backpacks and satchels, over purses and briefcases. Brad was relieved that he hadn't tried to bring his gym bag into the courtyard.

A live feed from downtown bleeped onto the large-screen TV. On the steps of the Capitol, the governor and his wife stood, along with a horde of interdenominational clergy, donning T-shirts that read: "Pray for Rain, to Sustain!" The enormous TV showed images of congress-men and -women smiling broadly, shaking hands with rabbis and preachers, priests and clerics, a sea of sweltering opportunists.

Brad looked sleepy-eyed over the crowd, spotting Julie near the podium; she was pinning a button on Toby's shirt, then another onto Watson Sr.'s lapel. They looked completely cool, unaffected by the heat and drought, the mass of people, and the overwhelming television. How could they look like an ad in some homey southern living maga-zine, Brad thought, while he was so hot his ass was wet, the hairpiece dampened thoroughly?

Brad's arms ached and he wanted nothing more than to sleep. He wiped the last of the bear claw from his lips and moved slowly around the perimeter of the crowd, thinking of Gina. His account at the bank was fine, nothing stolen, his credit card held only recent purchases of the hairpiece, billed over several months, and countless liquor store purchases that Brad had a hard time remembering.

He couldn't help thinking of Gina alone in a jail cell in the freezing air-conditioning. Maybe she really did love him, or at least had started to like him, while the other men were just a way for her to try to keep her house. He knew he was rationalizing her crimes, feeling the same duped embarrassment he had felt sitting with the deputy two days earlier, but still.

As Brad sidestepped two Food and Convenience researchers, the men responsible for developing "tastier foods with faster store visits," he caught a glimpse of a familiar hairdo bobbing among the crowd.

Sheila was in the center of a group of sober accountants, their faces scrunched up, eyes squinting against the sun. She wore a yellow sundress with white straps, one he hadn't seen before. Brad followed her at a distance.

She mingled with people who were eating Watsons prepackaged gourmet weenies, complete with dipping sauces. Cilantro Ranch and Bilberry Mustard. Brad wished there was an open bar, a keg, anything. He watched as Sheila nibbled and chatted and moved on to a small vacant area, a sidewalk that led to electronic doors and to a hallway inside. She swiped her security card and slipped in. Brad searched and thankfully found his own card in his damp shirt pocket. He tried it once and the light blinked red, then he slid it through faster and the green light blinked and the doors clicked open. He walked through and saw Sheila disappear into the ladies' room.

He stood by the drinking fountain and waited, the hallway spookily quiet compared with the dull thrumming sound outside. Brad heard the toilet flush, the sink splash on. He straightened his shirt collar and licked his teeth, swallowed with a gulp. The sink went silent, the yank of a paper towel, and another.

Brad shoved his hands in his pants pockets. Sheila pulled the restroom door open, her head down, looking at her feet. Brad stepped in front of her.

"Hello," he said.

Sheila let out a quick yelp, startled, and slung her large purse over her shoulder. A strong wave of alcohol lifted off Brad; it wasn't just his breath but his whole body. He carried the smell of a functioning drunk, sweat and cologne, spearmint over hot air. "What do you want?" she said, heading back outside.

Brad rushed to get in front of her. She swerved around him.

"I just want to say I'm sorry is all. Things have been so . . . " Brad refrained from rubbing his head, afraid that the piece might crumble and float off into the air like furry patches of helium.

Sheila put her hand on the door to the courtyard. "Sheil, wait," Brad said, holding the door shut. "Please. Can't you just listen?"

"Don't," she said sadly, not looking at him.

Brad was stuck. He couldn't keep her, but letting her go seemed more desperate than praying for rain. His palm against the door was sweaty. Sheila turned the doorknob and started to push through. "Compton got married," Brad said to the back of Sheila's brown hairdo, the broad curls tickling her neck. "She's pregnant." He waited. Sheila turned slightly. He could see the outline of her nose.

"He calls her Jesus, but her name is Peaches. That's why you thought it was funny he was so concerned about some peaches. He was washing her, not a carton of peaches. She's a person."

A faint simper passed over Sheila's mouth as she turned a little more.

Brad let go of the door. He felt like sobbing. She was his best friend, he thought, and he'd treated her horribly.

"Is that it?" Sheila asked. From outside, on the huge TV, came the sounds of a congressman warming up the parched crowd for the governor's flood of words, his holy dousing. They'd apparently missed Watson's live opening speech.

Brad's face was sweaty, and he focused on a droplet of sweat falling from his nose onto the marble floor.

Sheila stood waiting, silent. "Brad, is there anything else?" she asked finally, her voice softer, her shoulders dropping.

"No. I don't think so," Brad said, slowly exhaling, a strong, sour smell of alcohol pushing past her face.

A round of applause exploded outside, the courtyard teeming with Watsons followers. Brad caught a whiff of the sandwiches they made in the stores; he'd always hated the thick, savory smell, the way it mimicked real food.

When Brad looked up from the floor, the doors to the courtyard slowly closed, and there wasn't anything left of Sheila, except for a mild trace of her perfume.

He snaked through the crowd, his drunk dipping even further into sickness, a queasiness settling throughout his organs. Brad stepped on a small yew bush; it crackled under his foot like bones. People began bowing their heads as the show on the Capitol lawn—the turf as green as spring—leapt into full gear. On the plasma TV, the governor clutched his wife's hand, and the entire stage of elected officials and assorted clergymen, funded under faith-based initiatives, linked themselves arm-in-arm, trying purposefully to appear as a string of paper dolls, God's thirsty, thirsty children.

Brad moved past people, some of them in deep prayer, others glancing up at him and smiling, encouraged, maybe, by his lack of belief, emboldened by his movement.

Brad stopped at the edge of the stage. Something strange pulled at his insides, and a little deadened voice urged him to act. Julie and Toby stood like a wedding cake couple, aligned shoulder to shoulder, even though Julie seemed to wear the expression of a woman who'd recently been seriously pissed off. They bowed their heads. Now Brad could see their healthy scalps, the sunshine highlighting their dense hair. Toby's was almost bushy. He was one of those guys who has to have it cut every three weeks. Julie's hairdo was all sheen and gloss, the long ends framing her lovely face, curving toward her heart. Brad squinted against the brightness. The image on the huge television was crystal clear; the prayer was over and now the stage at the Capitol became alive with photo ops, hand shaking and teary-eyed revelations. The governor's approval ratings would soar for at least two days.

Watson Sr. approached the microphone; he, too, was choked up. He said, "Let's give our great, faithful governor a round of Watson applause, y'all!" Watson actually turned toward the large screen and delivered his thunderous clapping, as if the governor could see his appreciation, hear his benediction.

Brad clapped as if his hands were in mittens, as Watson walked back to the microphone.

"Now, folks. This is a day to tell your children about, and their children. The only way out of this water mess is through faith in the

Good Man above. Continue to pray to our Savior and the rain will come." Toby and Julie embraced, but it was slight, not very prolonged. Mary Lee, mother of Toby, wife of Watson Sr., who rarely came out to the company celebrations, stood politely clapping. Hers was the only hairdo Brad could relate to; she had alopecia, and her scalp always shone through the brittle patch of yellow-white hair she wore in a sort of modified pin curl, the meager loops tight against her head. Brad had always wondered why she just didn't wear a wig—maybe Watson Sr. had found a passage in the Bible that forbade it.

Brad watched Toby and Julie, peered at them, trying to see if they might actually be oozing wedding cake icing. They stood behind the elder Watsons as the crowd grew more restless; the area inside the courtyard had gotten hotter, and people were ready to head back inside to their cubicles, bask in the air-conditioning. Brad's skin, however, seemed to cool off and let go of all the heat, of all the feverish attempts he'd made to make his life resemble something meaningful. His eyes cleared. The drunkenness now turned toward a calm reassurance, purified and true. He climbed one step to the stage and no one noticed.

Watson Sr. was going on and on about the myth of global warming, how science had betrayed them and how every single person would have to change their ways or be burned up, brought to their knees by an almighty God. "We're thirsty folks! That's for sure," he said, taking on his pastor's tone, no doubt. "But it's not for water. It's the water of life we're in need of!" Some of the more rabid, job-fearing Watsons staff clapped loudly, but many others, chewing sandwiches under the noonday scorch, simply wiped their brows and waited for it to end.

Brad was on the stage before he knew it, before he could even decide for sure what to do. He stood briefly in front of Julie and Toby. They both seemed to give him a sad little glance, as if they'd known all along he would appear, as if it were on the event program. Toby seemed to be gesturing at someone in the back of the crowd where the security guards also ate their choice of Watsons premade gourmet sandwiches.

Brad moved toward the podium as the crowd silenced nearly instantaneously. He could make out Sheila rushing through the multitude, trying to get to him. Watson Sr. took a step back and put an arm over Mary Lee. Once his hand was wrapped around the mike, Brad felt worse than he had in months; his body ached and the pit of his stomach felt like it was outside of him, under his feet, pinched, naked for the whole crowd to point at. The top of his head was burning under the hair system, where dry skin had gathered, shedding itself, trapped between the toupee and Brad's sweaty scalp, forming a paste.

Brad found Sheila in the crowd, his eyes locked with hers. She shook her head slowly, purposefully. For a moment, the sadness left Brad, and he thought he saw a real smile fold over Sheila's face, then recede. Instead of making him change his mind, however, her smile encouraged him. He grabbed the mike with more force, even as he saw that the security guards were waiting for the go-ahead to move in. Brad knew he was being allowed a little leeway; Watson Sr. didn't want to blow the purchase of the Orville property. For that, Brad knew he could get away with more than most, but not much.

"I can't think of a sadder time to be working at Watsons," said Brad, head bowed. For a second, his mind drifted: he imagined all the pills he hadn't taken, the ones that were prescribed but sat on the shelf at the CVS, or ended up in someone else's stomach, coursing through their veins at the appropriate clinical levels, preventing them from doing what he was doing right at this very moment. He saw a mound of pink ovals, ingested and passed through urine. All of his medicine was in the Whitchfield County sewer system.

Brad looked to his left at the guards standing on tiptoes at the end of the stage. Toby said from behind, "Man, don't be an ass, Orville." He heard Julie sigh. What did they care? They had their anniversary cruises and special date nights, their matching wristwatches and cute vacation home in the north Georgia mountains; they couldn't know what it was like to feel like this, out of control and inside a deep well, alone and buried underneath betrayal.

The microphone stem felt like an asp, something about to strike, poison him. Brad leaned into it and made sure his voice grew louder. He huffed into the mike. "God isn't responsible for our actions, we are. Science is science. We're the ones causing global warming, not our sins." His mind latched on to some clarity, some old humor. "Asking for divine intervention for rainfall is like asking Watson here," Brad said, motioning toward the old man guarding Mary Lee, "to give up his SUVs. Neither one of them is going to happen." Brad thought a second and added, "President Watson thinks he's God, so he's actually asking you to pray to him." There was a vague muttering as the crowd started to scatter and move from the courtyard back into the office complex, expecting, probably, that any employees who didn't act outraged to be culled. Sheila leaned against the brick wall, a kind of proud smirk playing over her face.

Brad saw Watson Sr. summon the guards, his face red; Brad knew if Watson could get away with it, he'd strangle Brad and pray that the governor would commute his sentence. As the guards grabbed him and pulled him off the stage, Brad heard Julie whisper, "He's clinically depressed. That's what it is. It's medical." As he was hauled away, Brad watched as Mary Lee joined her husband at the podium. "This lovely lady," Watson bellowed, apparently taking the "ignore the crazy man and no one will even know he was ever here" tactic, "is going to lead us in our national anthem before we go back to work." In the parking lot, a guard led him to a long car. "Get in," said the security guard. He'd once played first base with Brad on the Watsons softball team. Skinny kid; couldn't catch a ball if you handed it to him. He held the car door open.

"Where are we going?" asked Brad. "You don't have the authority to arrest me, do you?" The security guard looked at his partner. They both shrugged.

"No," he finally said.

From the courtyard Brad could hear as the ceremony continued. Mary Lee Watson was a poor singer, amplified by the expensive sound system; the motionless air held her off-key soprano like the squeal of an injured shoat.

"So I don't have to get into the company car?" asked Brad, his head sloshing with adrenaline.

"No, but you should definitely leave," said the guard, and Brad noticed that his sideburns were perfectly etched, his thick hair glued with gel. "I'm pretty sure you're fired, dude."

Brad turned and walked toward his own car, as Mary Lee butchered the bombs bursting in air. He pictured her thin hair quivering under the relentlessly hot sun and worried that her scalp might burn, just like his.

thirty-three The roads were shrouded in thick smoke. Brad blasted through them, driving the car at speeds he'd never reached before. He was surprised the Sentra could even achieve them without overheating. At the corner of Old Blather and Old Pilcher roads, he pulled into the parking lot of a Watsons franchise. People dashed in and out, over and over. It was one of the most highly trafficked Watsons stores, and there were always plans in the works to buy it back from the franchisee, but the legal department cautioned against it, saying it would create very ugly, very unneeded press. "It's best to keep it as a shining beacon to other would-be franchisees."

Brad walked slowly toward the store entrance, stopping every few steps to adjust his hair and itch at the spot underneath. Inside the store it was freezing. Brad bought two cases of beer and heaved them onto the counter. The girl ringing him up didn't look at him, just punched the buttons and went on to the next person, all the while holding her hand out. The odor of pine cleaner gave the place the smell of something useless, the waiting room for another waiting room. Brad paid but didn't wait for his change.

In the car, Brad turned on the a.c. and downed one beer, then another. If he didn't know better, he'd swear that fog hung outside the windshield, not the smoke of forest fires; it drifted lazily, forming thicker pockets along the culverts. Just outside the store, a person selling Watsons' Pizzazzy Pizza stood. He wore an American Idol outfit: a T-shirt with a musical note and staff glittering upon his chest and a "Simon" mask. He waved people in from the street to sample Extra Cheesy Cheese Explosion for $6.99 a medium. Brad watched as people walked out of the store, balancing towering boxes of the pizza back to their cars.

He tried to find the NPR station but couldn't and gave up, finally shutting off the car altogether. It was instantly hot. Brad rolled down the window, then opened another beer and drank half of it. He tilted the rearview mirror down and inspected the hair system, pushing a pencil underneath it to scratch. It felt glorious to get to it, orgasmic even, and a shot of pure relief simmered throughout his body. The spot now burned even more, though, the skin no doubt razed. He tossed the pencil in the seat and slugged back the rest of the beer. He thought of driving to the

Whitchfield County jail and posting Gina's bail, but for the first time in a long while Brad thought he could sleep, really rest. He could use the cell phone to call the jail or even try to get in touch with Commissioner Birdsong and see what he could do, but even thinking about talking to anyone made Brad's mind fizzle, short out, and withdraw. If he could just sleep for several days straight, everything would be okay.

The American Idol guy had now changed masks into "Randy," and he was dancing a sort of tribal jig in front of the store. Racist, Brad thought. That was just plain wrong. Brad sat up some and strained to watch as the guy started strutting what was obviously a pimp walk. Brad hit the horn in protest, but the guy interpreted it as encouragement and pretended to moonwalk, poorly, essentially just walking backward, dragging his feet, dust kicking up.

Brad's eyes grew heavier, and the tedious hum in his body acted as a gentle lullaby. In a fitful sleep, he dreamed of Compton, of pushing him down a steep hill. At the bottom, Sarah and Milo caught him and looked up toward the summit where Brad still stood, his face melting off, hanks of stringy hair coming off, too, as his family waved him forward and back again, telling him to come on and stay put, all at once. Brad held a clump of the singed hair up in the air, trying to show them, but when he finally got their attention they all turned and walked away, their backs to him, each of them limping, just like Compton.

Brad woke up with the sun lower in the sky. The pizza guy was gone, but his sign still leaned against a telephone pole, the American Idol T-shirt drooped over it. People scurried to their cars carrying Watsons take-out delights and gallons of milk that cost $4.99. Brad sat up and sniffed. His head sat loosely upon his neck, wobbly, as if some crucial muscle had disintegrated. Brad's gloomy bully had come back full force, heavy on his chest, a weight so grave that it felt he might stop breathing altogether. He thought of the pills, how much energy it would take to actually start taking them again, all that unpredictable farting and belching.

Where was Sheila now? Maybe she was home with her husband, going on and on about the stupid thing Brad had done. Or maybe they were out for an early dinner, chatting about new patio furniture and a cable television series they would watch when they got home. A man chirped the doors to his Hummer and climbed inside. Something about the way the guy walked reminded Brad of Compton before the accident. His thighs, that's all women ever talked about, Compton's thighs, his muscular thighs. Brad imagined measuring them now, especially the bad one, knowing for certain it had dwindled to just a little bigger than a calf.

The car was stifling hot, even with his window open, but Brad withstood it. He couldn't go home, couldn't stay here in the parking lot of Watsons' most profitable store either. Brad was stuck, sweating and drunk. He dialed Sheila's cell number, but it went straight to her voice mail, so he hung up. Out of desperation he called Gina's cell. It rang only four times then clicked off. Overhead, helicopters whapped against the smoldering sky, ocher along the dreary edges, a real painting: The Last Decent Evening on Earth Before It Burnt Up.

Brad imagined the soil under his car, or rather under the pavement, the dirt that most likely held the microscopic DNA of Confederate soldiers, a splice of hair, a fleck of bone, tiny bits of cloth from an undershirt, all of it paved over, sealed tightly. It was the uselessness of life he pondered while sitting watching a woman carry two fat children on her hips, both of them sucking on large fountain drinks, filled from the beverage island inside called, Brad knew, Big Watsons Watering Hole. His cell phone rang, and a shot of hope raced through him, thinking it might be Gina or Sheila.

"Hello?"

"You've got to get over to the hospital, Brad. Now." It was Ratchet. Brad sat up straight.

"Why?" He heard how slow his voice sounded, how everything about him had slowed down. Speech, walk, eating—all of it was like he'd had his own brain injury, his own trauma to the head.

"Because Peaches went into premature labor. Compton rode in the ambulance with her. I'm shutting up the house and heading over there now, too." Brad could hear something wail in the background.

"What the hell was that?" he said.

Ratchet sighed, irritation exhaling into the phone. "It's the chicks. One turned out to be a rooster," she said, rushing through the explanation. "Now get over to ThriveStar Care Center. It's the one off the square on Sixty-one."

Brad tossed the cell phone on the seat and cracked his neck. A haze surrounded the car, moving some now, a slight wind kicking up, then dying. He smelled his own sweat and couldn't remember how long he'd been wearing his shirt. He started the car and chugged out of the parking lot. All the way to the hospital, Jennifer kept coming to him in the form of fleeting images scattered across the windshield. He waited at a four-way stop where his parents had once lived, near the campus. After moving to the farm, they'd driven the boys back there to show them the "Married Housing" where they'd first lived together. The name had captured Brad's imagination; it sounded as if the little brick barracks were actually wedded to one another, a foundation obliged to stick together.

Signs boasted a new development coming. The construction had been halted due to the drought, read an official Whitchfield County posting, but it was clear what was happening. "Married Housing" would be demolished for Fir Hills Enclave. Brad pulled over and jumped out of the car, moving faster than he had in weeks. He shoved the sign one way then another, working to get it out, not making a lot of progress. Brad walked quickly back to his car and steered the nose of the Sentra and edged forward against the sign. Brad stopped the car and sat back, half grinning.

A construction trailer sat just opposite, and Brad watched as the door opened and a man walked onto the decking, an orange vest over his shirt and tie. He was looking in Brad's direction, clearly angry. Brad pulled out quickly, in the direction of the hospital.

On the road, he took in a long breath and let it out. He sped up and stuck his hand out the open window, feeling the air rush over his sticky fingers. He wasn't sure if the man had taken down his license plate, but Brad was certain a transformation had taken place. He was Compton now, hating the developers, acting impulsively. Brad reached for his head, allowed his fingers to feel around. He wouldn't be a bit surprised to find a scar there, or even a fresh gash.

thirty-four Ratchet's hair seemed to have grown even more as Brad looked at her in the waiting room at the ThriveStar Care Center. The length of it moved like silk thread, almost luminescent, as if tiny solar filaments filled each strand. Brad watched its shimmering gloss instead of paying attention to the OB/GYN, now saying something to Ratchet. The woman seemed to know Ratchet well, as if they'd formed some significant bond. "As you know, Mrs. Orville is at a high risk for pregnancy complications." Ratchet nodded. Several of Compton and Peaches's assorted friends were sitting in the waiting room, too; Brad thought he recognized some of them from when the sheriff had taken him in. The man with the wheelchair, Roth, and his wife, Sally, were there; Brad vaguely remembered hearing something about the fact that they'd recently been married for the second time in fifty years, and now in the waiting room they held hands, listening intently. Apparently they'd grown very close to Peaches and Compton, and Brad was struck with how much he had missed over the summer, a shot of panic throttling through him. He shook his head as if to clear it and tried hard to tune in.

"She's fine right now," the doctor was saying. "We've stabilized the contractions and given her an ultrasound. The babies are fine."

Sally sighed and made the sign of the cross. "Thank the good Lord," she murmured. The old man, Roth, was trying to speak but had difficulty. His face was palsied and his right arm hung loose. Brad assumed it was this condition that had brought Compton and Roth together; in fact, if Brad squinted and tried to picture his brother thirty years from now, it was easy to see Compton much like Roth, well loved and incapacitated.

"Will she be able to go home today?" asked Ratchet, giving Brad a sidelong glance.

"Yes," echoed Brad. "Can they ride home with us?"

The doctor looked at him intently, perhaps thinking of something she wasn't going to say. "You're the father's brother, right?" she asked, putting both hands on her hips. She was clearly tired. Brad noticed her perfect mouth.

The question tripped him up. It sounded like the confusing riddle their father told them as kids: "Brothers and sisters have I none, but this man's father is my father's son." Brad never had understood it, while Compton had figured it out easily.

Ratchet spoke up. "Yes, Dr. Munro. This is Brad Orville, Compton's brother. He works for Watsons."

"Not anymore," Brad said blandly.

"We'll have her home by nightfall for sure," said the doctor. "She'll be on bed rest of course until she's full term. Our job now is to make certain Mrs. Orville doesn't deliver these twins early. You'll have to excuse me now," she said, walking briskly backward. "A nurse will be with you soon." With that she turned and nearly sprinted through the swinging doors.

Ratchet reintroduced Brad to the older couple. "Brad, you remember Roth and Sally," she said.

He stood up and offered his hand. Roth raised his arm with help from Sally and they shook hands.

"Hon, you look awful," Sally said to Brad, real concern in her voice. "Haven't you been sleeping?"

Brad sat back down and looked to Ratchet before answering. He really wasn't sure. Yeah, he'd been sleeping, some. Real rest, it sounded good.

Ratchet shrugged and got up. "I'm gonna get a Pepsi."

Brad tried to answer the question, but he was still buzzed, cloudy. "Oh, no. I just haven't had the time . . . " He stopped and noticed that Sally was looking at his head. She darted her eyes away from the lopsided hair system. She smiled and took her husband's hand again. "You just need some sleep, hon. Anybody could see that. If you're having trouble going to bed, you should see a doctor." Sally winked, and Brad nodded, somehow unable to speak. He felt like if he did, he might just break down in tears, bawling like a big old baby right here in the waiting room of the ThriveStar.

Sally stood up and patted Roth on the shoulder, then moved to sit down next to Brad. She put her hand on his thigh. "Things'll get better," she said cheerfully. "We've been trying our whole lives to get it right. Our first time around married, I screwed things up, but look at us now." Across from them Roth beamed, blowing her a fumbled kiss. Brad attempted a smile, one that would relay his appreciation yet make Sally understand he wasn't interested in advice, but it came out more like a snarl.

"Oh, I know you must be angry, hon," she said, tightening her grip on Brad's leg. "But just give things some time. Our daughter Kari is still trying at being happy. She went away to lose weight at one of those clinics, and her husband, well, her sort of husband, Hobbie, he's having some work done, too. He's met your brother, by the way. They all went fishing together after Roth decided that day program wasn't for him either. Anyway, you just have to remember that nothing is permanent, hon. You have to believe . . . "

"Thank you," said Brad, curtly. He removed Sally's hand, as if it were a lobster pinching his leg. He placed it in her lap and said again, in a low voice, "Thank you, though."

Sally nodded, her face tranquil. She patted him on the shoulder and returned to sit with Roth, the two of them holding on to each other as if they were in a capsized boat. It bugged Brad. He counted the time he might have to stay at the hospital. It would be better once he was alone, away from people, and could think through his next steps.

Ratchet came back, holding a Pepsi and flicking it with her nail. She seemed to have grown taller; her long legs were clad in tight, faded jeans and she wore high heels. Only now, after he'd seen she was wearing them, could Brad also hear the shoes tapping the floor. She sat next to him.

"Compton's in the small break room. There's one for families. It's right through that door," Ratchet said, pointing toward the receptionist area. "He wants to see you." Ratchet slurped from the can of pop, lipstick moist over her ample lips.

"I can't," Brad said, clutching his head, bending over in the chair. "I don't feel very good."

Ratchet put her can of pop on the floor and turned to Brad, took his arm. She whispered, "Go see your brother, Brad. You haven't spent any time at all with him lately. He's scared."

He didn't want to argue, and if he was ever going to get out of this place, he'd have to make an appearance, show Compton he was there. Brad rose slowly and scuffed across the floor. He looked back to the row of people. Sally winked again, and Roth looked as if he were bowed in prayer.

Compton sat in a plastic chair, blowing on a cup of coffee. He didn't hear Brad come in, engrossed in looking out a large window. The world outside was smoggy, as if dry ice percolated under the landscape. Compton's hair was perfectly combed as always, and the tremor in his hand made the paper cup jiggle. The room smelled like the rest of the hospital, an alloy of rubbing alcohol and burned popcorn. Brad noticed that Compton had a red Gideon Bible resting open on his legs; the bad one wobbled and the Bible fell to the floor with a whap. Compton bent to pick it up and caught a glimpse of his brother. For several seconds they stared at each other, Compton's big watery eyes almost floating. A floor lamp made a broad circle of yellow light that spread over Compton's feet.

"Are you okay?" asked Brad, moving slowly forward.

Compton placed the cup down. Brad stopped moving; it was all he could do not to run right out of there. His exhausted body, his fatigued mind—all of him—wanted to be anywhere but here, anywhere but in this nine-by-twelve room, trapped by the future, arrested by the past, the hum of the pop machine the loneliest sound ever heard. If he could throw himself out the window, he'd do it, take a running leap and smash through glass, fall six stories, and hope that the fires would come and cremate him, leave nothing but ash drifting over Whitchfield County until the end of time.

"It's a complication, the pregnancy," said Compton, now standing, trying to make his way to Brad, using the idle chairs as crutches, wending forward, the chair legs scraping the floor.

The sound grated on Brad. "I know," he forced himself to say. "But it'll be okay. The doctor said Peaches can come home," he went on, so weakly that even he didn't believe it.

Compton pushed himself up to Brad, stood there as red-eyed as a pigeon.

Brad nodded. "Anyway, it's going to be fine, Comp," he mustered. He started to turn back, head out of the break room, and just jump in his car.

"Forgiveness," said Compton, as if it were an entire sentence, as if it might just fix everything.

Brad's head spun. He moved toward the door, but Compton had built up his determination and rushed forward using all his energy; he nearly flopped onto Brad's back, pawing, trying to keep Brad from leaving.

"Stop it," Brad said, swatting, as if he were trying to keep a raccoon from attacking. Compton heaved and pushed a shoulder into Brad's back, pinning him against the wall. Brad flung around, and they were face to face, Compton shorter but fierce, his eyes clearer than ever, fixed. He sucked in and swallowed, focused so much that his temples pulsed. He braced both arms on either side of Brad and stood as erect as his bad leg would allow. "I did this thing to you."

"Shut up, Compton," said Brad, low.

"You will listen to me, Brad," said Compton, his voice shaky. "I did this thing to you and I'm so . . . "

"Get out of my way," said Brad, pushing at Compton's arm, but Compton only moved in tighter, making his body compact, harder to move.

"I'm sorry, Brad. This thing was wrong. I didn't mean it," said Compton.

A rush of hatred poured through Brad; he felt his head clear. If he was going to burn it all down, there was no better time. Who'd give a shit about a guy who could abandon his disabled brother in the midst of fear?

Brad grabbed hold of Compton's shoulder and shook him. "If you're going to apologize, brother, then get it right for once," Brad said, spittle flying. He moved in as close as he could to Compton's face, making sure to leave room between each word for the hurt to hit Compton square in the gut. "You fucked my fiancée, brother!" He drew back. "You fucked the woman I loved, Compton. Do you understand what I'm saying? It's not that complicated, asswipe. You fucked her while I was in the same house!" Brad pushed Compton away and yanked the door open, rushing through the larger waiting room, dazed. A nurse pushing an empty wheelchair stared after him, while Compton moved as quickly as he could, the bad leg dragging with so much force that it made one long, continuous chirp, his rubber sole leaving a snaking tread mark.

Compton yelled, "Brad, Brad, Brad!" He was crying. Ratchet jumped up, tipping her soda can over at her feet. Roth and Sally looked at each other, as Brad did stop, halfway down the hall, his back to Compton. He purposefully waited until he could hear Compton panting behind him. Brad turned slowly. A handful of other people waiting for loved ones to die or get better looked on.

"I'm leaving, Compton. But you should know this. I've sold the house, and the land. There's nothing you can do about it either." He said it loud enough that others could hear. A man eating from a jumbo bag of M&Ms stopped chewing.

"You better not. Are you being kosherish, Half Pint?" said Compton. "I plan on raising my babies there, so you shouldn't upset the peaches cart."

"Oh, it's sold, Compton. Start looking for a place where you can keep all these . . . " Brad looked at Sally and Roth and Ratchet and three others who'd showed up. They, too, looked sort of familiar, their names long forgotten under booze and depression. "These friends of yours."

"Stop it, Brad," said Ratchet. "Stop it and go home and get some sleep." She looked lovely in the light, pale but healthy; it made Brad want to make her miserable, make them all empty like he was.

"Shut up," he said, not looking at her, his eyes still trained on Compton. "You've got to admit Comp, Mom and Dad would find this mess the perfect social study. They'd call it: 'Brain Damaged: The Rise and Fall of Compton Orville.' Brad sneered, tears hot in his eyes, stinging, talking through thick-throated emotion. "I used to think you were a god, you know that? But now all I can see you as is a traitor. You'll never make it, Compton. They'll take your kids the first time you forget and put one in the freezer instead of the crib."

Compton's lip quivered. He reached out and snatched the hair system off Brad's head, the adhesive tape finally giving way under Compton's surprisingly firm grip. Brad didn't flinch, although he felt pain rip through him, deep and steady.

"Now I've got your Chia Pet, Half Pint." Compton stood holding it, the thing dangling from his hand like something from a clogged sink.

"Boys," said Sally, getting up. "Come on, now."

Ratchet chimed in. "Give it back to him, Compton."

"Brad, I think Compton simply wants . . . " started Sally.

"Shut the fuck up," hissed Brad. He reached out and took the hair-piece from Compton's hand. He walked out of the hospital, out into the smoke.

thirty-five   On the way to the house, Brad pulled into his old thinking place. The Dumpster was gone and the store was now open for business. He parked and stumbled around the back of the store, looking for Preston, the homeless guy. The new black pavement was soft, tugging at his soles as Brad shouted, "Preston! Preston!" He wasn't sure why he needed to see him, maybe he'd buy the guy another sand-wich, make sure he was hydrated under the hot sun, even drive him to the Paradise Club and let Mrs. Tantum work her magic.

Brad circled around the building again as a few customers came and went. He yelled, "Preston!" and stood still. An old woman said, "You looking for a dog? There's a cocker loose on Fourth Street." Brad shook his head. She shrugged her shoulders.

He sat down on the curb and thought back to the scene at the hos-pital. It felt good to confront his brother, even if it meant making a fool of himself. Maybe it was fear all these years that kept him from saying exactly what he finally said to Compton, words that Brad now realized were the key to moving on, freeing him. The idea that he'd finally moved past it all made him want to stand and find a new place to be.

The house was completely silent. Brad walked to the door that led to the basement. He stared down the steps, each one harder and harder to see; he thought he could make out the bottom one, maybe some water there. For all the cleaning and repairing, all the planting and trimming, Compton and his gang hadn't been able to fix what was wrong with the foundation.

As he'd driven up the lane, more aware than he had been in weeks, Brad inspected everything that had been done outside. The little chicks, now moved from the pantry to the outside, had grown into pullets, and their black feathers shimmered emerald in the strong sun. They pecked the dry dirt, moving from one spot to the other, a banty rooster guarding them, his head tilted in the hot air as if listening for danger. An entire row of rosebushes had been planted around the crisp white fence. There were new shutters, a dark green, and the porch had been repaired, new steps laid, with rows of petunias in boxes along the walk. Birdhouses were tacked to birch saplings, nailed to the towering pines. Brad had a vague feeling of seeing the improvements before, but he couldn't remember whether he was recalling his parents' work or Compton's.

Brad closed the basement door behind him and trudged up the stairway toward his room. He stopped before the heavy oak door to Milo's den, opened now just a crack. He pushed it slowly, afraid of what he might see, bottles strewn everywhere, their father's hobby consumed and pissed out with vengeance. The door squeaked farther open. The desk was clean and neat, polished even. Papers were straightened and aligned in stacks, and Brad realized that Peaches or Ratchet must've been in here, cleaning up his mess. The wooden floor had been swept and was spotless. Brad's eyes moved from object to object, cups and platters and mementos from student trips abroad, a stone pestle from a kid who'd gone to Malta to track the migration of the pallid harrier. Everything in the room looked complete and orderly—just as it had before Brad wrecked it with his sloppy drinking—except for the liquor cabinet. It sat empty. All the trash was cleaned up, labels and corks tossed away, the bottles and cups removed. He would've preferred the room to still be in shambles, not tidied up, which was a clear message that he was unable to recognize his own messes.

Brad went to his bedroom and packed, tossing suits on hangers into a trunk. In the bathroom, he sorted through a shaving kit, adding toothpaste and deodorant, a bottle of cologne. He'd live better, or at least clean up more often. He picked up the bottle of prescription pills sitting in the medicine cabinet. He examined the label, studied the warnings. He would start taking them again, maybe see if the doctor could prescribe something for the gas, maybe get back to jogging.

In the mirror, he scrutinized his head. Without the hair system, he thought he looked even older than just a few months ago. The red spot on his crown made it appear as though several bees had stung him or a spider had been living under the piece. Brad jumped in the shower, working fast, washing his head, careful not to rub the washcloth too hard over the irritated area. He patted dry as he walked to his room. He dressed quickly and retrieved the hair system from his suit pocket, where he'd stuffed it after Compton ripped it from his head. In the bathroom cabinet he found the other, earlier toupee and tied them together with a long strand of floss, wrapping the hairy mess until it looked like it was in a partial cast. Brad tossed the bound hair into the toilet and flushed it, picking up the plunger just in case. It went halfway down, then bobbed up again, floating obscenely in the blue water. He put down the lid and shut off the light.

In his room he piled jeans and T-shirts into the trunk, topping it off with running shoes and three more pairs of dress shoes. He packed his laptop. From his desk he pulled together his savings account booklet, the phone numbers to Watsons' HR department, and his passport.

He stood and surveyed the room. It had been cleaned, too, by Peaches maybe, or Ratchet, and the bed looked as soft and welcoming as a bed on a television commercial. For a moment, Brad thought of simply climbing in and drifting off to sleep, but he knew that if he didn't leave now, before Peaches and Compton and the whole group returned to the house, he'd die. His cell phone rang. The digital name ran across the screen: Randall, Climko, and Jefferson, Attorneys at Law. Brad flipped the phone shut. Downstairs he heard a door creak and footsteps in the kitchen. Brad shoved the trunk down the hallway with his foot, clutching the briefcase, tilting to the side so the shoulder bag wouldn't fall.

At Compton and Peaches's room, he noticed that a crib had been set up, and the corner of the room was halfway painted, yellow and pink and blue. He pulled the door shut quickly.

The footsteps below had stopped, but Brad could sense that someone was standing in the living room, probably just one of Ratchet's friends. He stooped and picked up the trunk by the leather straps and heaved it down the stairway. If it was someone sent to talk to him, anyone, he'd throw the trunk at him.

Gina appeared at the end of the stairs. Brad was breathless as he lugged the luggage past the last few steps. She smiled at him.

"What are you doing here?" he asked.

She shrugged. "I made bail. Thought you might like to get a drink with a wanted woman." Gina looked surprisingly good for someone who'd been arrested and interrogated. Her hair was clean, just washed; Brad could tell by the way it fluffed around her face, the scent it gave off, flowery herbal essences. It looked thick, but entirely weightless, too. Jennifer Hunton's hair had looked that way at times, so perfect to his eye. Gina didn't seem to mind or even notice that he was bald now, that his hair system was nowhere to be seen.

"Should I call you Sharon or Gina?" asked Brad, not a note of anger in his voice; he was truly curious.

"Call me either one. If the cops had looked closely they would have found out that my middle name is Genevieve. Looks like you're going somewhere," she said, nodding toward the suitcases. "Want some company?"

Brad wanted to answer; the idea thrilled him actually, but someone knocked on the back door, and before he could think how to say yes without desperation the knock came again, light but persistent. Brad pulled the bag from his shoulder. "Just a second," he said, holding a hand out to halt Gina, but she followed him anyway, through the kitchen and to the mudroom.

Old Man Tyler stood on the step, with a black eye, yellowed and purpled at his temple. He was whiskery and seemed older than just a few days ago. He held a large box, handles sticking out of the top; one almost poked him in the same bruised eye. Behind him, Brad noticed the first signs of autumn, tinges of yellow and orange, dusky reds in the trees.

"Hello, Brad," Tyler said, a little cap on his head. His voice was smaller, too, as if part of him had simply drifted away on the hazy smoke. Brad held the door open, Gina's warm body behind him.

"Are you okay, Mr. Tyler?" Brad said, standing aside as the old man came in.

"Sure, sure, son." He walked ahead, and Gina and Brad followed him into the kitchen. He sat down right away at the table and smiled up at them.

"And who are you, miss?" he asked, standing again, offering his hand.

Brad wondered what name Gina would use.

"Hello," she said, tossing her hair. "I'm a friend of Brad's. That's an awful-looking bruise. What happened?"

"You know," Tyler said slowly, not answering right away, "I think my boy would've been a lot better off had his mother lived. I think he could've used a brother or sister. 'Course, maybe that would've made things even worse, I don't know." He pulled the flap back on the cardboard box, his weathered hand marbled with prominent veins, skin as dark as roasted turkey. Most of his nails had dark purple spots, as if he'd hit each one with a ball-peen.

Brad moved to sit down, too, pulling a chair out for Gina. Still, he was eager to leave, to get out before things became more complicated. "Mr. Tyler," he said, "did you have that looked at?" Brad noticed the bruise also had a gash in the center, and when he studied it more closely, he could see the bristly knots of more than a couple of stitches. The old man pulled a croquet mallet from the box, its wood shiny from use, lighter where hands had grasped it. He smiled as he took the balls one by one from the box. His little cap was slipping off, but he didn't seem to notice. His face was red and he grunted as he put the balls on the kitchen table.

"You boys sure loved to play with these back then." Finally, he had all the balls on the table, his arms around them so they'd stay put. Some were maple, reddish and smooth, with blue and yellow bands, while others were cracked, made of hard oak, nicked, too, but with the maroon paint still on, orbiting them as if they were model planets.

Old Man Tyler looked up and rolled one to Brad. Brad had forgotten the idle autumn days when he and Compton rode their bikes up the road to play at the Tylers'. Sarah and Milo had encouraged them to go, and although sometimes they would come along, too, Brad now realized that it was a break they were after, and maybe Old Man Tyler knew this, that he'd understood how a married couple in love might spend a languid afternoon while their boys were down the road.

Brad rolled the ball back. "Where's Kyle, Mr. Tyler?" Brad stood up and started gathering the balls, placing them back in the box.

Gina didn't move, her large eyes and sympathetic frown trained on the old man.

"He's somewhere out there," said Mr. Tyler, his left hand starting to tremble. He pulled his cap down farther.

Brad squatted next to him. "Tell me what happened to your face," he said. His head felt naked, obscene even, and he felt a stir of impatience and irritation. If Gina weren't here, he might not even have let the old guy in. He was leaving, he told himself. Not sticking around in the kitchen with Old Man Tyler. He sighed. "Is Kyle in trouble?" he asked, dreading the answer.

The old man touched his battered face. His eyes grew distant, then tightened as he cleared his throat. Something smelled rotten to Brad, as if Tyler hadn't scraped his shoes off after working in the paddock.

"You boys sure are lucky to have each other," he said, looking up as Brad stood again. "The place looks good, Brad. It really looks so damn good. Just like your parents used to keep it. I worried about you two when you first moved back. God knows Compton needed some help. And you gave him that." Old Man Tyler straightened in the chair. He rose from the seat. Gina stood, too, and Brad wasn't entirely surprised when she gave him a little hug.

Tyler gave her a half smile. "I'd like for you boys to keep those," he said, pointing to the croquet set. "Compton is all excited about being a daddy, so I thought you'd get some good use out of them for the twins. Not right away of course, but . . . " It occurred to Brad that Old Man Tyler most likely had been helping with the improvements on the place, and he envisioned the newly troweled concrete steps, tightly hung shutters, the patched roof, and repaired gables, Old Man Tyler's dull hands, neck veins pulsing, expertly correcting them all.

"Thank you, Mr. Tyler. We'll let him know you stopped by," said Brad. Gina nodded, her neck long above a tight blouse.

"I'll let you get back to your afternoon," said Tyler, moving toward the mudroom. He was nearly in his pickup when Brad called after him.

"Thanks again," he said, a part of him wanting to run after Tyler, ask him to stay for dinner; maybe he'd be able to broker some deal between them all, settle things up. But the old man rattled down the drive in the truck, bent over the steering wheel. Brad felt the silence in the house again.

"You think he's okay?" asked Gina.

Brad didn't want to turn to her. He faced the door, peering through the screen and glass toward the old swing set. It'd been fixed up for two toddlers; painted, reinforced, welded, probably by Tyler. He said, "If you want to come along, I won't stop you."

"Just for the record," Gina said, "I didn't even think about stealing from you. I'm guilty of bouncing checks, and making horrible money decisions, but I'm not a thief."

Brad wanted to tell her it didn't matter, but the words wouldn't form in his mouth. "Okay," he said.

thirty-six Brad braked in the middle of the road. Across the four-way stop, foreclosed signs stood in front of some of the enormous homes in the Canterbury Eagle Landing subdivision.

"Did you see that?" asked Brad.

"They must've gotten ripped off with an ARM loan, too," Gina said, pulling down the visor to check her lipstick. "It's my fault, but still, they should tell you how much the dang things balloon."

"No, I mean did you see that person running across the field?" Brad felt more alert than he had in many months, a low-grade anxiety thumping throughout his body.

"Nope," said Gina, looking over her shoulder. The Tyler place was a mile behind them, but Brad thought for sure it had been Kyle, his bushy beard and flapping clothes unmistakable. Smoke drifted over the hood of the Sentra. "You think the fires will make it out here?" she asked. Brad couldn't answer; it hadn't been more than fifteen minutes since they'd loaded up the car and took off, first stopping at the new Watsons store for gas and beer, then backtracking, stopping off at the house again to get Gina's house keys from her car. They moved forward, the late afternoon sun more and more like autumn.

"Maybe, if the winds change. They say it might even rain a little."

"Because the governor asked God for a little downpour, a torrential blessing?" Gina licked her lips and smiled. It occurred to Brad that this was the way you found things out about people: you spent time together and, in passing, shared views about current newsmakers. Surely Gina wasn't a rabid supporter of the governor. Brad smiled back.

"Maybe he should've asked for a specific amount," said Brad. He mimicked the governor's drawl, "Please, y'all, send down five inches of rain, y'all."

Gina grinned.

Brad drove on, without any idea at all where they were headed.

They stood next to each other, not holding hands, but the backs of their fingers brushed. Kennesaw Mountain was closed, but Gina and Brad had hiked up the rear outcrop. The smoke seemed to thin out as they swept aside aster and goldenrod, their damp shirts snagging on dry brambles. The temperature had dropped, enough to feel for the first time since spring that the earth wasn't made up of hot coals. Brad thought of autumn football games, of the sandwiches their mother used to prepare, packed in an old Westinghouse cooler, hunter green, the silver handles worn just right. The four of them would bundle up, wrap hand-knitted scarves around their necks, and set out to the Bowman stadium to watch spindly boys get the tar knocked out of them.

Brad took Gina's hand in his; she seemed surprised and widened her eyes. He didn't know what to do. Brad thought of weightlessness, of space and the absolute certainty that his feet were planted on granite made up from a colossal collision, earth as cosmic leftovers.

"I'm tired," he said. The car sat at the base of the mountain, packed with his things. They'd driven around Whitchfield County for hours, stopping to eat, drink a beer or two. Gina smoked while Brad watched. He'd thought of calling the hospital or the house, but something made him switch the cell phone off and toss it in the glove compartment. The sun eased slowly down the sky, a little breeze ruffling Gina's hair.

"We should go then," she said. Brad wondered where. A line of orange lightning seemed to etch across the valley floor miles away, but it was a forest fire, small and insignificant from the top of the mountain.

"Sure doesn't look very dangerous from here," he said, pointing out the fire to Gina.

Gina laid her head on his shoulder. "I've got six more weeks before they can evict me. Let's go there. If you don't mind a house without a single piece of furniture, that is." She looked up. Brad nodded. He pictured the place, empty as a realtor's walk-through. For some reason he thought of his MegaWell pills—the ones that were now in his suitcase. He could see them on the empty, clean counter in Gina's barren, foreclosed home, the morning light clear and cold. He could taste the smooth capsule on his tongue, bitter but solid, there to swallow.

Gina was still asleep, quiet on the floor; they'd slept for four days on a pallet made of blankets. True, the house was empty, but Gina had an entire bedroom chock-full of new stuff. "From the third time I refinanced," she'd said, opening the door. "I know it looks like a lot, and it is, but most of this stuff is high-end, all bought on sale." She'd held up a cashmere trench coat. "This would've cost me two thousand dollars, but I bought it at Macy's in the summer for nine hundred." Brad had marveled at all the clothes and kitchen pieces, a top-of-the-line bread maker and cappuccino machine, more than a dozen containers of cutlery and pots and pans. "So you cook a lot?" he'd asked, but Gina shrugged. "Nope, but this set here would've been nearly a thousand. I got it for less than half that."

Brad crept into the empty bathroom. He still wasn't used to how the water coming from the tap echoed. In fact, the whole house echoed. He stared into the mirror. His head had healed, and now only a little dry spot of skin was there.

Brad tilted the bottle and watched as the pink pill rolled into his palm. He tossed it into his mouth and ducked his head to the faucet, slurped and swallowed. He brushed his teeth and shaved. Something about having sex and sleeping, eating pizzas, and drinking water from the tap had given him a foundation to work from. At nights, lying on the stack of blankets, the house seemed to disappear, and Brad dreamed of being at the farmhouse, Compton perfectly healthy, and Peaches, too. But in the dream, Gina and Jennifer Hunton were somehow the same person, interchangeable. When he'd awaken, Gina next to him, curled into a ball, Brad would ponder the reasons he'd made Gina and Jennifer the same woman. He knew it wasn't something he could stop himself from doing. He'd drift back to sleep and wake again a few hours later, early dawn creeping up, light spilling in from the curtainless bay windows.

Brad lifted his bulky car keys from the kitchen island. He tucked them into his jacket and tiptoed toward the front door. Outside, the cool air had held, but the smell of smoke still clung to it, as if they'd become the same thing, too, just like Gina and Jennifer.

He started the car, half afraid it would wake Gina and she'd bound from the house and want to ride along. Out on the road, Brad drove slowly, looking around, watching the trees, noticing the idle construction sites, the piles of lumber, the machinery frozen in time. Signs posted warned of trespassing and spelled out the fines and imprisonment numbers for breaking the watering ban. Brad felt like he'd woken up from a lazy afternoon nap and was behind everyone else, that they'd already known about something he didn't.

He switched on the public radio station in time to listen to an agri-economist lay out the dire circumstances of the drought on Georgia peaches, peanuts, and pecans. "The three p-crops will take a beating. It will end up near the half-billion point in lost revenues for the state." Brad looked at himself in the rearview mirror. He realized how accustomed his own eyes had become to the hair system. He ran his hand over the baldness. He'd read that hair transplants had gotten better, that they no longer had to look like seeded crops.

He turned into a Watsons store. He worried that the franchisee would recognize him and phone security, but everyone was too busy to notice, the cashier hollering "Welcome to Watsons, home of hospitality" to every customer who barged through the glass and silver doors. Still it made him nervous even to be in a store; a few days back, the HR department at Watsons had sent a letter to Gina's at Brad's request, which simply stated his 401(k) balance and contained his last paycheck, plus twelve weeks of unused vacation time and a letter he was supposed to sign that stated he'd never, ever tell any Watsons trade secrets. Brad had deposited the checks, and yesterday he threw the Restrictive Covenant into the trash.

Brad went to the Watering Hole and mixed a ginseng and carrot juice smoothie, with an extra squirt of B_{12} and a dash of lemon spritzer. He stood in line and waited to pay, a calmness settling over him. Someone tapped him on the shoulder.

"Hi," she said, holding a gallon of milk and her familiar-looking car keys, a little world globe attached to a string of other trinkets.

Brad stood holding the health-nut smoothie, his hand freezing cold. "So you still shop here?" Sheila said, smiling, not awkward at all.

"Oh, yeah," said Brad, a little tentative. "I prayed for a whole storm and it came. Big time." Sheila giggled.

"I guess you could say I am a tried-and-true Watsons supporter," said Brad, sniffing, acting tough and loyal.

"Geez," said Sheila. "You look so much better than just a couple of weeks ago." She looked him up and down and whispered, "And you're not even drunk."

"Well, I don't start binging until eleven a.m.," said Brad. "It's just ten now."

Sheila let the smile drain from her face. "How's Compton?"

Brad stepped forward in line, placed his drink on the counter, and fished around in his pocket. "Just fine," he said, "I'm sure just fine."

Outside, they stood and laughed about Watson Sr. and the look on his face when Brad climbed onto the stage. For a moment Brad wanted to ask her about work, but he didn't. Sheila gave him a little hug. "I hope this means we're still friends," she said.

It threw Brad. "I don't deserve it, but yes. We'll always be friends, Sheil." He watched her walk away and disappear around the corner of the building. Brad crawled back inside his car and headed out.

Along the ditch, just before he passed the Tyler place, two sheriff cars leaned into the culvert. He stopped and pulled off the road, clambering out of the car. Brad jogged up to the first cruiser. It was the same deputy who had found him passed out in his own yard and taken him in for questioning. The two deputies rested against the bumper of a cruiser.

"Everything okay?" asked Brad, standing on the shoulder. He looked toward the Tyler place.

"You're the guy that lives up the road, right?" asked a deputy, removing his shades.

"Yeah," said Brad, sheepishly. He shrugged his shoulders, smiled some. The cop nodded.

"You sure look a helluva lot better than the last time I saw you." He poured coffee from a thermos into the screw-on lid and sipped from it. The other deputy listened.

"Thanks. Is Mr. Tyler okay?" asked Brad, antsy.

"Yep, but his kid isn't. If you see him, make sure you call us. He's got three outstanding warrants. And for the record, he's armed and dangerous." Brad thought of the times they'd played cowboys and Indians in the Tyler hayloft, how Kyle seemed to be really shooting bullets from the end of a broken-off pitchfork handle.

"All right," Brad said, a little depleted. "I guess I'll be going. Is it okay if I stop by and visit with Mr. Tyler?"

The other deputy spoke. "Sure, but he's not home. The whole place has been sealed off. The meth force is dismantling the lab. We're just hoping his kid tries to come back."

"Where's Mr. Tyler now?" asked Brad, his depression resurfacing, pecking at his earlier clear mind, tattering its edges.

"He's up at that new place near the hospital." The deputy looked to his partner.

"It's the one they just built, has glass walls, kind of tall. I think it's called Whitchfield Manor Care."

Brad nodded and stood still.

"There anything else?" the deputy asked, putting his shades back on.

Brad hesitated, started to turn back toward his car, then stopped. "Have either of you been up the road? I mean, have you been to my house at all?"

"Your brother and his friends helped Old Man Tyler move. He says he's going to be a father soon." The deputy didn't seem to find it odd.

"Okay, thank you," said Brad. He slipped into his car and drove farther down the road. Everything outside the car windows seemed brittle and dead, but as he neared the driveway he saw that the Orville home stood like an outpost in the desert, the pastures browned for sure, but from the road the whole place seemed better than ever, verdant trees and shrubs, clean lines of paint and siding, all etched like a drawing.

Brad saw that Compton was struggling to push Peaches in a wheelchair through the orchard, while the couple Brad had met at the emergency room, Roth and Sally, sat at a new picnic table near the creek. Ratchet and her friends were cooking on a grill while another couple strolled toward the road. Brad maneuvered the car into the ditch and watched.

The couple held hands and chatted, kind of shyly, Brad thought, the woman dipping her head, almost as if they didn't know each other very well. A wiener dog on a short leash trailed behind them, sniffing billowy dandelions. The woman was a little overweight, but beautiful, and the man was skinny, with a full head of brown hair. Brad could see, though, even at this distance, that the guy's face was somehow marred; it was red, even a bit swollen, like he'd recently recovered from a serious burn. The couple paused, waiting on the little dog to finish peeing. Then the woman called to the dog, "Come on, Terry."

For nearly a half hour Brad watched from the car. Everyone had reassembled at the table by the creek, and they were toasting something, holding their glasses high into the air, laughing. Sally and Roth stood with the couple that had been on a walk; they hugged over and over, and Brad decided the woman must've been their daughter.

Brad started the car, hoping the noise wouldn't give him away. It didn't, and as he pulled out of the ditch he heard their voices trailing toward him in the smoky air. Compton clapped and bellowed, "And many more!"

Brad paused and watched, his hands clenched tightly on the steering wheel. In the strong sunlight, everyone looked so cheerful that Brad couldn't even think of interrupting, of telling Compton about how the house and the property would be Watson's before long, the closing date just a month off. He just couldn't tell them all, not today.

He backed up and made a U-turn. He started the drive back to Gina's empty house, content and pleased that Compton was well. And satisfied that he could finally be happy for him.

thirty-seven Brad sautéed the onion and drizzled the red peppers with truffle-infused olive oil before adding them to the pan. The garlic sizzled in a skillet with pecan halves, the pepper and onions filling the air with the robust smell of savory cooking. Brad had said to Gina, holding an armload of groceries, "If you're willing to break out some of those pots and pans I'll make something for you. I'm pretty good at it. Our mother taught us how to cook. I'll have to show you the cookbook she wrote. Besides, I'm getting kind of tired of Domino's."

Gina was upstairs getting dressed. She'd told Brad they would make it a romantic night, complete with candles she got for nearly 75 percent off at a crystal sale at Parisians. Brad heard her blow-dryer droning, as the chops broiled in the stove, lightly popping. He had the built-in satellite radio playing, the speakers hidden somewhere in the ceiling. The kitchen was tricked out with all sorts of modern amenities: a pizza oven in the wall over a superheating convection stove, everything stainless steel, fingerprint proof. Gina had told him that, usually, she kept only yogurt in the fridge and vodka in the freezer.

On the counter sat a stack of mail, some opened. Brad hesitated to look but spotted a letter from the mortgage company. He picked it up and read it over. Gina owed nearly $15,000 in missed payments and overdue fees. In less than four weeks she'd be evicted forcibly. Brad placed the letter back, trying to make certain it didn't look like he had been snooping.

He finished the blue cheese salad with the garlic and sugary pecans, adding the red peppers and onions, the truffle oil. He plated the veal chop and added a chive and parsley Chasseur sauce on the side. Another story about Georgia's drought played on the radio as Gina's perfume trailed down the stairs. For the most part, the fires had been put out or contained, and although every day held the possibility of a pop-up blaze, started by a spark from the road or a discarded cigarette, the real problem was the lack of drinking water, the lakes at all-time lows. Brad changed the station in time to listen to the last half of a new Tom Petty song. The music sounded good turned up, the low bass and clear treble highlighting guitar riffs and crisp vocals. Brad poured wine and sat down at the glistening counter. He'd prefer a table, but it would do. Maybe he'd buy one tomorrow and surprise Gina.

She emerged from the shadowy stairs, wearing a tight burgundy dress and high heels. She smelled so clean and flowery that Brad thought he'd inhale her completely.

"You look beautiful," he said, turning in one of the four high-back chairs affixed to the counter.

"Thank you, Mr. Orville," she said, tucking her dress underneath her hip as she sat down. "The food looks delicious. I could smell it when I was taking a bath. I just about ate the herbal soap."

Brad poured Gina a full glass of wine and placed one of her Ralph Lauren cloth napkins on her lap. They sampled their salads, a little awkward at the counter.

"Would you mind if we took this out to the deck. There's a table out there and chairs, too. That way we can see each other's faces," said Gina.

On the deck the cooler night air made the food taste even better. Brad told Gina about his parents, how they'd been in love all their lives. He talked about Compton's accident and the months that followed, how scared he'd been, but the story stopped there. He asked Gina about her family. She said her parents were alive, living in California, where they ran a wine cellar business. They'd grown up without much and finally bought into a business that seemed to provide them a good life, two houses, one on the coast and another in Colorado Springs.

"That was so good," Gina said, smacking her lips. Brad liked the way she ate, without pretending she was dainty or barely hungry. He smiled.

"You know," she said, "you look better without the hair thing." She sipped her wine and winked. "Really, I mean it wasn't bad, but I think you're handsome either way."

Brad felt a blush hit his face. "Thank you. I was thinking about maybe checking into hair replacement surgery, you know, do it right. They can really do a lot with micrografts now," he said, adding, "Sorry, I guess I've been Googling it too much lately."

"You should do what makes you feel better about yourself." Gina drank down the rest of her wine.

"Right," he agreed, his voice faltering. Brad sipped a drink of water and then gulped another one, putting the glass down too hard. "I mean, I'm fine. Either way," he said, shrugging, offering a smile. He got up, taking her empty plate. "Okay," said Brad. "I wanted to talk to you about something. Do you want to come inside?" Gina rose and hugged him, as Brad held two plates behind her back, trying to hug her, too, without getting anything on her dress.

They stood in the sparkling kitchen, the lights on, the satellite radio, too. Brad scraped the plates and ran the disposal, wiped down the counters, and put away spices. It saddened him to watch as the kitchen returned to the look of vacancy. Gina poured another glass of wine and took a call on her cell phone.

"Really?" she asked. "And they're only four hundred bucks?" She bit her lip, raising her eyebrows at Brad, who stood against the stove. "Sure, save two for me and I'll be in tomorrow." She clicked the phone shut.

"Now, what did you want to talk about?"

"I hope you don't think I was going through your mail, but I noticed the mortgage company letter."

Gina smiled, her hip jutted out; she flipped off her heels, which made Brad think of a walk in summer rain, the two of them side-stepping night crawlers, pants legs rolled up to the knees. "Of course not," said Gina, motioning toward the stack. "Most of the time I just shred it without opening it." Her nails were perfect, carmine red, shiny as she drank more wine.

"Well, I was thinking. How about if I help pay your back mortgage payments and we live together?" Brad watched for a reaction as she lowered the wineglass from her mouth. He added, "Here, I mean. Live here together."

"Oh," she said, as if it had never occurred to her that they were already living together. "I hadn't thought of that. But still, I'd just rather let the bank have it back. The new payments are so much."

"How much?" Brad asked a little too eagerly. "If you don't mind me asking," he added, trying to sound more offhand

"The payment was twenty-one hundred dollars when I got the loan in 2004. Now the monthly minimum is a whole lot more. It's just not worth it, plus, like I said, I've refinanced a lot, too."

The kitchen grew quiet as Gina chinked the glass with her nails and the radio aired another story about the vanishing lakes.

"Maybe we could move to another place. Find something we both like." Brad sounded whiny even to himself.

Gina placed the wineglass on the counter and walked over to him. She put her hands on his hips and planted a kiss on his forehead, much more like an aunt than a lover. "I really like you, Brad. I do," she said, her perfume tantalizing. "I just don't know what I'm going to do next. My parents have offered to let me move in with them in California, and I've got a girlfriend who just got divorced, so we might get an apartment together in Buckhead."

Brad couldn't raise his head to look her in the eye. "Okay, sure," he said, looking at the travertine floor, scuffing the toe of his foot.

"Hey," said Gina, "I thought we were going to have a romantic night." She kissed his neck, her hand behind his head. She stood back some. "It's just that I'm not sure yet if we're good for each other. Maybe we're only supposed to help each other through a bad time in our lives. It might be more than that, but things are way too complicated now to know." Brad nodded, staring at the tile, using an index finger to rub at his eye.

They slept on the floor after making love, which had been awkward, legs knocking into knees, a mashed lip from banging teeth. Brad woke up and stared at the ceiling. He'd left the radio playing in the kitchen, and something droned on, a voice mumbling, never quite materializing. He fell asleep again in the predawn light, gray and steady. His dreams were fitful, and over and over Gina morphed into Jennifer, their faces melding and melting, turning like pages until they stopped and Brad jolted from sleep. Gina was awake, standing over him, still clad in her staticky dress. Her hair was mussed, eyes sleepy.

She handed Brad his cell phone. "It's someone about your brother. The babies have come early," she said, groggy yet energized, like a kid up early on Christmas Day.

Brad took the phone and listened to Ratchet tell him about preemies. He thought he heard her say two pounds, and neonatal and intensive care. Gina was already upstairs, putting on a new outfit from her stash.

thirty-eight The sounds in the hospital reminded Brad of the cashier dragging cans of food over the scanner. It never stopped, just bleeped, bleeped, bleeped, a never-ending tally of health-care bills, amounts that when printed on paper would seem too absurd to even

conceive of; he tried to block out the noise by reading a sports magazine he wasn't interested in. He wasn't sure where the noise was coming from, maybe a jammed electronic door or security system hidden under the nurses' station, but it put him on edge, as if something was about to detonate.

It was almost nine a.m. and they still hadn't been able to see Compton or Peaches and the babies. Roth and Sally read from a Bible while Ratchet played hostess, asking everyone if they wanted coffee or a snack. She seemed to have come to the hospital with a sack full of quarters. Gina was introduced by Brad, as Sally smiled warmly. Brad thought he saw Sally wink at him.

Brad excused himself and went to the bathroom. He locked the door and took out his MegaWell, swallowing one without water. He'd thought his mood would've been blunted by Gina's rejection to live together, but something had risen in him, moved past an obstacle, and he felt as if he'd made it through some test. He looked into the mirror, got closer to it, and examined his eyes. Brad took a deep breath and then another. Compton's need for him seemed less now, as others had stepped in. Brad nodded at himself in the mirror, somewhat embarrassed. Needing someone, he thought, could be just as fine as being needed.

When he returned to the waiting room, everyone was standing, circled around a doctor in light blue scrubs. She was the OB/GYN from before, Dr. Munro, hair pinned back in a tight bun. She caught Brad's eye as he approached. "I was just telling your family here that the babies are in critical condition, Mr. Orville." Brad thought of his father, "Mr. Orville," and he almost looked around to see if somehow he was there.

"They are premature by about twelve weeks. The little boy weighs two-point-two and the little girl about two-point-five. Things will be hectic and intense for some time." Dr. Munro rubbed her chin. "Mr. Orville, the father, your brother that is, he's in need of some support right now. I guess the best way to say it is he's overwhelmed." She looked at Brad, her eyes tightly fixed. "To be perfectly blunt, the parents are going to need as much help as they can get. Now and in the future."

Ratchet took Brad's arm. "Do you want me to go see him with you?" Out of the corner of his eye, Brad saw Gina step back, out of the circle.

"No, I'll be all right." Brad followed the doctor through the swinging doors.

They walked down a shiny hallway, the trill and dull thuds of machines working, the smell of rubbing alcohol as potent as if it were under Brad's nose. He wondered why, with all the advances in medicine, rubbing alcohol was still the prominent smell in hospitals. Still, the scent of babies, their wipes and lotions, climbed over the other smells. New life was here, abounding even, though each room they passed contained another set of parents, heads bowed, the lights dimmed; Brad thought he could actually feel the mumbling of prayers, the energy of hope. The doctor led him around a nurses' station and pointed, then disappeared, her shoes squeaking.

Compton sat near the door of the chaplain's room. Brad watched his brother. As Compton sat there like that, legs together in front of him, blowing over a cup of coffee as if to heal it, it was possible to believe he'd never suffered any kind of injury. Brad thought Compton would be in tears, but instead he'd taken on the same stoicism as their father. He was much smaller, of course, and certainly not as strong, but Brad saw Milo in Compton's eyes, his steady, patient gaze.

Brad stood still, somehow not wanting to move. Perhaps if he stayed put, everything else would stand still, too—the babies, Gina, the fires, the sale of the house and land—all of it would not move until he did, a kind of musical chairs set to the rhythm of cooing incubators, ventilators breathing to the tempo of heartbroken parents. So he resisted the urge to move, to jog to Compton and lift him into his arms, hold him like when they were kids on a cold night in a twin bed. The thought of a drink—a warm shot glass of one of his father's whiskeys—fluttered across his mind, unbidden, and was gone just as quickly as it came, nothing more than a harmless thought, come and gone. He had no idea how long he'd been motionless when Compton stood up, his bad leg wobbling under his weight, and hauled himself in Brad's direction. There was no place to hide, no cubby to duck into, not even a job or lover to run to.

Compton caught sight of Brad and stopped. They stared at each other across gray linoleum, Compton's gaze steady, knowing.

"I'm sorry," said Brad, his voice wavering, thick at the back of his throat.

"I'm apostle apologetic," Compton said as he pushed toward Brad. He shook his head, swallowed, his bad eye flickering. Brad could tell Compton was concentrating hard. "I mean I'm really, really sorry, Brad." He lugged the last step to Brad.

They stood, holding each other, for a long time.

"How are they, Comp?" said Brad, sniffling, sucking in air.

"Half Pint, they're perfect. Little and perfect," said Compton, smiling through the shimmer of his tears. "The little boy is Justice and the baby girl is Sarah. The names of their grandparents, one from each side." He took a deep breath.

"And your wife, Comp, how is she?" asked Brad.

"Peaches is fatigued out, really bushed. But I got to eat with her, so she's sleeping now." Brad nodded and patted Compton's back.

"Would you come in to see them?" asked Compton.

Brad kissed his brother's head, the bangs tickling his lips. "Of course. I'd like to meet my niece and nephew."

Brad could hear the material from the scrubs brushing together as he suited up. He stopped for a second, the nurse holding up the sleeve of the jumper, waiting for him to slide in. Brad helped when Compton got a little tangled up in his, guiding his arm through the sleeve.

Inside the NICU complex, computerized instruments took up most of the space. Monitors beeped and whirled, and the entire room seemed far too intricate for only five pounds of life. Compton reached and took Brad's hand. They walked together toward the incubators, lit up with a warming light; it reminded Brad of a tiny greenhouse. He felt Compton's hand through the surgical gloves.

Compton stopped a few feet before the incubator, peering over the mask, his eyes wide. He squeezed Brad's hand as he nodded toward two nurses, who wore cheerier scrubs, pink and blue, with storks printed on them. They stepped aside, giving Compton a thumbs-up. He pulled Brad to the incubators, which sat higher than a normal crib, perched above an intricate digital underbelly, silver and white, digits ticking up then down again, temperature and heartbeats, blood pressure.

Compton's eyes smiled. Inside the incubators Justice and Sarah lay motionless, tape and tubes up their tiny noses. They wore oxygen masks that looked entirely too bulky for them. A nest of tubes and patches clung to their chests. Brad let out a small gasp that he hoped his brother hadn't heard. The pitiful little babies were so tranquil that Brad had to squint to make sure they were actually real. Another set of patches wrapped around the twins' miniature feet. Brad decided that pinky toes that little, smaller than pebbles, had to be proof of science and God working together.

"They're beautiful, Comp," said Brad, his voice muffled through the mask.

Compton put a hand into the incubator through an opening that turned into a glove. He gently picked up Justice's hand. Brad stood, holding his breath. A part of him felt he didn't deserve to be here; after all, he'd been such a jerk for so many months.

"Put your hand in, Half Pint," said Compton, a proud, anxious lift in his voice. Brad hesitated and looked to the nurse, who was busy prepping more tubes and patches. She smiled and urged him on with a nod.

Brad's hand slipped into the gloved hole. He took little Sarah's hand, the itty, biddy fingers so weightless and foreign they reminded Brad of something exotic, a translucent sea creature found on the beach, hollow but full of life. He noticed now how perfectly brown the babies' skin was, a lush caramel, lighter around their sweet temples. They each had very low hairlines, and the little girl, to his amazement, had a single curl the size of a Cheerio on the crown of her head.

It was as if Compton had read Brad's mind. "Look at little Sarah's hairdo," he said, elbowing his brother. They laughed nervously together, and Brad felt a sense of pride, something building him up.

A tangle of tubes and wires knotted over Justice's midsection, and Compton expertly moved them aside. He whispered, "Look at those legs, Half Pint. Have you ever seen a nicer pair of little legs in all your life?"

Brad nodded, unable to speak. He leaned toward Compton and kissed the side of his head.

Compton said, low, "After this, let's take a walk outside and chew some gum."

"That would be nice. Just like old times, huh?" said Brad, Sarah's tiny fingers curling around his gloved thumb.

"Maybe," said Compton, "or we could call it all brand-new. Make up something else to do. I can't wait for these babies to play where we used to." Compton's voice broke, and he shook his head, as if he couldn't imagine his babies ever making it to the point where they'd play in the creek.

Brad almost winced and shifted his legs. The lawyer had Breathalyzed him to protect the sale of the place, that was comforting, but still, it would require money and time to stop the Watsons.

"We'll see, Comp," said Brad. He looked through the hyaline glass at the twins. "They are gorgeous."

"Yep," said Compton. He turned to Brad. "When they get out of there," nodding toward the incubators, "I'd like a photo of you holding them. Put it on the refrigerator in the kitchen." Justice kicked his feet some, which made little Sarah yawn.

"My goodness," said Brad.

"Goodness," said Compton. "Goodness for sure."

Brad heard Ratchet's voice inside the chaplain's office. He stepped to the door and waited until she caught a glimpse of him. Roth and Sally and Ratchet all sat around the clergyman's desk.

"Pastor Wilhelm, this is Brad, Compton's brother," said Ratchet. Brad stepped inside and shook his hand.

"We were just talking about organizing volunteers to help out with your brother's situation, you know, people to form a kind of circle of support. It'll take a lot of prayer and resources, energy, too, to get these little ones to their first birthday party." The man's vigor sort of drained

Brad, but he smiled and looked around the room and said, "Thank you all."

Brad said to Ratchet, "Can I see you outside for a second?" She followed him out the door and over near the snack area.

"Thanks again for calling me."

"You look so much better, Brad," said Ratchet, touching his elbow.

"Oh," he said, "I've been getting that a lot lately." Brad looked around, searching. He said, "Did you see where . . . "

"Gina told me to let you know she'd see you back at her place," said Ratchet, rocking on her heels. Brad knew then that he wouldn't stay another night there, and although it was dismal to acknowledge, he also felt as if a stone had been lifted off his chest.

"Sorry," said Ratchet, as if she, too, knew how it would play out.

"Sorry?" he asked. "For what? Putting up with me? For taking care of my brother and Peaches?" Brad leaned forward and took Ratchet in his arms and squeezed her softly. She kissed him on the cheek.

"I'll see you back at the house then?" she asked.

"Seems like the place to be," Brad said as he watched her slip back inside the chaplain's office.

thirty-nine Old Man Tyler sat in a lawn chair, the loose leaves somersaulting over the brittle grass. Brad plopped down in the chair next to him.

"Not a bad day to be living inside the city limits," Brad said, patting the old man's hand.

"Well, Bradley Orville. Did you move in here, too?" teased Tyler.

"No, but I tell you, a fella could do a lot worse," Brad said, looking around. It was true; the place was neatly kept, clean, and orderly.

"Took a little getting used to, but I don't mind it."

"Good. I just wanted to stop by and let you know your neighbor had his babies. They came too soon, but they're here." Brad pointed to the hospital towering over the retirement community. "Right up there to be exact. I guess you and Compton are still neighbors."

"I'll be darn," said Old Man Tyler, looking up at the hospital, his eyes kind of searching the facade, as if the twins would be out there for him to see.

"Let's get some coffees and talk all about it," said Tyler. Brad had heard him say the same thing when they were kids, and he wondered how Kyle could've turned out so wrong with a man like Mr. Tyler as a father. A few weeks back a beer would've sounded better, but today a nice cup of java was perfect.

"I'd love some coffee," Brad said as they stood up and went inside, the smell of burning trees finally gone from the air.

In the car on the way home he thought of all the things the twins would need: their health care, food, in-home assistance for Peaches and Compton, clothes, dentists, braces for their teeth, and maybe even braces for their preemie legs. All of it would've bogged Brad down in the past, but something about the onslaught of needs, at least for now, stirred in him a firm purpose. He drove on toward the house listening to the radio, tapping the steering wheel and watching foreclosure signs whip past the window.

Brad switched on the light to the basement and stared down the stairs into the shimmering water. It appeared black, and he imagined the floor slimy with growth. He took the steps slowly and recalled a song their mother sang to them as boys, a ditty about sailing a dark sea for a bride with no name.

He stood at the edge of the water, hesitated only for a moment, then went in knee deep. The water was warm, almost comforting, as he stood still, listening for something he didn't know. Water lapped at the edge of the basement walls, little splashes like rhythmic ticks of a clock. Brad recalled a baptism they'd gone to as a family. For a while, he couldn't remember who the kid was, why the Orvilles had attended. He saw green water and a full creek, mallards moving silently along the bank, a group of ten or so people watching a preacher dressed in a large white robe. Then it came to him; Brad saw Kyle Tyler being dipped forward then backward, silver water dripping from his stiff arms. Old Man Tyler actually whooped when it was over. Afterward, Compton and Brad played with Kyle; he ended up hitting Brad so hard in the head with a fallen limb that Sarah seemed on the verge of punishing Kyle herself. In the end, Compton held a bag of ice on Brad's head, while they sat in the mudroom. "Don't worry, Brad. I'll take care of it for you." Kyle was spanked by Old Man Tyler. Milo told the boy, "You've started down a path of self-examination, Kyle," but the boy just ran off toward the woods.

Brad touched his head, the smooth skin hot. How could so much time have passed since Kyle's baptism? What instrument of measurement had delivered Compton's twins right now, right here in this time, where rain had been so scarce and the world was drying up? What would occupy this space in a hundred years? Would water even matter in a thousand? The very spot that Kyle had been baptized might be on the other end of the universe in a million years.

None of it mattered, and all of it did. Love, hair, water, and the memories of their lives on a county road; these things had the potential to hold him in hope, in a new, broken family, struggling at this very moment to breathe, to move this instant forward, blending it with the same ones Sarah and Milo had held themselves.

Brad sloshed toward the metal shelving on the wall and searched for some type of tool; he didn't know what he was looking for, but he was ready to fix their foundation. Down here, he told himself, is where I'll start.

Reader's Guide

1   Brad and Compton Orville are brothers with a history of betrayal, yet their sibling bond remains intact. Why is this? Have you had a similar experience in your own life or family? What makes the relationship between brothers and sisters so different than any other?

2   Depression is one of several issues Brad struggles with in the story. Does this complicate his decision making? If so, how? Medication is one solution he turns to. What are other methods of coping with depression?

3   Compton is not the same man he was before his brain injury. How does this play out in his life? What kind of love did he experience before the beating? Would he have fallen in love with Peaches before his accident? Does Compton experience a deeper type of love now? Is his love for Peaches driven by the heart or the brain, and what is the difference?

4   Did Compton deserve the beating? And who's right here, Brad or Compton? Can they both be seeking forgiveness?

5   What role does nature play in the novel? How is the suburbanization of Whitchfield County reflected in Compton? How about in Brad? The Watsons?

6   One of the themes of the novel is forgiveness. Compton, though, has trouble remembering what it was that he did to his brother. What does forgiveness entail, and can we ever achieve pure forgiveness? Is it a onetime effort or a longer process?

7   As parents, Peaches and Compton will need help and support in raising children. Is that okay? Should people with disabilities have the right to form families?

8   Brad begins drinking his deceased father's prized liquor collection. What does this symbolize? Can you put a price on family history? Do material possessions represent memories? If so, how?

9   Brad believes, at least in some part, that he is trying to stop Peaches and Compton from making a huge mistake. Does he succeed? What do you believe is at the center of his efforts?

10 The novel touches on several social issues: the environment, race, parenthood, housing foreclosures, and mental health. Which one do you think is most prominent? Which of these matters the most to each character?

11 Look beyond the final page of the novel. Where do you see Brad in five years? What about Compton and Peaches? What role will health care play in their lives? Where and how do you envision them all living?